JULIA

A Novel

FAIRCHILD

JULIA
A Novel
FAIRCHILD

The future seemed so clear...until lightning struck

LOUISE GAYLORD

NATIONAL AWARD-WINNING AUTHOR

Beverly Hills, California

JULIA FAIRCHILD: A Novel by Louise Gaylord

This is a work of fiction. Names, characters, places and incidents either are the product of the author's imagination or are used fictitiously, and any resemblance to actual persons, living or dead, business establishments, events or locales is entirely coincidental.

First Edition

Published in the United States by Little Moose Press®, a division of Smarketing, LLC, California.

ISBN 10: 0-9786049-7-0
ISBN 13: 978-0-9786049-7-4

Library of Congress Cataloging-in-Publication Data

Gaylord, Louise.
  Julia Fairchild : a novel / Louise Gaylord. -- 1st ed.
      p. cm.
  ISBN 0-9786049-7-0, Cloth, First Edition
  I. Title.

  PS3607.A986J39 2006
  813'.6--dc22

                                        2006020955

Book Design: Dotti Albertine
Editor: Brookes Nohlgren
Cover Photo: Getty Images

This book is printed on acid-free paper and manufactured in the United States of America by Sheridan Books, a member of the Green Press Initiative (www.greenpressinitiative.org).

For Ted

CHAPTER 1

JULIA FAIRCHILD peered into the inky depths smeared with stars. To have Mac Brantley's body wrapped around hers gave enormous comfort.

Her fiancé had kidnapped the clinical psychologist from her office at Piñon Mesa Hospital and whisked her to the Las Cruces airport, where his Beechcraft Bonanza packed with a double sleeping bag and coolers filled with food and wine had been waiting.

Their destination, a dusty landing strip at Prewitt, New Mexico, two hundred miles to the north where a four-wheel-drive waited to take them into Ojo Redondo Campground in the Zuni Mountains not far from the Continental Divide.

And now after two bottles of wine, a thick, juicy steak, and potatoes baked over the fire, she was lying skin to skin in a sleeping bag with a man she never expected to know, staring through thick pine boughs that touched the sky, a million miles and a lifetime away from her wealthy and highly respected family with homes in Manhattan and on Long Island.

Their coming together after days of separation was intensified by Julia's desire to assuage her nagging doubts about their future. Would she be able to leave her eastern roots behind to cleave to a family so alien to her own?

All thoughts died when Mac's lips covered hers and their union took on a power of its own, pushing them to another compelling dimension.

It seemed as if each were trying to disappear into the other and, by doing so, protect themselves against . . . against what?

The distant call of an owl drifted through the pines, sounding more sad than urgent, and Julia clasped Mac's hand to tighten his arm around her, needing to feel his warmth and the steady drub of his heartbeat against her back.

She smiled into the darkness. This impromptu trip had turned out to be the perfect remedy to release the threads of doubt so tightly coiled at the bottom of her stomach.

MAC STARED at the fading embers through the red-gold screen of Julia's curls. The night was so quiet he could hear her soft, drawn breaths as her back caressed his chest then sighed away.

There were no words to describe his new happiness. Finally, he was complete for the first time in his life. And though Julia came from a world away—one filled with old-school ties and yacht clubs—Mac recognized and appreciated the part she played in this now-perfect equation.

He had whisked Julia out of Las Cruces to this remote rendezvous, plied her with wine and food, then taken her to bed. But instead of the long, lazy loving he planned, the moment their lips met the pace accelerated and took on an urgency that thrust them together until each seemed lost in the other's passion.

Afterward, Julia had clung to him until she fell asleep and now she lay curled inside the protection of his arms, her hand strangling his in a death-grip.

Mac kissed the nape of her neck, relishing the cool slide of her skin beneath his lips, then gathered her closer into his curve as a lazy tickle of desire stirred.

He shut his eyes and silently groaned. Why hadn't he told Julia about Emaline Pierce when they first met? Explained his broken engagement? Gotten it out of the way? There was no one to blame but himself for his cowardly omission, which now would require a major announcement accompanied by a string of reasons for his failure to mention this woman.

Mac shook the thought away. He was blowing things out of proportion. After all, his relationship with Emaline was finished—part of the distant past.

WHEN HE heard the first low rumbling in half-sleep, a sound as familiar as the rush of the stream outside his bedroom window, Mac scrunched beneath the covers, sure that in the next few minutes he would hear the beginning ping of raindrops against the tin roof above his bed.

A flash and sharp crack followed by the first cold freshet preceding the descending storm brought him to, and he shook Julia awake.

"We've got to get out of here. Try to make it to the car. Too many tall trees. Perfect lightning rods."

Mac pushed his way out of the sleeping bag toward his discarded clothing just as the advance squall-line picked up the camp stools and tumbled them to one side of the clearing. "Hurry. It's a big one."

He started to retrieve the stools but realized time was running out.

In the next flash Mac saw Julia dressed and trying to hang on to the wildly flapping sleeping bag.

"No. No time. Head for the car. That way. I'm right behind you." He was shouting over the roar of the wind and hoped she understood. When he saw her veer toward the narrow cut in the rocks he hurried to follow.

There was still a difficult descent ahead. Even though the four-wheel-drive was less than half a mile away, the drop to the parking area was almost vertical and the path composed of slippery shale. Bad enough to negotiate in dry weather, but treacherous in wet.

Lightning strobed the forest in almost continuous flashes, allowing Mac to monitor Julia, who was several yards ahead. He saw her slip twice, then slide, and was flooded with relief each time she rose and plunged onward.

He fell only once, cracking his left knee against a boulder, but in spite of the excruciating pain he pressed on through the assault of wind-driven pine needles spearing his face and neck.

When he reached the clearing he saw Julia huddled against the car on the lee side of the storm. Keys. He jammed his hands into empty pockets and cursed as the first pelting drops fell. It was too late to go back and much too dangerous. The only thing he could do was try to protect Julia.

Mac hurried to kneel beside her and shouted above the churning winds. "We have to crawl under the car."

He saw her nod and start to slide under the car when ozone stuffed his nose and the forest exploded around him, sending electricity surging through his body, throwing him backward into unconsciousness.

CHAPTER 2

A BIRD'S CHIRP filtered through his haze and Mac opened one eye to see diamonds sparkling on pine boughs beneath a bright, cloudless sky.

He tried to roll to his side but something held him to the ground. Thinking Julia must have fallen on top of him, Mac opened the other eye and strained to look down his body. When he saw nothing, the sickening realization brought a stone to his throat. He was paralyzed. He fought his panic, pushing it to one side as his physician's mind took charge. The paralysis could be temporary. He'd read of such cases. He was able to breathe. His heartbeat was accelerated but regular, his brain seemed to be functioning well, and he could move his eyes.

He made a second attempt to move his head and when his neck accommodated the sent signal, hope surged and the stone dissolved. He was going to be all right.

Mac's thoughts flew to Julia and his panic doubled.

"Julia? Can you hear me?"

Nothing.

"Julia?" His voice, hoarse with fear, cut through the silence as his heart zoomed. "Are you all right?"

Nothing.

Mac willed himself to roll to his right side and saw he had been knocked a good ten feet from the car and Julia's crumpled body. She was on her stomach, face away, her right leg and arm extending at crazy angles as if some giant had flopped a rag doll to the ground.

"Oh, God—oh, God." He tried to move his legs but they refused to respond. Some sensation had returned to his arms and he was able to raise them and flex his fingers.

His arms would have to do the job.

Mac rolled over and began to inch his body across the ground, each effort becoming a hell, as insignificant pebbles turned to flint grinding into his tender forearms and stomach.

It seemed like a lifetime before he reached her, and when he did and felt for her pulse, there was none. He stanched a groan, pulled himself closer, and pressed his ear to her back. Nothing.

"You can't. I won't let you." The terror in his voice startled him.

Mac's effort was finally rewarded by the flutter of a heartbeat, and tears pushed at the back of his eyes. "Thank God."

He struggled to a half-sit and with every effort available checked Julia's breathing. Her eyes were shut and her mouth open, but he couldn't be sure she was getting oxygen.

"Breathe, Julia. Please. I don't have the strength to do it for you."

From the tug at the base of his skull, Mac knew he was close to losing consciousness. "Not yet. Not yet." He made his heavy hand move in one last effort to moisten a finger and put it to her lips. A faint flush of breath was the last thing he felt before exhaustion won and he collapsed.

CHAPTER 3

"DOCTOR BRANTLEY?" Someone was calling his name. Why couldn't he answer?

"Wake up, Doctor Brantley." That someone's voice carried authority. Was he still interning? He cracked one eye. A white coat. Overslept. He'd get it now.

It took every bit of strength to mumble, "Just let me splash some water on my face and I'll be right with you."

"No need to do that quite yet." A cool hand pressed against his forehead as a thumb peeled back his eyelid to let in the bright pierce of an ophthalmoscope. "You're one lucky man. No sign of optic damage."

Mac willed his other eye open to see an attractive woman with wide, dark eyes staring back and recognized his colleague at Chaco Point, Dr. Sylvia Chee.

"Sylvia?" he muttered.

She shook her head and laughed. "Very good. We can add this to your long list of medical miracles."

Both his arms were bandaged to the wrists, but before he could ask, she continued. "Not much damage, Mac. Mostly superficial cuts on your forearms and chest from dragging yourself across the ground. You're going to be real sore for a while."

Chee stepped back. "Thank heavens Joe Pinto found you."

"Joe? The airstrip guy?"

Then Mac remembered. Joe had helped him tie down his plane the afternoon before. Helped carry supplies to the waiting four-wheel-drive. Made a kind remark about the beautiful lady.

He sent up quick thanks for his many good friends among the Navajos. Through the years he and Joe had shared more than a few pots of coffee in the tiny lean-to next to the packed-dirt runway at Prewitt.

Sylvia nodded. "Joe knew the storm was bad. After it passed through he drove into the parking area, and when he found you both unconscious he radioed for the EMT."

Mac shot up, almost colliding with the doctor. "My fiancée . . . ?"

Chee frowned. "Not quite as lucky as you, I'm afraid. They took her to Albuquerque."

Mac's stomach fell away and he crashed back to the pillow.

"Hold on there," Chee said. "I didn't mean to scare you. Before I came in here, I got in touch with Pavilion in Albuquerque, and from what they tell me Doctor Fairchild will be fine. It's just that when the EMT arrived, your vital signs read much better than your lady's. She sustained a few exit burns, her EKG was erratic and her breathing shallow. So . . . they took the extra precautions."

"I've got to get there . . . be with her." Mac swung his feet over the side of the bed, then slid backward as black rose to meet him.

CHAPTER 4

WHAT WAS WRONG with her hands? They wouldn't move. Julia tried to open her eyes and winced. The glare from the sun was too painful. The storm must be over. They were safe.

A shadow brought brief relief. A cloud. More rain? Julia let out a small moan and heard a deep, "Welcome back."

"Where am I?" Her voice seemed like it was coming from another person.

"You're in the Emergency Room at Pavilion Hospital."

She cracked an eyelid to see that her hands were swathed in gauze. "What happened to my hands?" she gasped.

"Exit burns."

"Exit burns?"

His laugh filled the room. "You're getting it now. I'm Doctor Duke. Do you remember what happened?"

Julia closed her eyes to see Mac crouched next to her. They had gotten under the car. A bright light, then silence. "Lightning. We were hit." Her eyes flew open. "Where's Mac?"

The doctor put a restraining hand on her shoulder. "Don't get upset. He's in good hands. They took him to the reservation hospital at Chaco Point."

Julia scrambled to recollect where she had heard the familiar name. That was it. The hospital at Chaco Point was run by the Indian Health Service.

"If he's there, why did they bring me to—where did you say?"

"Albuquerque. Pavilion Hospital. Mac wasn't as badly injured as they thought you were and, of course, he practices at Chaco Point."

As the doctor bent over to pass an ophthalmoscope in front of both eyes, Julia smelled the pleasant scent of Dentyne chewing gum. He stepped back and nodded. "There's not much more I can do here."

She fought to keep awake. "Why am I so drowsy? Did the lightning . . . ?"

"You're okay but you'll probably be drifting in and out for a while. Don't worry, your brains aren't fried. Vision's good and, except for those exit burns, you're as healthy as you were before the strike. Well, almost. For the next couple of days you're going to think you've been beat on with a ball-peen hammer."

The doctor removed his white coat to reveal a plaid cowboy shirt and faded jeans.

He turned to the nurse. "She can take solids, so remove the IV. Put her in a room for overnight observation. I'm going to grab myself a longneck and a burger. It's been a busy day."

Julia shoved up on one elbow. "What time is it?"

"It's just past three and two hours into my free time. The nurse will take over now."

He handed a chart to the woman. "I'm on call until seven tomorrow morning, and if everything seems okay I'll release her then."

He was almost out the door when Julia called, "But, wait. I have to find out about Mac."

Duke stopped to face her. "I told you he's okay. Now, get some rest." Before she could say anything else, he was gone.

Julia sank back to her pillows. "Well, that one's certainly all business."

"Doctor Duke?" The nurse lowered her voice. "I guess you could say that. But if I weren't a happily married mother of four, I'd jump his bones in a New York minute."

Julia shrugged away the endorsement. From what little she had seen, the prickly Dr. Duke didn't appeal to her at all.

She held up her useless hands. "What in hell are exit burns?"

"Guess you were struck by a stray current or else you'd be dead.

The current has to get out of the body some way, in your case it left through your hands."

Julia flipped her bulkily bandaged hands to one side and back again. How would she be able to dress herself? Feed herself? Drive to work? The thought of having to depend on someone else was exasperating. "How long will I be like this?"

The nurse shook her head. "I didn't see your hands before the doctor dressed them, so I can't say. But they can't be that bad since he's discharging you tomorrow."

She slid the IV from Julia's vein, swabbed the area with alcohol and slapped a piece of adhesive in its place. "Hungry?"

"To tell you the truth, I'm more interested in reaching my fiancé."

Fifteen minutes later Mac's deep voice came through the receiver Julia shouldered to her ear. "What a hell of a weekend."

She closed her eyes and felt his body curled at the back of hers. "I didn't mind the beginning one bit. But you might have canceled the extra entertainment."

To hear Mac laugh was a welcome relief. "Guess I should have. How are you?"

"Hey, I called you first. How are you?"

"I was blinky for a few hours, but I've recovered. Now, you."

"I'm fine, I guess. Except my hands are encased in giant balls of gauze and I've been at the mercy of some doctor named Duke."

Mac's tone lost its lightness. "I thought I'd lost you, Julia. Thank God you're all right."

Sudden tears filled Julia's eyes and she swallowed twice before she could make a sturdy response. "You'll have a hard time getting rid of me, Mac Brantley."

"That's the best news I've heard since last night. I'll fly in first thing tomorrow to pick you up. Okay?"

"Sure," she mumbled. Why couldn't she remember? What day was it?

Julia pushed out of her dreams to the static and glare of the television. One o'clock. She managed four hours of sleep, but the night was hardly over.

Though the bandages impeded her efforts, she finally silenced the television. In its place came the low murmur of the night-shift personnel drifting down the dim corridors, their muted exchanges punctuated by soft laughter and the slap of the metal cover against paper as someone shut a chart.

Julia came to with a start, then realized she must have dozed off again, since the clock now read one-thirty. She raised one hand and carefully pressed against her arm, searching for any pain, when a low voice at her side startled her.

"Are you in pain?"

Julia turned to see the cowboy doctor sitting by her bed.

"Not really."

"Good. The wounds weren't too bad and I probably used too much gauze, but better that than an infection. Lay low for a couple of days and have someone remove the bandages. By that time, a band-aid should be fine."

She grinned. "That's great news. I'd hate to be married looking like the Bride of Frankenstein."

"Married?" Duke's eyes cut to her bandaged left hand. "That Navajo is an engagement ring? I've never seen a ring with such refined totems. The turquoise is incredible."

"I love the color too. It was my fiancé's mother's."

"Sorry I had to remove it to get the bandage right. It's in the safe at the nurses' station. Don't get away without it."

"Don't worry. That's one thing I won't forget."

The doctor pushed back in his chair and lazily trailed his eyes over her face and down her body.

Julia glanced away from his gaze until she heard his voice close by her ear. "When's the big day?" His face was only inches from hers.

She edged to the middle of the narrow bed before she stammered, "First Saturday in May."

"That's not far off." He stood and reached above her. "Mind if I turn on the light? It's not too bright."

She nodded, and a dim light on the wall behind the bed added a glow to the room.

The doctor sat, then leaned forward, giving Julia a chance for closer inspection.

His narrow face, ending in a square, stubborn jaw, was framed with a mane of longish black waves and featured shaggy eyebrows shading deep-set sable eyes. Two distinct lines bracketed his mouth—an unattractive feature on some faces, but on his they added strength.

Julia chalked one up for the nurse. After closer inspection she agreed that the woman was right on the mark.

Duke took her hand and carefully sandwiched it between his palms. "So you're Mac's lady."

"You know him?"

"Doesn't everybody?"

"I've only known him since last July."

"The man works fast, doesn't he?"

"Does he? I never thought too much about it."

"How come Brantley's such a lucky jackass?"

Resentment crowded out Julia's initial interest and she echoed, "Jackass?"

"Well, he's luckier than a jackass, I guess. Usually a man is allowed only one beautiful woman in his lifetime."

"One? I don't understand." Her words slurred as an overwhelming urge to sleep blunted her curiosity. She focused what concentration remained on retrieving her hand from his, but gave up when she couldn't seem to find the strength.

"I'm afraid I'm going to have to sleep now."

His voice drifted through the haze. "Go right ahead. Don't mind me."

The last thing Julia heard before she floated away was Duke's whispered, "Too bad I didn't see you first."

CHAPTER 5

JULIA AWAKENED the following morning half expecting to see Steve Duke still seated by her bed but the chair was empty. She shoved aside a small twinge of disappointment and directed her attention toward getting a quick release from the hospital.

Her initial efforts brought no success, and she was about to have the nurse contact the doctor when Mac walked into the room.

Once she was in his arms, Julia sighed, "Thank heavens you're here. They won't spring me."

Mac shook his head. "I can't believe they let you get dressed."

"They didn't."

Her fiancé pointed toward the bed. "You're worse than a kid. Get under those covers while I go check on your status."

Before long, Mac returned with the Charge Nurse, who reported that Dr. Duke had written Julia's discharge early that morning and she was free to go.

They were rolling past the nurses' station when Julia thought of the ring. "Stop. I almost forgot it."

"Forgot what?"

"Your mother's ring. Steve—Doctor Duke—removed it to dress the wounds last night."

Mac gave her a thoughtful look. "Hold on."

He stepped to the counter and retrieved a small, brown envelope. "All safe and sound. I sure hope this isn't a bad omen or anything. I thought you were never supposed to take it off."

"Lightning strikes don't count," Julia said.

"Glad to hear that." Mac stored the ring in his hip pocket, wheeled her to the front door and helped her into a waiting cab.

Once they were headed for the airport, Julia asked, "How do you know Steve Duke?"

"It's a long story."

"He's a good doctor, isn't he?"

"Steven Duke is one of the best triage doctors in this state."

"Emergency only?"

"Yep. Duke's saved more lives than I can count. Heads a crack team of ER doctors." He lowered his voice. "It's just that he's not a good friend."

"What do you mean by that?"

He frowned. "Not now, okay? I'm too tired to open that can of worms."

Julia didn't have the strength to pursue the mystery any further. Instead she put her head on Mac's generous shoulder and shut her eyes.

Mac shook her awake to make the short distance to the waiting plane, and once she was buckled in she slept until the aircraft touched down on the broad mesa west of Las Cruces. The nap didn't begin to alleviate Julia's fatigue and she struggled to keep her eyes open during the drive from the airport to her townhouse.

Once inside, she collapsed against Mac and asked, "What on earth is wrong with me?"

"Don't worry, it's a natural reaction. To be honest, I'm not up to par myself. Let's get to bed."

Julia read the weariness in Mac's face. "Oh, Mac, you don't have to do this. You're worn-out and so am I. Go home."

"How will you get ready for bed?"

She peered at the cumbersome bandages. "Are you sure you want to take this on?"

His arms went around her. "Hey, enough of that. I can't think of a place I'd rather be."

Mac led her past the insistent blink of her Caller-ID and up the stairs, where he helped her undress, then settled her in bed.

When she stretched out, she stifled a groan. Just as the doctor predicted, her body felt like someone had beaten it with a huge hammer.

Mac took her hand. "Hurt?"

Julia nodded. "Much worse than yesterday."

"That settles it. I'm sedating you."

The shot was quick and painless, bringing relief almost immediately.

Mac tossed the syringe into the wastebasket. "Only bathroom privileges and complete bed rest for you today and tomorrow."

Julia's weak protest came through a cottony mouth. "But, you can't stick around here for two days and wait on me. What about your schedule?"

He placed a kiss on her forehead. "Don't worry about a thing."

Through a gauzy daze Julia watched Mac slip off his shirt, step out of his jeans and crawl into bed to curl around her. She struggled against the invading sedative just long enough to wonder why Mac disliked Duke, but before she could make any sense of it she was asleep.

CHAPTER 6

FOR THE NEXT two days Julia lay in her darkened bedroom sedated by low doses of Seconal, coming up long enough to take care of her basic needs before sinking back into euphoria. Through her haze she heard the telephone ring but soon realized the answering service was catching her calls. Mac seemed to come and go, leaving her to sleep for long pleasant intervals, but he was always there for her meals and to curl around her each night.

Wednesday brought Julia into the day refreshed and eager to resume her duties. She rolled to greet Mac and realized he had left sometime around midnight after changing her dressings. She flexed both hands and was relieved to see that she was able to use them again despite the thin layers of gauze covering her palms and wrists.

Julia headed for the coffee she smelled rising from the kitchen but stopped at the Caller-ID. Twenty calls. Most probably from her mother. She arched her back to relieve the sudden tension buildup and decided a steaming mug would give her the strength to face the music.

Julia took a few soothing sips and dialed the number to retrieve her messages. Her mother's voice rose with each frantic call. By the time they ended, Julia was hunched between aching shoulders and reluctantly punched the speed-dial number to the house in Sutton Place.

Lucia Fairchild's agitation was still evident in the first part of the conversation and reached a fevered pitch when Julia told her about the weekend.

"Did you say you were struck by lightning? Oh, dear heavens, you could have been killed."

"I'm fine, Mother. Really. I just have a couple of exit burns on each hand that are hardly visible."

Lucia's voice was shrill with frustration. "As far as your father and I are concerned, you might as well be living on another planet."

Julia hated that her mother still possessed the ability to reduce her to a small child and was about to apologize for nothing when Lucia continued.

"This hurry-up wedding of yours is driving me crazy. I raced to put together the invitation list so I could make the trip to England, and what have you done with it?"

Julia's retort was sharper than she meant it to be. "This hurry-up wedding is almost two months away. Besides, we're sending announcements. So, go on to England and have a good time."

Her mother's verbal onslaught turned to entreaty. "Oh, darling, just this once couldn't you humor me and change your plans? Why not make it a June wedding at Saint Bart's? A small reception at Sutton Place if you want. It would sound so much better in the *Times* write-up. No one in our crowd has the slightest idea where Las Cruces, New Mexico, is."

Julia squelched her impatience. "I want a small wedding here because this is where I plan to live. Besides, I don't think Mac's family would be comfortable coming east and having social stuff crammed down their throats."

Lucia sniffed. "This is happening much too quickly. Are you sure this is what you want? And just who are the Brantleys, anyway? They sound like a bunch of yahoos."

There was a too-long silence, then the coup de grace was delivered in a soft, "Maybe it would be best if Ian and I didn't come."

Julia couldn't help her wail. "Please don't say that. I can't get married without you. Besides, a trip west will be the perfect antidote for an English spring. Remember how much fun we had on your last visit?"

"Oh, Julia."

"I won't take 'no' for an answer. All you and Dad have to do is show up. I'll take care of the rest."

"What about Perez-Gasca?"

The pain in Julia's shoulders was already excruciating, but the thought of Jorge Perez-Gasca added an extra twinge.

Two months had passed since their last dinner meeting in the private room at Café Quentero. He had been called to the Mexican interior, and she had gone to Albuquerque with Mac.

Julia didn't want to think about her feelings for her birth-father, or about what part he should have in her wedding. It would be difficult to include him, not only because the Perez-Gasca family knew nothing about her, but also because she wanted Ian to give her away. In her heart, Ian Fairchild was her father, not Jorge Perez-Gasca.

"I haven't talked to PG in a couple of months. He was out of town, then I was. But I will." Julia glanced at her watch. "Got to run, I'm late already." The receiver was in the cradle before her mother could reply.

The phone rang again just as Julia hung up and twice more before she picked up.

"Julia, this is Steve Duke." The ER doctor's voice brought a warm rush to her cheeks and she laughed, delighted to hear from him again and so soon. "I was calling to see how you are."

"Well, thanks. You were right on target, Doctor. Every muscle I own was in spasm."

"Sorry about that." His voice carried a slight drawl that added an interesting inflection. "But you should be over it by now."

"I am, thanks to two days in bed."

Julia heard the hospital sounds behind his silence and was flattered that he'd taken time to leave the Emergency Room for her. "You're nice to call. I'm sure you must be very busy."

"Just doing my job." After a long pause he said, "I'm coming to Las Cruces next weekend. How about meeting me for coffee?"

"You're not working?"

"I've served more than my time. I need a break."

"Well, if that's the case, we don't have to meet for coffee, why don't you join Mac and me at Radium Springs that Saturday? Our good friends Bob and Myrtle Sandoval are giving us an engagement party, and I'm sure they wouldn't mind an extra eligible bachelor."

Steve laughed and the sound was round and deep, as if coming from the bottom of a well.

"What's so funny?"

"I'm already invited. Bob didn't say what the occasion was, just that he and Myrt were giving a party."

"You're friends with the Sandovals?"

"Why, yes. Bob was at Sandia here in Albuquerque until he was hired by Piñon Mesa. I was the one who recommended him for the job. I was raised in Las Cruces."

"It's a small world, isn't it? We'll play catch-up when I see you."

"Please don't hang up, Julia. I have to ask you something." There was an urgency in Steve's voice that held her.

"Ask me what?"

"Tell me what you've heard about Mac and Emaline Pierce."

Julia was surprised by her fluttering pulse at the mention of a name she'd never heard. "Not a thing. Should I?"

"Yes."

She struggled to speak around the sudden anger that swelled her throat, hating that she had been attracted to Steve and flattered by his call.

Mac's words echoed: "Not a good friend" and she immediately regretted her hasty invitation.

"I don't want to hear about Mac and whomever, and certainly not from you."

"You're angry."

"Of course I am. You're trying to cause trouble."

"No, I'm not. I brought up Emaline out of genuine concern."

"Oh? Out of your friendship for Mac?" Julia didn't try to keep the ice out of her voice.

"I'm sure that by now you're aware that Mac and I aren't friends. It's just that I don't want you to get hurt."

"Why can't I seem to find it in my heart to thank you for your interest?"

She slammed down the receiver and stood in the silence, suddenly cold, her trembling hands clasped together; the trauma of the lightning strike two days before diminished by the doctor's news.

At last. The "whatever-it-was" she felt between Mac and herself finally bore a name. Emaline Pierce.

Julia slowly sank to the chair and glanced at her watch. It was seven-thirty. If she called Mac now, she would be late for her staff meeting. Mac would have to wait.

CHAPTER 7

AS FAR AS Julia was concerned, Sunday came much too quickly. Though the lightning strike had been a traumatic incident, the thought of finally meeting Mac's family loomed over her like a dark cloud.

As Mac pulled his Jeep up to the Square B's massive iron gate with a large block "B" welded in the middle, Julia's heart rate zoomed.

Though she had lived in Las Cruces for over a year, she hadn't met any of Mac's family. She supposed it was because her life centered around her job at Piñon Mesa Hospital and, as Mac had once mentioned, the Brantleys seldom left Hatch.

Julia sighed and hunched into her shoulders. It was too late to turn back. The white stucco hacienda, sprawling beneath a large stand of gnarled cottonwoods, lay ahead.

Mac pulled into the already crowded parking apron and slammed the Jeep to a stop behind a dusty black truck sporting a well-stocked gun rack in the back window.

"Too damn many vehicles in this family. There's never anyplace left to park."

Julia heard Mac's irritation and wondered if he was as nervous as she, but there was no time to ask.

She glanced down at her left hand to admire four slender lines of deepest turquoise bound together by hammered silver.

Under a full moon, dead white in a sapphire sky, Mac had slipped the ring on her finger saying, "This was my mother's."

He had blessed the tips of her fingers with his lips then found her mouth for a long, sweet kiss. "Now, at last, we are *Nizhoni*. In Navajo that means 'walking in beauty.'"

With that memory came a slight wrinkle of regret as Julia realized she would never know the woman who had first worn the engagement ring. Selma Brantley had been dead for some years, her abrupt end still a mystery.

Julia shook away the thought and ran her forefinger carefully across the smooth stones, unable to believe the sudden turn her life was taking.

What would the old-line Fairchilds of Sutton Place think if they could see their daughter at that very moment? Clad in denim down to rough-out work boots, her already lithe, long body defined by daily jogs along the high mesa. Her once-heavy mane of auburn replaced by a curly crown that glowed more gold than red.

Unchanged were her large tawny eyes that startled at first glance— tiger eyes.

The man responsible for the new direction in her life stood, hand extended, a Stetson covering his close-cropped sandy hair and most of his high forehead. The crinkles edging his soft azure eyes revealed humor, kindness and an awareness that had immediately drawn Julia to him.

Though Mac's eyes were his best feature, his hands ran a close second. They were powerfully sculpted, with prominent veins running across smooth tanned backs to long blunt fingers—perfect hands for a dedicated physician.

Mac had told her everything about his mother, and spoke with loving pride of his father, but his only mention of his brother, Frank, was that he had broken Selma Brantley's heart when he returned home from Arizona married to a Mexican several years his senior. A woman very pregnant with their only child, Allen.

Julia felt more than a little intimidated by this powerful Valley family. Everyone from Truth or Consequences to El Paso knew and respected the Brantleys; no one knew a thing about the Fairchilds of Sutton Place. She hated that she felt so insecure—doubly so, because there was no need. She had grown up surrounded by servants in a stately home on Manhattan's fashionable East Side, spent summers in a rambling clapboard "cottage" on Long Island, and sailed out of the most venerable yacht club on the North Shore. Then, too, she was a highly competent clinical psychologist with degrees from Wellesley and Harvard and had the added prestige of a short internship at Payne Whitney Psychiatric Hospital.

Mac helped her from the Jeep, then took her in his arms. "Hey, they're just people."

"I know. I know." She gave him a quick kiss. "Where to?"

He pointed toward a double door off the side verandah. "We're having cocktails in the library. But first." He grabbed her hand and led her down a gravel path lined with pampas grass.

After several steps Julia glanced back to see the verandah. Though the drop wasn't precipitous it was enough of a contrast to set the area apart.

The path turned and Mac squeezed her hand. "This is it. My secret place. Now it'll be ours."

Julia let out a small gasp. Before her was a dark pond filled with water lilies and to her surprise and delight a colony of goldfish darted here and there beneath the flat green pads.

"It's lovely. So peaceful." Julia looked into her fiancé's reassuring eyes, took a deep breath and drew herself tall. "Thank you for sharing this with me. It's exactly what I needed."

CHAPTER 8

AS THEY WALKED away from the pond and up the path, Julia recalled Mac's description of the room they were about to enter. Behind those thick adobe walls, cool tile floors gleamed in muted earth tones and deep leather chairs begged one to melt in their comfort.

Julia knew the room still evoked a jumble of emotions in Mac. The library was Selma Brantley's favorite haunt, where she could always be found reading, mending, or playing piano.

Those were the happy times. Too long gone for Mac to remember well and tainted by the shock of having discovered his mother's body in the very room he connected to her life.

The sound of the opening library door ended Julia's thoughts. She saw a rangy but stooped outline accompanied by a gruff and unceremonious, "You're late."

"Dad, this is Julia."

Mac's father started forward then stopped, mouth open, for a long, silent moment before he swept her into a fierce hug.

"Welcome, my dear. Welcome to our family."

Mr. Brantley led her into a brightly lit room and shoved her hand into that of an attractive, powerfully built man sporting a thatch of salt-and-pepper hair and transparent blue eyes.

"My oldest son, Frank." He clapped his arm around his son's shoulder and beamed.

Julia found herself standing toe to toe with a man who, after closer scrutiny, bore not the slightest resemblance to father or brother.

She wasn't the only one making an inspection. Frank's vulpine eyes were touring her face and body with the speed of an expert assessing a piece of horse flesh.

"Miss Fairchild." Frank's gruff voice echoed his hard eyes. "Seems Mac has brought home quite a prize."

Julia squelched her initial displeasure beneath a smile. "I'm pleased to meet you, Frank. Mac has said so many . . ."

Frank stepped out of the close quarters and gave a curt nod to the woman standing beside him. "My wife, Dolores. The love of my life." Sarcasm slithered through each word.

Dolores Brantley's quick response was brittle with malice. "How sweet, my precious."

The woman's cheeks were badly pitted, but uniform teeth sparkling between thick, sensuous lips, and large slightly upturned obsidian eyes gave a balance to her detraction, creating an offbeat, almost animal beauty.

Julia extended her hand to thin air as Dolores narrowed her eyes, stared past her and crooned to Mac's father, "The resemblance is truly remarkable."

He nodded. "Yes, isn't it? A few minutes ago when I saw her in the half-light, I thought . . ." He shrugged his shoulders apologetically. "Please forgive me, dear. But you remind me so much of my darling Selma." He pointed to the portrait above the fireplace.

Julia followed his gaze to a face that could easily have been the reflection she saw in the bathroom mirror each morning, except Selma Brantley was a stunning brunette with wide eyes, the same soft blue as Mac's.

He had told Julia of the resemblance when they met at Radium Springs and often referred to it. Still, she didn't expect to be a clone.

Julia was about to turn away when something stopped her. She cut her eyes to Frank, then to his father, then back to Selma's portrait. Frank's face was the same shape as his mother's—the same small ears set flat to his head—but bore not one characteristic of his father's. Was she the only one who saw it?

Frank broke the spell. "Enough of this worship service. Let's get on to the important part of the evening." He strutted to the bar and wheeled to give Julia a second piercing once-over, sending another unpleasant shiver to tour her body.

"Join me?"

Before she could answer, Mac stepped to her side. "I'll take care of Julia." His hand was at the small of her back steering her across the room to the hall.

"Let's hit the kitchen. My wine stash is in there. Besides, I want you to meet the most important person in the family."

They traveled down a dark wide hall, across a spacious dining room with a long bare table set for six, and finally through a broad swinging door into the aroma-filled kitchen.

On a wooden platform in front of an enormous black commercial gas stove was a small round brown woman dancing from pot to pot, stirring—sniffing—poking. Repeating each move so quickly she almost seemed a blur.

Mac lifted her screaming into the air. "You bad boy. Put me down. How can I ever get your dinner ready if you throw me around like this?"

A pleasant oval face peered around Mac's arm at Julia, then the woman gasped and made a poor attempt to cross herself.

Mac carefully placed the cook back on her makeshift stage and took her chubby hand in his. "No, Cuca, she isn't a ghost from our past."

He gathered Julia to him, eyes bright with love. "But she's the angel of my future. This is Doctor Julia Fairchild."

He motioned her forward. "Julia, this is Cuca, my second mother."

Julia had barely recovered from the encounter when the kitchen door swung wide to reveal a younger version of Frank Brantley except for Dolores's jet-black hair and eyes. Same build, same swagger, but the anger contorting his face blunted his dark good looks.

Mac swung to greet him. "Hey there, Nephew, it's good to see you."

The boy's frown broke momentarily then resumed. "Just came up from the barn. Last-minute look-see to make sure things were set up right for tomorrow, and damned if I'm not sent packing back here like some servant."

He held up an empty ice bucket and shoved it against Cuca's arm. "*Estupida*. Pop expects this bucket filled and on time."

Mac grabbed the bucket and jammed it back at his nephew. "Hey, boy. Can that attitude. Get the ice yourself. Cuca has enough to do."

Julia saw a flicker of resentment before Allen's patent-leather eyes darted to slide from her head to her toes. He addressed her in the same voice as his father's. "You must be the new . . ."

She held out her hand. "I suppose I am. And Julia will be just fine. I'm delighted to meet you, Allen."

One dark brow shot north as the young man bared his teeth in a wide grin that dripped with charm. He grabbed hers with his free hand and pumped. "Wow, Mac. She's a hottie."

As quickly as the tension developed, it evaporated. Cuca was back at her pots, humming and stirring, and Mac's arm was once again around her waist as they watched Allen saunter into a back room.

After a moment he returned, carrying the bucket brimming with ice cubes. "Don't stay out here too long. Grand Pop wants to make a toast." He eased past them to disappear through the swinging door.

Julia relaxed into her fiancé and forced a shaky, "That's everyone, isn't it?"

"Yes. Now you've met the whole 'fam damly.'" Mac's eyes darkened. "I'm sorry about Allen. Spoiled rotten from first breath. Bright as the devil but won't hear of college. Wants to be a chile farmer like his dad. Naturally, Frank is thrilled."

In contrast to its awkward beginning, the cocktail hour continued with reasonable civility. Even though Frank protested that he hated "sissy fizz," Cuca poured champagne for everyone and Mac's father made several toasts to the happy couple's future.

That done, the group made its way into the dining room, where Julia was seated to the right of her future father-in-law.

Dolores sniffed and slumped into the chair across from her, making it plain that she had been demoted and resented it.

During the first course of a steamy, spicy tortilla soup, Julia took time to observe each Brantley. Mac's father, with his craggy face and silver mane, was every bit the family scion and displayed a courtly manner, a pleasant echo of his Virginia forebears.

Frank's heritage remained a puzzle, but Dolores was an enigma—dark, coarse and angry but displaying an edgy humor, which Frank immediately put down. It seemed as though they were frozen in some timeless dispute so deeply embedded in their past it could never be resolved.

Allen, the classic disaffected teen, played the unhappy role of a child trapped in the middle of his parents' war. He kept his face flat with boredom most of the evening, signaling his departure from the conversation by eyeing the massive wrought-iron chandelier above.

Throughout the rest of the meal an underlying tension pervaded the room, causing the conversation to spurt and suddenly come to a halt until someone thought to begin again. Even Cuca's succulent chiles rellenos failed to ease the strain.

After one long lull, broken only by the sounds of silver meeting china, Mac's father patted Julia's arm, raised his glass and spoke. "Tonight is not only special because we welcome a new member to our family and eagerly anticipate your wedding, but, as everybody at this table knows, it's planting time. At first light tomorrow, ten trucks filled with contract workers will arrive."

Dolores nodded. "We're ready. The tables are set up for breakfast, and as soon as the men hit the fields we'll clear and prepare for lunch."

Frank drained his wine glass and reached for the bottle. "And the seeds are all set to go."

Mr. Brantley nodded. "Only the best. Right, Frank?"

"You got it, Pop." He looked to Julia. "We take the seeds from the best peppers grown last year and that's what we'll be planting tomorrow. That way the crop gets better and better."

Allen suddenly came to life. "Yeah, if we don't get pounded by hail the size of golf balls, or if the chile-wilt doesn't creep on the fruit or if the bees don't cross-pollinate from the field down the road. Hell, if nothing like that happens, raising chile's a snap."

There was a dead silence as every head swerved toward the boy. Dolores crossed herself and mumbled some incantation and Frank drained his full wine glass, but the elder Brantley's low laugh eased the moment.

"Everything you say is true, Allen, and no telling what might happen this summer. But let's not forget our little ace in the hole south of Old Mesilla. Red Stone Pecan Grove has been our cash cow for over fifty years."

Frank raised his glass. "I'll drink to that. And some day—well, anyway, here's to Red Stone."

"Hear, hear," Dolores and Allen chimed in as Julia and Mac raised their glasses.

Mr. Brantley scowled at Frank and his family, then slowly raised his glass.

Julia waited a moment to break the awkward silence, then turned to Mac. "Did you tell your father about the latest outbreak of Hantavirus?"

Mac nodded his relief. "We're afraid we might be fighting an epidemic in the Four Corners."

For the next few minutes Mac described the mysterious flu-like illness that had already killed twelve and threatened the lives of seven others.

"The problem is most of our victims are young adults under thirty who have been healthy up until the symptoms strike. They come down with a cough, muscle aches and a high fever and the lungs fill so quickly, there's no way we can save them."

Allen put his hand to his throat. "I knew it. I'm sure I got it."

Mac shook his head. "Let's hope you don't. It's not a pretty death."

His father interrupted. "I'm not going to put up with this kind of talk. This is supposed to be a celebration."

Mr. Brantley patted Julia's hand for the third time in as many minutes. He had downed several glasses of Port in quick succession and Julia noticed his words were slurred and his eyes rheumy.

"Your resemblance to her is . . ."

The old man shook his head as his eyes filled. "If only my Selmie could be here." He grasped Julia's hand in his massive, rough paw. "What a shock. Seeing you like that. All soft . . . soft like my . . ." He lowered his head as his shoulders began to heave.

Dolores jumped up. "Frank. Allen. Do something."

Father and son helped Mr. Brantley to his feet and started to move him out of the room.

He briefly resisted, turning toward Julia. "Will you kindly accept the apologies of a brokenhearted old man?"

Julia read the sadness in his eyes and felt tears at the back of her own. "Of course. Of course. Thank you for the lovely evening. I'll see you soon."

CHAPTER 9

THE THIRTY-MINUTE ride from Hatch to Julia's townhouse in the Missions development was silent for the most part except for her question about Red Stone Grove. "You never mentioned your family was in pecans."

"We're not. I mean, not on a day-to-day basis. The grove is handled by a large Texas producer."

"When Frank made that toast, I couldn't help but notice your father. What was all that about?"

"You don't miss a thing, do you?"

"Well, it was hard to miss the expression on his face."

"Dad's always been a little funny about that grove. In one way he treasures it because it brought my mother to him. But for some reason he hates it just as hard.

"It belonged to my maternal grandfather's brother, Sterling Allen. When he died suddenly Joel Allen moved Mom and her mother to Las Cruces. Bad news is they had a head-on just outside of Marfa, Texas, and though Mom was thrown free, both parents were killed.

"My dad helped her settle the estate and they fell in love. Frank is positive he and Dolores will inherit Red Stone."

"That seems fair since Frank is the oldest."

"True, but Dad has devoted his life to developing the very finest chiles in New Mexico and he's afraid Frank will let the chile farming slide in favor of the pecans." Mac let out a long breath. "And he's right; the grove is such a money machine, Frank wouldn't have to lift a finger for the rest of his life."

Julia focused on the white median dashes flashing past. Something didn't quite add up. Frank was Selma's child, but plainly the son of another man. Why didn't she insist her property be left to him? After all, Frank was her firstborn.

Mac walked Julia to the front door, then took her in his arms. "Want some company?" Then his lips asked the same question.

Julia wanted him. She desperately needed his physical reassurance to make the evening seem right. Instead she said, "I would love it, but tomorrow is a heavy day. There's the usual staff meeting and new patient presentation. As a rule we have only one, but tomorrow I've scheduled two."

"I understand." Mac's voice, filled with concern, was soft against her ear. "Are you okay? My family's pretty hard to take."

"Your father's a love and the others were just fine—especially Cuca."

"You mean it?" She heard his relief at her acceptance.

"Yes. Really. Now go." Julia gave Mac a gentle shove, afraid if he stayed a minute longer she'd give in.

She waited until the Jeep's motor faded, then sighed. In just a little under two months, on the first Saturday in May, she would exchange wedding vows beneath a stand of cottonwoods on the bank of the Rio Grande.

Julia peered down at the Navajo ring, remembering how her heart somersaulted when Mac slid it on her finger.

Raised to expect a diamond solitaire from Tiffany, with a lavish wedding at St. Bartholomew's on Park Avenue, it gave her a start each time she saw the opaque blue mineral confined by silver etched in totems.

She remembered when she met Mac, eight months before at an outdoor dance in Radium Springs. A full midsummer moon silhouetted the tall man standing before her. When he asked her to dance, she moved into his arms to be surrounded by the redolent smells of hay and starched cotton. She felt so comfortable in his embrace that she closed her eyes and let herself flow with him.

When the music finally stopped, they were alone under an arbor on one side of the building and he whispered, "Check that moon. It's pure magic."

She didn't look at the moon but into Mac's eyes, as their lips met for the first time.

Julia set aside her treasured memory. In the beginning, their relationship seemed so simple—just the two of them wrapped in each other's love, facing a hope-filled future together.

But now there were the Brantleys to consider. Mac's family, so different from hers. A family riddled with petty jealousies and animosities that were more than evident at dinner. A dinner so foreign to the evenings Julia was used to.

She missed the forest-green dining room where elegant meals were served on crisp linen set with glittering china and crystal. She missed the intelligent conversations. At that moment she ached to be back in New York.

And this woman Emaline Pierce.

Steve Duke's words echoed, "Tell me what you've heard about Mac and Emaline Pierce."

A chill rolled through her. What had Emaline meant to Mac?

CHAPTER 10

EMALINE PIERCE stared north across the Golden Gate toward Sausalito. From her office on the thirty-second floor she enjoyed an unlimited view of San Francisco Bay, its electric blue spotted with white sails. It was a gloriously clear day, one made even more agreeable by the exit of the three-day marine layer of fog that shrouded her windows.

Her father, "Big Ed" Pierce, was shouting through the phone. "I thought I told you to get back here, Emmy."

She grimaced at his use of his pet name for her. He used it only when he wanted something, and now that she was one of the most successful real estate agents in San Francisco it hardly seemed proper.

"I hear you, Daddy, but I just can't drop everything and come home."

"This is an emergency. I can't believe you're going to let that choice piece of beef walk out of your life and into the arms of some Yankee bitch."

Emaline's heart skipped a beat at the thought of Mac Brantley. Though his face was hard with anger the last time she saw Mac, he had belonged to her since they were children, and until this very moment she was positive he always would.

"It's impossible to do anything now. I'm in the middle of a huge shopping center deal."

"You and that damn career. What a waste. You're more interested in some dad-blamed piece of property than in planning a wedding to the man of your dreams. If you have to run something, come home and run Pierce Pecans."

She laughed. "But Dad, you're running Pierce Pecans and there's not room for both of us."

Her father's voice filled with excitement. "Did your mama tell you I finally got Ben Barney's grove? Took me almost forty years but I just bided my time. Now, we own every pecan tree in the Lower Rio Grande Valley except for Red Stone."

"Congratulations on the Barney tract. You're one patient man." Emaline swiveled back to the Golden Gate, suddenly glad she was distanced from her too-small family. Even now, after years of separation, she hated the thought of facing her father again. So much had happened in the past, and to think of it was still too painful.

Ed's voice came back to entreat, "It doesn't mean a thing without Red Stone Grove. I'd hoped maybe . . . come home, Emmy. Come home and put a stop to this ridiculous move Mac Brantley is making."

Emaline sighed, wishing her father were a little less transparent. For some unexplained reason Ed Pierce was sure Red Stone Grove would go to Mac and had pushed for an alliance as soon as they started dating.

"I wish that were all there is to it, but it's plain Mac doesn't feel the same way about me . . . anymore."

"It's just because you got your feathers ruffled and flew the coop. You lived with him for a year. The least he could do is make an honest woman out of you."

Before Emaline could lodge a protest against his chauvinism, her father took another tack. "Your mama and I just want what's best for you, and we both think that's a life with Mac Brantley."

"It's too late."

"No. No it isn't." His voice was back at full decibel strength. "There's a party for Mac and this lady in a couple of weeks. The Sandovals are giving it out at Radium Springs. I'd be willing to bet once he lays eyes on you, she'll be put out to pasture in no time."

"Sandoval? The administrator at Piñon Mesa Hospital?" Emaline had heard the name before, but she couldn't recall exactly how.

"Yep. This Fairchild's some sort of shrink out there."

"Oh?" Emaline's heart plunged as she realized her rival shared a lot more in common with Mac than she did. Mac would heal the Indians and this woman would fix their psyches. It was too, too perfect for words.

Ed plowed on. "And Emmy, there's one more thing. This gal's the spitting image of Selma Brantley, except for the flaming red hair."

"She's a redhead?" Another sliver of uneasiness nudged its way into Emaline's already wobbling self-confidence.

"I'm telling you, she's real competition. You better come home and protect your assets."

Emaline knew she was doomed. Her father would continue to call until she capitulated. "I'll try."

Ed paused, then played the trump card. "Trying won't do it. Selma Brantley's ring is already on that woman's finger. What we need here is a desperate measure."

Emaline flinched. She had coveted that ring from the first moment she saw it glinting in the afternoon sun as she, Mac, and his mother shared a summer lemonade in the gazebo next to the fish pond Selma Brantley had built as a refuge.

Emaline had asked to try it on—a cheeky request for a ten-year-old. And though the refusal was polite enough, Emaline knew in that instant that Selma Brantley didn't like her and never would.

After that, she received no more invitations to visit the hacienda. And even though Mac tried to cover up by insisting he'd rather play at the barns, Emaline realized she had made an enemy. When Mac's mother died several years later, it was the best news she'd ever heard.

"Are you there?" Her father's gravelly voice pulled her to the present.

"I hear you, Daddy. I'll see what I can do about taking some time off. I promise."

CHAPTER 11

EMALINE PUT the receiver down, sat back in her chair and shut her eyes. The last time she saw Mac he was leaning against the front post of the little house they had shared for almost a year. She had shouted, "I won't be back."

He had shouted, "Thank God for that."

Those were the last words they spoke.

Had her stubborn refusal to accept Mac's new career cost a future with him? Had she been too involved in her own budding real estate career in Las Cruces to give the wall rising between them the attention it needed?

Mac's announcement that he was giving up his share of a well-established medical practice to join the Indian Health Service had thrown them into a pitched battle.

To her mind, Mac's bright future was about to dissolve into a thankless, low-paying job with no prestige. Worse still, he'd be gone for days, even weeks at a time, and with little or no access to a phone.

Emaline tried reasoning, then cajoling, then arguing, and in a last desperate move she dragged Mac to bed, but even their lovemaking became a contest of wills. Finally, when she saw that she couldn't win, she ran.

While attending Stanford, Emaline worked at the Palo Alto branch of a major real estate firm based in San Francisco. After graduation she refused their offer to take a spot with the firm, but when she called to say she was available they took her immediately.

During the next several years Emaline became one of the major money earners and was honored by being asked to join the prestigious Realtor's Roundtable. Her elation was short-lived when she realized there was no one special to share her triumph with.

Now this. Just as she had been almost ready to return to Las Cruces, settle down and bear the children she knew Mac craved. It never occurred to her that he wouldn't wait.

"Oh, Frank. Did I wait too long?" The sound of her voice startled her. She uttered the unutterable. All visions of Mac faded at the sound of Frank Brantley's name.

Emaline closed her eyes to replay the morning of her fourteenth birthday. She had ridden her horse Ahab from her ranch to the Square B in search of Mac but was thrilled to find his handsome older brother, Frank, slouched on the top rung of the wooden fence of the Brantley corral. She had been attracted to Frank from the first moment they met and was heartbroken when he returned home trailing a pregnant Mexican wife.

When Emaline learned that Dolores had tricked Frank into marrying her, she hated her rival even more.

But that day, when she turned fourteen, everything changed.

She watched Frank ease his taut, well-honed body off the railing. "Your boyfriend's gone."

She hitched her shoulders back to show off the new curves she had acquired during the spring and lowered her voice. "Who said I came to see him?"

"Didn't you?" Frank grabbed the reins and reached for her hand to help her down. When she landed beside him, he held her to him and her legs had turned to rubber as unaccustomed warmth rushed between them.

"I hear it's your birthday."

She wanted to make some smart reply, but her heart was pounding so, she couldn't answer.

Frank pushed her away a little as his silvery eyes traveled over her. "All grown up now, aren't you?"

"I guess so." She seemed to be throbbing in every part of her body, even parts that had never throbbed before.

Then they moved inside the barn and she was in Frank's arms, his mouth mining hers, his hands sliding around her rump to lift her to him.

He moved her slowly toward the tack room and pushed her onto the rough blanket covering an old iron cot that squeaked with each move they made.

First her shirt disappeared, then her bra, then her jeans, but she didn't care. Frank's mouth was covering each part of her willing body, bringing sensations she had only dreamed about.

Emaline knew "something else" was going to happen. That same "something else" that had happened so long ago.

She shoved away the frightening memory in her eagerness to have it happen again. She must move against Frank to make it happen—yes that was it. For a moment there was no sound other than Frank's rapid breathing, as she suspended in air, then met ecstasy again.

The afternoon following her birthday Emaline initiated an unwitting Mac, taking him as ruthlessly as Frank had taken her. Through the years Mac never questioned her widening experience since she had always been the leader. Together they practiced each new move she learned from Frank and it wasn't long before Mac became her slave just as she was his brother's.

It really wasn't Mac's decision to give up his practice that drove them apart. Frank Brantley was the problem. She had belonged to Frank ever since that first encounter, allowing him to take her whenever he wanted, and until she was about to go away to college she had deluded herself into believing Frank would leave Dolores.

As a present for her graduation from high school, Frank took a room in a small Juarez hotel for the night. It would be the first time they would spend an entire evening together, and he promised a night she would never forget.

Emaline was finally able to sneak away using a friend's invitation to a slumber party for a cover, and the evening was everything Frank promised until Emaline drank too much champagne and begged him to divorce his wife.

To her dismay Frank waffled, saying it was against his religion, and she had sobbed he was a coward to blame the Church.

Only then did he admit that Dolores had threatened to leave him and take his son with her if there ever was a divorce. He took Emaline in his arms and begged her to try to understand that he was trapped and wouldn't be free as long as Dolores lived.

Years later Emaline would learn the truth about Dolores's hold on Frank, but that night, as she lay in his arms, she made the decision to settle for second best. When the time came, a marriage to Mac would at least give her father access to Red Stone Grove and she would live only yards away from the man she truly loved.

CHAPTER 12

JULIA'S DAY TURNED out to be as frustrating as her sleepless night. Mac had called before sunrise to say he was headed to Albuquerque this morning to meet with the CDC on the Hantavirus outbreak and her afternoon schedule, which seemed so bare the week before, was completely filled.

It was past six and Julia was just shutting the door behind her last patient when the telephone buzzed. She quickly checked her watch, positive it would be Mac calling from Albuquerque.

Her brow puckered at the sound of Dolores Brantley's voice. "Julia? Could you come out to the Square B tomorrow? Since it looks like you're going to join the family for sure, I'd like to get to know you a little better."

Julia hesitated. "Oh, dear. I'm really busy this whole week. Could we wait a bit on this?"

There was a long silence on the other end, then, "I don't think we can. I'll see you tomorrow around four."

JULIA'S STOMACH tightened when her Range Rover passed through the big gate to the hacienda. She took a deep breath to dispel the anxiety compounded by Dolores's abrupt and discourteous summons. If that woman thought she was going to hold all the cards, she was sadly mistaken. No time like the present to establish the proper boundaries.

Cuca opened one of the sky-blue front doors and bustled her into the large living room, where a small blaze crackled in the fireplace.

"The Señora is coming. Please. Sit." Cuca motioned her to a chair and disappeared.

Julia peered up at the ceiling of dark massive logs supported by smaller wooden crosspieces.

"Vigas and latillas," she whispered to no one, pleased that she was retaining some of the vocabulary of New Mexican architecture.

The furniture in the room was contemporary, but the smooth white stucco walls featured several fine religious paintings on tin flanked by several fine wooden crosses.

The chests placed about the room were old, probably Spanish if she read the provenance correctly.

How different this was from her family home in Manhattan, where high ceilings were bordered in crown molding and Scalamandré drapes puddled on either side of tall, narrow windows.

Julia rose to study the nearest artifact and noticed a small door opening into a greenhouse attached to the outside of the living room wall.

She was almost to the door when Dolores's voice stopped her. "Julia. Welcome. Please, won't you join me?"

The two women sat in silence for a moment, each contemplating the other. Today Dolores seemed softer, somehow more relaxed, and in response Julia followed suit.

Her hostess smiled tentatively. "I'm afraid Frank and I behaved rather rudely the other evening and I want to apologize."

Julia shook her head. "There's no . . ."

"Oh, but there is." Dolores paused, then continued. "It seems our little family's forgotten how to behave in front of strangers. We seldom meet new people and our close friends have come to overlook our bad manners."

Cuca's return with the tea tray gave Julia a moment to reappraise Dolores. She had sized her up as a probable adversary, but in the light of her latest statement Julia felt a surge of hope.

"I appreciate your telling me this. I must confess I was a little uncomfortable at first."

Dolores took a sip of the steaming liquid. "I guess Mac told you that Frank's and my marriage isn't exactly perfect."

"No. He hasn't discussed the family much."

"That's because he bolted as soon as his mother died. He hated that I took over his mother's bedroom so soon after her death. Frankly, Mac has never been very fond of me."

"Oh, I'm sure that's not . . ."

Dolores waved aside Julia's attempt to cover for her fiancé. "Don't even try. I know exactly where I stand in this family. Mrs. B would have cashiered me the minute she saw me and my bulging belly, but I have to say, Mister Brantley was wonderful to me from the very beginning. Oh, by the way, thank you for being so sweet to him the other evening. He tends to drink a bit too much whenever he thinks of Mrs. B, and Port makes him a little maudlin."

Dolores picked up her cup, then sat back. "Now, tell me about yourself."

"Not much to tell. Born and raised in Manhattan. College at Wellesley. Master's in Clinical Psychology at Harvard and a stint at Payne Whitney Psychiatric. I came here to escape a romance gone sour and because my biological father lives in Juarez I wanted to get acquainted with him."

Dolores sat up. "Your father? He lives in Juarez?"

Bits and pieces of her mother's tearful and shocking confession replayed. An unhappy first marriage—anxious to end it. Had gone to Juarez, Mexico, where once a person could get a divorce in one day. Her Mexican attorney Jorge Perez-Gasca had been very attractive— very charming. Somehow they ended up in her hotel room.

Dolores's voice filtered through the painful recall. "Did I hear you right? Your father lives in Juarez?"

Julia nodded. "Yes. He's a prominent attorney there. His name is Jorge Perez-Gasca."

"You're a Latina?" The shock on Dolores's face was almost humorous.

"Well—yes. Now that you mention it, I suppose part of me is."

"Can you beat that? A sister under the skin." Dolores slapped her thigh and guffawed.

The blood traveled up Julia's neck to flood her face as she realized how embarrassed she was to admit the truth about Lucia Fairchild's one "slight indiscretion."

Ten years, two degrees and an internship later, Julia had come west to escape her mother's stifling domination and a love affair gone bad. The magnet that had drawn her to the El Paso area was the desire to reconnect with her birth-father.

Though their blossoming relationship was one of two adults with separate pasts, until that moment Julia never really considered herself to be Perez-Gasca's daughter. To her mind she was an Easterner, an Episcopalian and a Brahmin with all the attendant pedigrees.

"Have I made you uncomfortable?" Dolores's voice shattered her thoughts.

Julia jerked her head up. "Oh, no. Not in the least."

"What a hoot. In spite of their differences, Mac and Frank do seem to have the same inclinations."

Julia, filled with too many mixed emotions to properly sort them out, diffused the electricity of the moment. "I consider that a compliment coming from you."

"And I meant it as one," Dolores said. "You're okay, Julia Fairchild. No wonder Mac's so smitten." She bent forward. "I must confess, I never thought he'd fall again."

"Again?" It was Julia's turn to come to attention as Emaline Pierce's name echoed. At last here was someone who would tell her everything she needed to know.

But before Julia could form the first question, Dolores jumped up. "Would you like to see my babies?"

"Babies?"

"My plants."

"Well, yes. I suppose." Julia reluctantly put down her cup and rose to follow.

The damp warmth of the greenhouse felt like a mountain leaning against her lungs. "My goodness, it's warm in here."

"My babies can't live without the moisture." Dolores stopped in front of a potted plant bearing purple-black berries. "This is Azuncena de Mejico. Do you know it?"

Julia went cold in spite of the oppressive heat. "Can't say that I do."

"Does 'Deadly Nightshade' strike a bell?"

Julia shrugged.

"How about Belladonna?"

"I've heard of that."

"Yes. Lot's of poisons can be beneficial when used correctly."

Dolores caressed the leaves of each plant she named. "This is Banewort, and this . . . Jimson Weed. Do you like flowers?"

"I'm afraid I have a brown thumb. My only achievement is a poor corn plant that's struggling along in my front hall."

"Too bad. I thought we might have something else in common."

At another table, Dolores pointed to tiny pale-green shoots just pushing out of dark loam. "But these are my real love. Orchids. Finicky creatures. The seeds are almost microscopic and are the devil to coax to life."

"All these plants are so . . . exotic. What made you choose them?"

"I have to have something to occupy the long days. The Las Cruces ladies haven't seen fit to include me, not that I give a damn, and frankly, the men of the family don't pay me much attention anymore."

Dolores stared away for a moment, then sighed. "Well, enough of my depressing story. Let's get out of here."

She led Julia through the plants and back to the living room, where she took a quick sip of her tea. "Would you like to see the rest of the house?"

Julia followed Dolores toward the wide central hall.

"Old lady Brantley designed this place. Used the Southwestern Territorial for the exterior and this shotgun hall plan for the interior. She brought the idea with her from Louisiana along with her damned chicory coffee." Dolores laughed. "That's one more thing I don't miss."

They stopped in front of a large high-ceilinged room dominated by a dark mahogany four-poster.

"This is my room."

"It's lovely," Julia murmured. Mac had told her all about his mother's room and how Dolores insisted it be kept in its original state: pale-green walls, filmy sheers, light streaming in through slatted blinds. The only heaviness was in the furniture Selma brought with her from Louisiana.

"Mac says you've kept it just like his mother decorated it."

"Yes, I have. Even though she hated me, the old lady dripped class. No reason not to give the bitch her due. I really kept it like this for Mister B. I often find him in here. Sitting in that rocker, staring into space. Guess he gets comfort from it."

"He must miss her terribly."

"That was pretty obvious the other evening. I'm sure Mac's told you Mrs. B and I fought like crazy. It always seemed like I caused the trouble, but she was clever as hell. So damn subtle. Mac and Mister B think she hung the moon, but she wasn't all that . . ."

Dolores waved toward the other doors at the end of the hall. "The men's quarters. Not very interesting."

Julia remembered Mac saying how sudden his mother's death was and how helpless and alone he felt, unable to carry out his gut feel that her death was never properly explained.

Worse still, Dolores had moved into his mother's room the very day of her funeral. He made no mention of Frank's accommodations, but it seemed from Dolores's last statement that all the men roomed together.

"Mac's mother died of a heart attack?"

Dolores nodded and snapped her fingers. "Just like that. What a shock. But it was awful for Mac. He was his mama's favorite."

"Mac thinks she might have died from other causes."

"Oh? Really?" Dolores stopped and slowly turned. When she spoke, her voice was hard. "That damn Frank. Used to tell Mac I poisoned his mama. I guess it was just his sick way of covering up his own grief. If anything killed Selma Brantley it was her addiction to chiles."

Julia nodded. Mac had told her of his mother's weakness for the flat green fruit and her insistence that her daily intake was purely for the medicinal benefits from the capsaicin. Whatever the reason, from mid-August through September, Mac's mother and Cuca roasted sack after sack of Nu Mex Six chiles so the family would have enough to last the year.

"Mrs. B died the day after Labor Day," Dolores said. "The afternoon before, she'd been in the kitchen 'pickin' peppers' as she called it. Unfortunately she often ate as many Sixes as she peeled. She just couldn't help herself."

Julia laughed. "I've never heard of a chile addict."

"You have now. Anyway she ate a whole bunch that day and Mac found her body the next morning. There was no autopsy, but the doc assured the family it was her heart."

"Did she have a history of heart problems?"

Dolores's face darkened. "Are you playing detective or something?"

"Oh, not at all. It's just a hangover from my training. Clinical psychologists are supposed to ask a lot of questions."

"I see." Dolores thought a moment. "It all happened so fast. Poor Mister B. Poor Mac."

Julia remembered the sadness in Mac's eyes as he told her about the dark morning he had come suddenly out of a nightmare, washed in sweat, his heart threatening to leave his body. How something had drawn him down the dark hall to his mother's room to see her empty bed, its twisted covers trailing across the floor. How he hurried to the library, where he found Selma Brantley sprawled across her favorite chair, her hand at her throat, her unseeing eyes still wide with fright.

"That whole experience must have been terrible for him," Julia whispered.

Dolores nodded. "I guess he's never gotten over it."

The two women stood face-to-face until Dolores broke her gaze and motioned Julia toward the front of the house.

Julia hurried behind, thinking they would finish their tea and she would have the chance to ask about Emaline Pierce, but instead of entering the living room Dolores headed for the front door.

She smiled as she opened it. "Thank you so much for coming. I really enjoyed our little chat."

"Yes. So did I." Julia made a quick detour to the living room to retrieve her purse, then slid past Dolores and into the sunshine.

Julia was halfway down the long lane before she realized Dolores's intention was to pump her for information, but when the subject changed to Selma Brantley she had been sent on her way.

CHAPTER 13

MAC WHEELED his Jeep into the last guest space in the Piñon Mesa Hospital parking lot. After Julia's strained introduction to his family the Sunday before, he felt an urgent need to nourish the bond between them.

There was little time to make up for Frank and his family's obvious hostility at dinner. The emergency meeting with the CDC in Albuquerque had lasted longer than expected and even though he phoned almost every night and Julia had sounded delighted to hear his voice, Mac sensed his fiancée's reserve on the other end of the line.

He was about to open the car door when he saw Bob Sandoval, the administrator of Piñon Mesa, emerge from the main building. He first met Bob at a medical conference in Albuquerque shortly after he had joined the Health Service, and over time Bob and his wife, Myrtle, a pretty, round-faced blonde, had become Mac's surrogate family, eventually filling the void created by Emaline's bolt to San Francisco.

At first Myrtle tried to fix him up with a few dates, but when none seemed to take, Mac begged off, saying he really didn't have time for women. He meant it, or at least he thought he did, until Christmas Day the year before.

That particular Christmas morning had begun like all the others since his mother's death. The ritual tree and presents no longer started the day. Instead the family rose just in time to greet guests for the traditional Open House featuring Selma Brantley's famous egg nog. It was a Hatch and Las Cruces "must do" and had been for close to fifty years.

After the last guests departed, Cuca reset the dining room table and the family rejoined for the usual mid-afternoon feast of roast suckling pig, smothered quail and their favorite side dish of posole.

Mac had never quite understood his sudden urge to leave the rest of the Brantleys, still seated around the table enjoying hot puffy sopapillas dripping with wild honey. Or why he had driven north to the Elephant Butte Reservoir instead of to the Sandovals' cocktail party. Or what prompted him to turn down that particular overlook. But there, at the end of the road, was a Range Rover. And in that car, sound asleep, was almost a carbon copy of his mother.

Mac stared through the raised window to memorize every inch of that face: long auburn lashes fringing closed eyes, heavy hair glowing gold-red in the low winter sun, full lips slightly parted, begging to be kissed. And, for the first time since Emaline Pierce had left his bed, he yearned to oblige that silent invitation.

Several months passed before Mac tracked Julia down. The day after the encounter at Elephant Butte he had departed for his winter circuit of the various tribes and stayed away from Las Cruces until mid-April.

Even though he had begun his search in earnest, he ran into several dead ends before mentioning the mysterious redhead to Bob Sandoval. Mac couldn't believe it when Bob laughed and told him there was no problem—he knew exactly who the woman was and where to find her.

But before Mac could meet Julia, an emergency in the Four Corners had taken him north for another two months of duty at the reservation hospital, Chaco Point. He returned the day before the July dance at Radium Springs.

Bob Sandoval's rap on his window startled Mac out of his reverie and he grinned up at his friend. Sandoval smiled back beneath his dark, neatly trimmed moustache. "Coming to see your sweetheart?"

"Sure am." Mac eased out of the Jeep. "Julia and I are looking forward to your party at Radium Springs next Saturday. You and Myrt are great to do this for us."

Bob's face flushed with excitement. "It's our pleasure. Can you believe everybody we invited accepted? I expect this little shindig'll be remembered for some years to come."

The man lowered his eyes and cleared his throat a couple of times. "Say, Mac, Ed Pierce called last night and . . ."

He took a deep breath and squared his shoulders before he launched on, "He asked if they could bring Emaline. Seems she's going to be coming in from San Francisco for the weekend and poor Myrt—"

Mac clapped his friend on the shoulder. "No problem at all. As far as I'm concerned, Emaline and I are history."

Bob's relief was immediate. "Boy, am I glad to hear you say that. You know Myrt and I wouldn't ever do anything . . . well, anyway, the party should be fun. Got a great band coming over from Silver City and Myrt's all puffed over that. Better get on my appointed rounds. See you."

Mac watched Bob walk away, then leaned against the Jeep.

Emaline.

At the first mention of her name the old familiar tingle marched through his body and he closed his eyes to see the lively dark-haired girl-child who could out-ride, out-shoot and sometimes even win the arm wrestles.

They had been best buddies until the summer of Emaline's fourteenth birthday, the day she changed from a tomboy into a woman. At least it seemed that way to him. One minute they had been playing Army Scout amid the cow barns, and the next Emaline was planting her first awkward kisses on his surprised lips as her hand found his crotch and she guided his to the warmth between her legs.

He replayed that stifling August afternoon when the horses had gone without their brushing down and fresh pail of water while Emaline had coaxed him up to the suffocating hayloft and dragged him reluctantly into manhood.

Mac took a deep breath and slowly let it out to ease the embarrassing rush that memory brought. Emaline was coming back into his life. Too soon. He needed more time.

He looked across the broad mesa to the foothills of the Organ Mountains suddenly thankful he and Julia would have this evening together. He wanted to tell her about Emaline before anyone else did.

When she mentioned having tea with Dolores, he'd held his breath. Dolores was just spiteful enough to drag Emaline out and parade her by Julia, but when the conversation ended without any reference to his past, he was sure he had been given a small reprieve.

Filled with sudden urgency, Mac strode toward the Piñon Mesa Hospital office complex of desert-brown two-story buildings surrounding a quadrangle landscaped with mesquite trees and quiet pools.

He headed for the sidewalk to Julia's building and covered the steps in one bound.

Mac knocked on the open door of Julia's waiting room. "Hi Phyllis, is the doc done?"

His answer was the door opening to Julia's office and a large woman towing a small boy brushing past him and down the hall.

Mac moved quickly to the entry and stopped to take in the view. Julia was bent over the desk writing in a chart, but all he saw was her crown of feathery copper haloed in a shaft of sunlight.

He crossed the room and bent to capture his first kiss in what seemed like an eternity. "Hey there."

"Hey, yourself." Julia stood and lifted her lips to welcome his.

Mac inhaled her essence, willing it to invade his whole being as Julia's breath quickened in response and her arms drew tight around him as their mouths met again.

"When did you get back?" She murmured against his neck.

"Late last night. Too late to call."

"It's never too late to hear your voice. You know that." She snuggled against him. "I've missed you. I have needs to be met—a nagging problem with my libido."

Mac laughed. "Well then, I'm just what the doctor ordered."

The words were barely out of his mouth when his beeper beeped. He looked at the number and sighed. "I was hoping I was off the hook. It's Albuquerque. That can only mean trouble."

CHAPTER 14

STEVE DUKE wound his way through the festive crowd toward the bar to order his second beer. As the four-piece band struck up Jerry Jeff Walker's "Redneck Mother," he checked his watch. Seven-thirty and not a sign of the "happy couple."

He was anxious to see Julia, but seeing her meant reviving his long-time rivalry with Mac Brantley. It still rankled that Mac had bested him each time they had gone head-to-head. Steve lost captain of the basketball team to Mac and was edged out as Editor-in-Chief of the *Bull Dog*. Worse still, though he and Mac had both been Merit Scholars there was only one basketball scholarship to the University of New Mexico available. Steve had counted on that as an escape from his abusive alcoholic father, but Mac the rich bastard had gotten it. And then there was Emaline.

Steve took a swig of his beer, concentrating on the frosty sparkle as it swished over his tongue. He waved to a familiar couple, then turned toward the entrance where the Sandovals stood greeting the arriving guests. A long line of cars still streamed toward the parking lot. Maybe there was still a chance to make amends, if only he could get to Julia in time.

When he saw the Sandovals again, Steve almost choked. Behind the couple the Sandovals were greeting stood the Pierces and Emaline.

Steve warmed at seeing Emaline's mother. Palatia Pierce, though in her late fifties, was a strikingly beautiful woman who bore the serene grace of her Amerind ancestors.

He would always be grateful to Palatia. She had saved him the day her snippy daughter left him standing in the kitchen holding a pathetic offering of sage and wildflowers. He was sure she remembered how the afternoon ended—and the many other afternoons they shared during his senior year in high school—he did.

When Mac received the cherished basketball scholarship, Steve realized that a stint in the service would be his only ticket to a higher education and headed for the nearest Army recruiter.

His interest in medicine pushed him to the medical corps, and it was there that he developed a taste and skill for triage. After serving the required stint, he headed for the University of New Mexico, this time backed by the GI Bill.

It was easy to pick up the relationship with Palatia, who came to Albuquerque for a visit whenever she could, and after they made love she would share the latest Las Cruces gossip.

Steve worked hard to cram four years into two and a half and graduated on schedule with his class. His father had been long dead when he was accepted into medical school, so Palatia was the only one he told—she was the only one who cared. She never talked about her husband or her daughter but offered Steve encouragement when he was low and praise when he succeeded.

Even now, he could hear her soft voice as her breath tickled his ear. "I'll always be here for you, my darling. All you have to do is pick up the phone."

They hadn't been together for years but the sight of her filled him with a rush of warmth. Palatia Pierce taught him what caring for someone else could mean. She had given him that gift and asked for nothing in return.

He couldn't help but glimpse Emaline, who was standing between her parents, and knew she wouldn't be glad to see him. Why was she here? Not six months before, she told him it was all over with Mac. Why would she want to put herself through the torture of seeing her old lover with his fiancée?

Steve had attended a medical seminar in San Francisco, called Emaline and was gratified when she seemed pleased to hear from him. After a drink at her apartment, they had shared a long, winy dinner trading memories and compliments. The evening was so successful, Steve had decided to sacrifice a coveted week of whale-watching off the Baja coast for a shot at spending some time in Emaline's bed. To his mind, he deserved to have her after standing by all those years while she mooned over Mac Brantley.

He was about to announce his intentions when Emaline told him about her breakup with Mac. At first he was flattered that she would confide in him, but as she continued he realized she would never put Mac away.

At her door he made a graceful exit, promising to call again, then cursed his way back to the St. Francis Hotel, thankful he hadn't canceled his reservation in Cabo San Lucas.

A drum roll drew Steve's attention toward the stage, where Julia, Mac and the Sandovals stood beneath the arch of bright paper flowers and Chinese lanterns swaying in the breeze.

Scattered applause greeted Bob Sandoval as he stepped forward with microphone in hand. "Welcome. Welcome one and all. Myrtle and I are so glad you could share this evening in celebration of my good friend Mac Brantley's coming marriage to the lovely Julia Fairchild."

Sandoval's voice faded as Julia captured Steve's attention. She was a vision in a loose chemise of turquoise that stopped just above the knee to showcase her legs. The dress was sophisticated and simple, accentuating her high ample breasts and narrow hips, its deep blue-green complementing her tawny complexion.

Steve swallowed and took a deep draw from his beer, hoping to wash away the desire that suddenly rolled through him. He wanted to take Julia in his arms, crush her body against his and cover her lips. He had wanted that from the moment he saw her in the ER.

HE WAS going off-duty when they brought Julia in, unconscious, hair plastered to her head, clothing covered with pine needles and bits of gravel. But even in her wretched condition she had stopped his heart.

He cleaned her wounds, bound her hands, and when she had

finally opened her eyes Steve drowned in their golden-brown depths, realizing that for the first time since he decided to specialize in trauma medicine he wanted to follow up on a patient.

He tore himself away from the hospital to stop at the diner across I-25 for a beer and two hamburgers, wolfing them down as was his custom. But instead of going to his apartment he returned to Julia's room.

When he saw that she was sleeping, Steve dragged a chair over to her bed and sat. He studied every line of her face, memorized her lips, her nose and the way her eyelashes splayed away from her lids, then concentrated on the rhythmic rise and fall of her breasts beneath the sheet. Was she real? When he touched her to make sure, the silky slide of her skin beneath his fingertips made him want more.

It had been well past two when his beeper summoned him to Emergency, but it had been too late—Steve Duke had fallen in love with Mac Brantley's fiancée.

CHAPTER 15

THE SUN WAS long gone, but a faint peach glow still filled the sky behind the Sandovals, Mac and Julia as they stood on the stage above the crowd.

Bob's welcoming words faded as Julia, clutching Mac's hand, gazed over the sea of faces searching for Steve Duke. Instead, she spotted the four Brantleys. Mac's father was beaming with unabashed pride, but his face appeared ashen, almost green. Julia wondered briefly if Mac saw it too, but before she could mention it, Frank Brantley's dark scowl captured her attention.

She traced his stare to three strangers. The man was tall and beefily handsome, his flushed face contrasted by large almost-colorless eyes and a thick mane of salt-and-pepper hair.

One arm circled the waist of an elegantly thin woman wearing a simple cerise tunic. Her dark, silver-streaked hair was gathered into a sedate bun at the nape of her long neck, and her square face featured huge ebony eyes framed by winged brows black as night.

On his other arm hung one of the most beautiful young women Julia had ever seen. A mass of jet-black waves surrounded the same shaped face, but mirror-blue eyes and a generous mouth took elegance and transformed it into a sensual vitality that was accented by a drop-dead body wrapped in a cobalt sheath.

Julia's heart stammered to a stop when she realized the woman was gazing at Mac with lips slightly apart, and to her horror those see-through eyes were filled with blatant adoration.

In the same instant, Julia felt Mac's hand twitch then release hers.

She turned and softly called his name, but he didn't hear. His eyes were locked on the woman below.

Emaline Pierce. The name now bore a face.

Adrenaline shot to Julia's every extremity as alarms jangled in her ears. It seemed as if Mac had drawn away, leaving her to stand alone above an ocean of upturned, smiling faces. When she faced Emaline again, those ice-blue eyes glared back, glittering triumph.

Applause brought back the reality of the moment and when Mac's lips found hers, a cheer went up. They hugged the Sandovals, thanked them for the evening and descended to the dance floor.

Once they began a slow dance to a country-western tune, Julia relaxed a little. Mac's arms were around her. That's all that mattered. In a few minutes, the pain of that frozen moment would fade.

"Mind if I cut in?" Steve Duke's voice was at her back and before she could protest Julia was in his arms and spinning away from Mac.

They made a few turns around the dance floor before Steve whispered, "Don't say anything until I finish. Okay?"

"You don't have to. She's here and she's gorgeous."

Julia peered over Steve's shoulder just in time to see Emaline step into Mac's outstretched arms. "I can't believe it. Now, he's dancing with her."

Steve laughed. "Cool it, will you? He's not going to run off with her tonight. After all, this is your engagement party, isn't it?"

Julia nodded and let Steve pull her to him, using the comfort of his embrace to stave off the panic that threatened to invade.

After a few minutes he asked, "What did Mac say when you told him you knew about Emaline?"

"I didn't tell him."

Steve stopped and stepped back. "You didn't?"

"He was gone all week and just got back. That's why we were late."

Julia hated that she felt compelled to make excuses to a man she was quickly learning to dislike. "I don't have to explain my fiancé or his actions to you or anybody."

"That's right, you don't. But please know I care about what happens to you."

At that her heart picked up an extra beat. She remembered how she had hoped to see the handsome doctor that following morning in Albuquerque and how disappointed she was when he failed to appear.

She murmured, "You hardly know me. How could you possibly care?"

Steve drew her close and they slid slowly through the other dancers.

When the song ended, Julia pointed toward the rest rooms, "Guess I better beat the line. Thanks for the dance."

Steve grabbed her hand. "Don't go yet."

"I have to get back to Mac." Julia tried to step away, but he refused to release her.

"He seems a bit occupied." Steve turned her toward the bandstand, where Emaline stood wrapped in Mac's embrace.

Julia turned her sudden rush of resentment toward her dance partner. "There's no future in a friendship with you. Mac isn't your best fan and I'm close to joining the ranks."

"I'm not exactly his, either, and if you're angry over my telling you about Emaline, I'm sorry." He cocked his head and gave her a winning grin.

Julia shook her head. "You just won't give up, will you?"

"It's not my nature."

She turned toward the narrow path beneath the arch of red bougainvilleas, but Steve's hand caught her arm. "I'll call."

CHAPTER 16

EMALINE SLID into Mac's empty arms. "May I?"

He took a step back, then realized how stupid that was. Emaline posed no threat. It was over between them. "Be my guest."

The brush of her hair against his cheek sent a shiver down his spine, and he took a deep breath to regain composure. His second mistake. Emaline's scent assailed his memory, evoking such nostalgia, he was afraid he might let the groan buried in his throat escape.

He shook his head hoping to clear the jumble of thoughts pouring through his mind. How could this be happening? He was so sure he had put Emaline away when Julia had come into his life, bringing a completion and happiness he had never known.

"In for the weekend?" He tried for noncommittal but heard the quaver in his voice.

"That's right. I'm leaving Monday." Emaline's honeyed voice caressed his ear. "Or depending on you— maybe never."

Her hand moved across his shoulder to smooth the nape of his neck. Emaline always did that when they danced, knowing how it aroused him.

"All my stupid hang-ups about money and position that stood in our way before don't matter anymore. It's important that you do whatever kind of work you want. All I want is to come back to Las Cruces, marry you and raise a family."

"Marry me? Raise a family? This is news. What about those long stretches of time when I'm up in the Four Corners? What about the poor pay? And how about your big job in San Francisco?"

"Nothing means a thing without you."

Mac shrugged her hand away from his neck. "Too late."

"You can't mean that." She nestled her head on his shoulder. "It's never too late where we're concerned. All you have to do is give us a chance."

"When did you ever give us a chance?" Mac saw her wince and softened his voice, hating that she could still get to him. "After you left, I nearly went crazy. I never thought I'd love anyone else until Julia."

"But you hardly know that woman—at least not like you know me."

Mac shook his head. "I'm in love with her. I was in lust with you."

"Mmmm. Don't remind me." Emaline nuzzled his neck and rolled her pelvis against him.

He jerked away, face hot with embarrassment. "What in hell are you up to?"

Emaline's eyes were hooded, but she was smiling. "Sorry. Old habits die hard."

"Our 'old habits' were over years ago. You and I both know it." Mac scanned the dance floor and was relieved to see Julia walking toward the rest rooms.

Emaline drew him back into her arms, eyes pleading. "Please. At least postpone the wedding for a few months."

Mercifully, the slow dance ended and the accordions began wheezing "Under the Double Eagle."

Frank Brantley's voice slithered over Mac's shoulder. "Hello, Emaline."

Emaline's eyes widened then grew wary. "Hello, Frank."

Mac turned to see his brother standing behind him, fists clenched, jaw engaged. Why did Frank seem so concerned with what was going on between the two of them?

Mac barely got out, "What's up?" before Frank stepped between them and spat, "What brought you home?"

Emaline smirked past Frank's shoulder at Mac. "I was invited."

"Don't give me that. Admit it, you've come back to make one last stand for my brother."

"That's not . . ."

Frank's eyes narrowed. "Why don't you let Mac off the hook? Tell him the truth."

Mac put a placating hand on his brother's shoulder. "Hey, Frank, we're having a party, loosen up."

"Get lost."

Emaline stepped back, her eyes icy. "Why don't you get lost? Mac and I were talking."

"That's the problem. You were probably lying, as usual."

Mac watched his brother grab for Emaline but she side-stepped to leave Frank's hand clenched in midair as he repeated, "If you won't tell Mac the truth, I will."

"The truth? When did you get so lily white?" Emaline's eyes filled. "Go ahead, I won't stop you. Just be sure you don't leave anything out."

She turned and hurried away, leaving the brothers in the midst of couples jumping past in a wild polka.

CHAPTER 17

MACKENZIE BRANTLEY SR. lurched down the path toward the men's room, then paused to lean against the side of the building to catch his breath.

The dull pain that had occupied the middle of his chest since late afternoon now traveled down his left arm, and, to add to his misery, his stomach was threatening to give up its contents any minute.

He hadn't felt this sick since the time he and Selma were on the tender headed from the Queen Elizabeth to the Cherbourg pier. She had held his head, wiped his face and offered sympathy. Not now. Now he was alone.

He plunged past the row of urinals and reached the only stall offering a sit-down toilet just in time to empty his stomach. Once that was done, the distress eased and he sank to the seat in relief.

"Something I ate, that's all," he said to the emptiness and silently thanked God it wasn't his heart. It couldn't be. He would know if it were. "Just let me see them married. That's all I ask."

He shut his eyes and Ed Pierce's face floated before him. Why was he here? Everyone in the Valley knew the two men barely spoke, but not the reason why.

Over the years he had made a point of avoiding the Pierces and cursed the day young Mac had brought little Emaline home to play. She was eight and a beautiful child, wild and fearless, filled with animation and joy. It hadn't taken long for her to weasel her way into Mackenzie's heart in spite of his enmity toward her father.

There had been a time during Emaline's teens when Mackenzie suspected she was attracted to Mac's older brother, Frank. That frightened him. But as usual, he had been mistaken. Anyone who hadn't taken the past into account could see Emaline was after Mac.

Selma, in her wisdom, refused to succumb to Emaline's winning ways. If she had known he was the one who encouraged the young couple to live together, she would have rolled in her grave.

Even so, he made the right move. In less than a year Emaline showed her true colors and was now out of the picture. Mac finally had met the right woman and they would marry in May.

Pierce might have made one last effort by bringing Emaline to the party, but it was too late. She didn't stand a chance. Not against the beautiful redhead from New York.

Brantley chuckled and shook his fist at the dark above him, "That should fry your balls, Eddie Pierce."

When some strength returned, Mackenzie pushed himself to a wobbly stance and stepped out of the stall.

"Under the Double Eagle" was blaring over the PA and, from the sound of boots shuffling against concrete, the dance floor was filled.

Since he was alone, he decided to take advantage of his trip to the men's room and was relieving himself when the door slammed.

Mackenzie heard the zip, then the stream hit the porcelain before the man spoke in a mocking tone. "Don't tell me I get the honor of pissing next to the great Mackenzie Brantley."

Mackenzie didn't look up. "Hello, Ed." He took a deep breath, zipped and began moving toward the exit.

"What's your hurry, Brantley?" Pierce's beefy finger poked his back, sending knives through his body. "Guess you heard I finally got Ben Barney's grove."

Mackenzie was able to get out a "Yes" before a new wave of nausea lurched through his innards.

Somewhere in the agonizing haze he heard Pierce bluster, "Now, all that stands in my way is Red Stone."

Mackenzie staggered a few steps searching frantically in the dim light for the edge of the wash stand wall. Once a hold was secured, he turned. "Don't count on Emaline to get it for you."

Ed stepped close to loom above him. So close, Mackenzie could smell his Bourbon-laden breath. "Now, don't you go counting my Emmy out of the race just yet. She's a mighty tenacious woman and gorgeous to boot."

Mackenzie ignored his enemy's bray. He needed oxygen and a place to sit.

"You okay?" Ed bent forward to search Mackenzie's face. "You're white as a ghost. Celebrating too much?"

"No, I'm fine. Must be the bad light in here." He moved toward the door, drawing his hand along the cool wall to steady himself.

Ed grunted, then continued as he fell in step. "As I was saying, Brantley, I want Red Stone and I intend to get it."

Mackenzie took his time before answering, hoping his voice sounded strong and steady. "It's not for sale and especially not to you. I made that promise over fifty years ago and I don't intend to break it now."

"Aw hell. Are you still stuck on that? Selma's been dead for years."

"Don't utter her name in my presence." Mackenzie's words were barely out before the pain returned full force.

Ed gave a slow, lazy laugh. "I'll say her name any time I please. After all, she was mine first."

"You sonovabitch. You raped her." The vise miraculously released, giving Mackenzie a chance to strike out at his enemy but he missed. Ed had stepped easily out of his reach.

"Is that what she told you?" He gave a sneer. "Why, Selma told me little Frank was our love child."

"Love child my foot. She told me how you got drunk and broke into her room at the hotel. Don't deny it. I saw the bruises."

"Bruised, was she?" Ed laughed. "She showed a lot of spunk, I'll say that for her."

"You bastard. Poor thing was barely seventeen. Too innocent to know about the likes of you."

"Don't kid yourself, Brantley. Selma wanted it. She begged."

"You're lying and you know it." Mackenzie longed to throttle the man before him but the pain in his chest chained him to his station. "It was years before she would let me touch her, she was so ashamed."

"Aw come on, Brantley, give your ego a rest. Selma probably wanted a real man."

Mackenzie fought his failing body and lack of air to mumble, "I should have killed you."

Pierce's voice was barely audible. "Why didn't you?"

There was no oxygen to give aid to his retort. All he could do was shake his head.

Pierce studied him for a moment. "Did Selma ever tell you about my visit? It was a couple of weeks before she died."

Mackenzie tried again for breath but none came.

Pierce must have taken his silence as weakness and gave a low chuckle. "I'll bet she didn't. I offered to acknowledge Frank as mine and take him into my business, but she called me names and kicked me out. Not that I blame her; she knew all I wanted was Red Stone. That's when I found out the grove was going to Mac."

The iron band around his chest released and his lungs kicked in. Mackenzie managed a gasping, "That was decided the minute Mac was born."

"Too bad you made that decision." Ed's eyes narrowed. "Maybe it's time everyone knew the truth about the high-and-mighty Selma Brantley and her spurious offspring."

"Why? What did she ever do to you?"

Pierce rose to his full height. "You never figured it out did you, Brantley? It's *always* been about Red Stone."

The nausea returned full force leaving Mackenzie to wonder whether it was his illness or his sudden fear that Ed Pierce might make his threat good.

"Why destroy Frank? He's your own flesh and blood." Mackenzie smirked through his pain. "His eyes? Dead ringers for yours."

Pierce flushed, then sputtered, "Damn his eyes. Frank means nothing to me." He pointed a finger at him. "But he's your Achilles heel and you'll do anything to save Selma's reputation and protect him."

"You're wrong."

"Oh, am I? You value your family too much to let me blacken the Brantley name. I want Red Stone and I'll do everything—say anything—to get it."

"What about your wife and daughter?"

Ed lowered his voice. "To hell with them. But it might be a real shock for young Mac to find out the gruesome truth. He's always worshipped Frank."

"You'll pay for this, you bastard. Someday you'll burn in hell."

"Long after you, old man." Ed was silent for a moment. "I'll give you until Monday to reconsider."

"Don't bother. There's a codicil in my will saying that if Mac marries Emaline, Red Stone Grove reverts to New Mexico State."

Ed's face clotted with rage. "You sonovabitch, you've thought of everything, haven't you?"

"I tried." The iron band clamped down and he gasped, "Get help."

Pierce took a few steps toward him and stopped. "The hell with you, Brantley. I hope you die right here on this cement floor."

In seeming response to Pierce's command, Mackenzie's legs gave way and panic took over. "I am dying . . . get help."

Ed stared down at him, pure pleasure filling his face. "Sure I will. Just wait here."

The last thing Mackenzie Brantley saw was Ed Pierce's back as he headed for the door. Then his world faded to black.

CHAPTER 18

EMALINE LURCHED through the dancers, searching for refuge. She needed time to think. Make a plan. She exited the dance floor at a narrow path beneath an arbor of red bougainvilleas where she stopped to catch her breath and wipe away her tears.

She'd made a fool of herself. Deluded herself into thinking Mac might still be in love with her. Worse still, for some unexplained reason, Frank was furious. Why did she ever let her father talk her into this?

She was sure Frank would tell Mac everything. All about the countless seedy motel rooms in El Paso, the furtive meetings in the hayloft, the hurried couplings stolen in the very bed she and Mac shared. Would he tell him about the trips to San Francisco, too?

At the thought of San Francisco, more tears came. Frank had just been in San Francisco. Over the past several years he was able to slip away from Dolores, using his soft spot for the gaming tables in Las Vegas as an excuse.

It had been so easy. Frank would announce his trip weeks ahead, producing the round-trip ticket on Southwest to back him up. He didn't lie about the gambling, because he played the slots at the airport while he waited for the next United flight to San Francisco and a non-stop orgy with Emaline.

Once Frank reached her apartment, he never left. They would fall into her bed and become two animals, unable to get enough of each other, coming up for air only long enough to eat from her well-stocked refrigerator.

Sunday morning she would drive Frank to the airport in time to catch the flight that connected with a Southwest return to El Paso. On his last visit he promised to return as soon as the chile was planted.

What happened? Why did Frank want to expose their relationship? And why now? The whole miserable situation was his fault. He had made her incapable of loving any other man.

Emaline pushed down the covered path and turned toward the ladies' rest room, tucked behind a shadowy trellis at the back of the pavilion. She was just about to reach for the door when an iron grip on her arm yanked her to a halt and she found herself staring into Dolores Brantley's anger.

The two women stood facing each other for what seemed to Emaline like a lifetime, then Dolores growled. "I know everything, puta. No use trying to fool me anymore."

"Puta? Calling me a whore is a little heavy, isn't it, Mrs. Brantley? Do you have proof that I'm taking money for sex?"

Emaline tried to keep her voice even; she needed to play it cool. Had Dolores found out about Frank's trips to San Francisco? Maybe that was it. Maybe he was putting on an act for his wife's benefit.

Dolores's voice was pinched with rage. "Whether you get paid or not doesn't matter to me. I have all the proof I need to make your life as miserable as you've made mine."

"I have no idea what you're talking about, but I'd think twice before starting something with me. I know all about how Selma Brantley died."

Dolores's grip tightened. "Selma Brantley died of a heart attack. It's on her death certificate."

Emaline laughed. "Sure, that's what everyone thinks."

"It's the truth, whether you believe it or not." Dolores's teeth gleamed in the half-light. "As for the rest of it, you don't know a damn thing, do you?"

Emaline's pulse picked up a few beats. Rest of what, she thought. Instead she said, "I wouldn't bank my life on it if I were you."

"I wouldn't bank yours on it either." Dolores began to twist Emaline's arm.

"Stop that." Emaline wrenched free. "Keep your threats and your hands to yourself, bitch."

She bumped past Dolores into the ladies' rest room, making an extra effort to slam the door in her enemy's face.

CHAPTER 19

TO JULIA'S RELIEF, the dressing room was empty when she first arrived. Even so, she headed for the nearest stall, sat on the lowered toilet lid and leaned back.

When the hum of the crowd drifting through the open window high above her head gave way to a brisk polka, Julia took a deep breath and closed her eyes. At least she would have a little time to pull herself together and make some sense out of what happened while she was standing on the stage and later in Steve's arms.

The picture of Emaline's pale-blue eyes glued to Mac and filled with love burned in her mind as did that same expression on Emaline's face when she stepped into Mac's arms only a moment after Julia left him.

It was obvious the woman was there to make one last stand for her lost love, but the unanswered question was did Mac still love Emaline? Julia should have asked Steve about Mac and Emaline when they were dancing. He would have been more than happy to volunteer the information.

At the thought of Steve, Julia smiled to herself. He was definitely attracted to her. He made that clear when she was in his arms. She couldn't help but be a little intrigued by the handsome dark-eyed doctor and maybe a little attracted to him, too.

When the crunch of approaching footsteps on the gravel path signaled the end of her privacy, Julia stood and was reaching for the door when she heard, "I know everything, puta."

The voice was familiar. Julia strained to pick up the reply, but couldn't make out a word until the other woman said, "Mrs. Brantley."

The only Mrs. Brantley Julia knew was Dolores. But who was she talking to? Who was she calling a whore?

She stepped on the lid of the toilet, hoping to see who it was, but the window was too high.

Below, she heard Dolores growl, "I have all the proof I need to make your life as miserable as you've made mine."

Julia got as close to the window as she could without falling off her perch and was rewarded with, "I know all about Selma Brantley."

Julia thought she heard Dolores say, "You don't know a damn thing." Then she lost her balance and by the time she regained her footing, all she could hear was a scuffle as the mystery woman yelled, "Keep your threats and your hands to yourself, bitch."

The outside door to the rest room slammed and Julia stepped down to stand for a moment, unsure of what to do next.

She eased the latch out of the eye and peeked out, but took a quick step back when she saw the unknown woman. Seated on one of the stools in front of the mirror was Emaline Pierce, intently rubbing an angry red welt just above her left wrist.

Julia's first thought was to confront her enemy and get it over with, but caution overruled. She carefully threaded the latch back through the eye and sat down to wait.

When the polka ended, the dressing room filled with chirping women and Julia slowly eased open the door. Much to her relief, Emaline was gone.

She stopped in front of the mirror to repair her lipstick, took a few minutes to chat with each well-wisher, then slipped out the door and hurried down the path.

Myrtle Sandoval waved her over. "What's the lay of the land in there?"

Julia laughed. "Only three stalls and at least ten women."

Her friend laughed, too. "Okey-dokey, I guess I'd better wait."

The two stood watching the dancers glide by for several minutes before Julia spotted the Pierces heading toward them. Ed Pierce, face dark with anger, held his wife's arm firmly in his grasp and she seemed to be pleading with him. His wife's frown dissolved at the sight of Myrtle Sandoval and Julia.

Julia's first impulse was to walk away and postpone the meeting, but it was too late. The couple parted a few steps from them with Ed Pierce veering off toward the parking lot, leaving his wife to come forward.

Palatia Pierce put her hand out to Myrtle. "Thanks so much for including us."

Myrtle beamed back. "Our pleasure, Mrs. Pierce. Leaving so soon?"

"I'm afraid so, Mrs. Sandoval. We're too old to keep up with you young'uns." The woman laughed and held out her hand to Julia. "Congratulations on your coming marriage, Miss Fairchild. Mac's a fine man."

Julia nodded her thanks and watched Emaline's mother float away. "She's beautiful, isn't she?"

Myrtle nodded. "And nice, too. Much too good to be married to a lout like him, or have a daughter like . . ." She began to fan herself with the small leather purse she was carrying. "Whoo-ee, it's warm. I hope it's just the excitement. I'm too young to be having hot flashes."

Julia laughed and pointed toward the rest rooms. "Talk about warm. I just avoided meeting Emaline Pierce in there a few minutes ago."

She started to tell Myrtle what she overheard through the open window but decided to wait until she got more information. Instead she asked, "Why didn't you tell me about Mac and Emaline?"

Her friend looked down and stammered, "I—I didn't think it was my place."

"Myrtle. You're my closest friend. Didn't you think I needed to know?"

Myrtle's eyes met hers to beg forgiveness. "I'm sorry about not telling you. Lord knows, there were plenty of opportunities."

Julia waved away her concern. "Oh, forget it. Maybe it's best I didn't know about Emaline in the beginning, but I could sure use a little background now."

"I guess I owe you that." Myrtle moved close and lowered her voice. "Well, I only heard bits and pieces of gossip when we moved here. After Mac and Bob became friends, he told us all about . . . are you sure you want to hear this?"

Julia nodded.

"Well, to tell you the truth, Mac told us he was pretty broken up over it in the beginning. He and Emaline had lived together a year and were planning to be married when he decided to give up his practice to join the Indian Health Service. He told us she was furious that he made the decision without telling her, so she left."

Julia's heart fell. It had been much more serious than she thought. "They lived together?"

Myrtle rushed on. "But Mac told us they fought all the time."

"And they were planning to get married?"

"Yes. But she broke it off. Mac didn't date anyone for a long time. Oh, I tried to fix him up, but he wouldn't budge." Myrtle patted Julia's arm. "But, all that changed the first time he saw you."

Julia sighed relief. Of course Mac wasn't interested in Emaline. It was silly to be so uptight over a past relationship.

"Say, if Mac didn't tell you about Emaline, who did? Dolores?"

"No, though I think she was on a fishing expedition when she invited me out to the hacienda for tea last week. Steve Duke told me."

Myrtle's eyebrows arched. "I saw you dancing with him a few minutes ago, but I didn't know you knew him that well."

"I don't, really. He was in the ER in Albuquerque when they brought me in. I thought I mentioned his name."

"No, you didn't, because I would have remembered. He's got quite a reputation among the ladies." Myrtle nudged her. "What do you think? Pretty sexy, huh?"

"I didn't really notice," Julia lied. "Frankly, I'm not sure if I like him very much."

"He might have a checkered history but he's always been real nice to Bob and me."

Myrtle pointed across the dance floor. "There's Mac."

She turned to see Mac striding toward her and hurried to meet him, hoping they might have a chance to discuss Emaline Pierce during their next dance.

His arms were barely around her when a man rushed from the direction of the rest rooms yelling, "Get a doctor."

"Oh, Lord, what now?" Mac groaned. "Wait here."

"What do you suppose is going on?" Myrtle asked.

"I have no earthly idea," Julia said, just as Mac ran out of the rest room toward a pay phone near the bar.

"He's going for the phone. Oh, honey, this is bad." Myrtle was barely finished when Bob Sandoval emerged to join Mac and, after exchanging a few words, turned to make squeeze box motions at the bandleader.

At the first strains of "Cotton-Eyed Joe," the crowd moved quickly onto the dance floor and soon the air was filled with whoops and screams.

Minutes later, the distant wail of a siren cut through the darkness and Myrtle moaned. "Hear that? It must serious. Let's go see what's up."

Julia put out a restraining hand. "I think we should wait here. We'll only be in the way. Besides, we'll find out who it is soon enough."

The ambulance, lights blinking, siren dying to a low growl, swerved through the crowded parking lot and jammed to a stop. Two EMTs jumped out, removed a gurney, then pushed past the women to disappear into the milling guests.

Minutes later a sorrowful murmur rippled through the crowd and it parted to reveal Mac and Frank supporting a weeping Dolores followed by the gurney.

When she saw that the body on the gurney was completely covered, Julia gasped. "Oh, Myrtle, it must be Mister Brantley."

She pushed through the crowd and was almost to the trio when she met Emaline Pierce face-to-face.

Julia saw the challenge in her rival's pale eyes and heard her hiss, "This is no place for you. Out of my way."

She shoved Julia aside to step in stride with Mac, crooning, "I loved him, too. And he loved me. You know that, don't you, darling?"

As they moved past, Julia called, "Mac?" and put her hand out to touch him, hoping to comfort him in some small way. "Mac, I'm here."

When he didn't respond, Julia stepped back into the crowd.

CHAPTER 20

BOB SANDOVAL'S voice came over the PA. "Folks, may I have your attention, please?" He waited for the crowd to quiet. "I regret to announce that Mackenzie Brantley, Senior, has just passed away. Myrtle and I thank you for coming and are sorry the party has to end this way.

Julia turned toward the exit and bumped into Steve.

He nodded toward the departing ambulance. "Must have been a coronary."

"I guess so. When Mac and I were standing on the stage, I noticed his father didn't look very well." She tried to walk around him, but Steve blocked her way. "Would you please move? I have to get to the parking lot."

"I'll be happy to drive you home."

"Thanks for the offer, but I'm going with Mac."

Steve pointed toward the parking lot. "I don't think so."

Julia peered around him just in time to see the ambulance followed by the Brantley Suburban leave the parking lot. Behind the Suburban was Mac's Jeep with Emaline Pierce at the wheel and Mac, face buried in his hands, slumped forward in the passenger seat.

She felt Steve's hand on her elbow. "Now, will you let me take you home?"

"I'll let you drive me to the hospital."

"What for?"

"If you have to ask, oh, forget it." Julia turned back toward the stage where the Sandovals were standing. "I'll ask the Sandovals to drop me off after everyone's cleared out of here."

Steve grabbed her arm. "Don't get so hot. If you want to go to the hospital, I'll take you."

"Let's go." Julia wheeled and hurried for the fast-emptying lot.

The trip turned into a high-speed race as Steve roared past the other cars, veering wildly into the oncoming lane every time there was an opportunity. By the time they reached the hospital Julia could see the ambulance at the Emergency entrance and the Suburban and Mac's red Jeep in the parking lot.

Steve turned into the doctor's parking lot and slammed on the brakes. "We made it just in time. He'll hardly know you weren't with him."

Julia couldn't help but laugh. "I don't know whether to thank you or report you to the police."

She turned to open her door and stopped. Mac and Emaline were walking arm in arm toward the entrance talking to Frank and Dolores, then she saw Emaline lean into Mac and slide her hand beneath his jacket.

Julia turned away, trying to make sense out of what she saw. Mac didn't appear to be in shock and he obviously knew who walked beside him. Yet only moments before he was called to his father's side, she had seen the love in his eyes.

She whispered, "Would you take me home, please?"

Steve smiled. "Sure thing." Then he sobered. "I wouldn't hang my hat on what you just saw. As you know, people in shock don't always react the way we think they should."

Julia nodded. "You may be right about that, but I think it's better if I stay out of the picture for now."

"Suit yourself." Steve turned the car around and headed for the exit.

The ride was spent in silence. Other than the brief directions she gave, Julia couldn't complete a thought, and there was something stuck in her throat that refused to budge.

When the car stopped in her driveway, she grabbed for the handle and found none. "I can't find the . . ."

"Here. Let me get it."

Steve started to reach across her, but she pushed his hand away. "No. I can do it myself."

He was out and around the car to open her door before she could find the handle.

They stood a few moments before she realized Steve was still holding her hand. When she tried to move away he held fast, and the tears of frustration and anger she'd held back for so long began to spill.

"Let me go."

"I can't." His arms went around her. "It's all right."

She relaxed into his embrace and wept, comforted by his hand softly stroking her back and the soothing lull of his voice.

When she was finally able to get a breath, she said, "It's not over between them."

His voice resonated against her ear. "No, no. Mac loves you."

Julia tried to see his eyes but they were blurred by the glare of the moon and her tears. "Does he?"

"How could he help himself?" Steve's lips touched hers in a soft caress and she felt his breath on her face scented with a pleasant mix of beer and Dentyne chewing gum.

He stepped away, took a folded handkerchief from his pocket and handed it to her. "Sorry."

Julia's thoughts were too jumbled to answer immediately, so she dabbed her eyes on the soft linen and strained, "Don't be. Thank you for caring."

He was silent for a moment. "I do, you know."

She stepped back. "Oh, Steve, don't . . ."

"Forget it." He straightened, and when he spoke again his voice was brusque. "Now, let's get you into the house. You're shivering."

"Am I?"

Steve steered her to the porch. "Do you have your keys?"

When he reached out in the darkness Julia jumped back, fumbling in the small purse that dangled from one shoulder. "Here they are."

Steve closed the small distance she made between them and touched her hand. "Let me."

"Oh—I—I'd better do it. Finicky latch."

She unlocked the door, then watched it swing into the stuffy darkness. "Goodnight."

Steve was standing so close Julia could feel the warmth flowing from his skin, and for one small instant she hoped he might kiss her again.

"Well, I better be on my way. Try to get some sleep."

"I will." She stepped inside and watched as Steve moved from the porch into the moonlight.

"If it's all right with you, I'd like to come by before I leave."

"That won't be necessary."

"Says who? Besides, you owe me a handkerchief."

"That's a pretty slim excuse for a visit."

He laughed. "Okay, I'm desperate."

"I'll make coffee." She waved the crushed linen in his direction. "And you'll get your handkerchief back in the same shape you offered it."

"You're on."

Julia waited until Steve backed out of the driveway, then shut the door. She picked up the phone and dialed the number for messages but there were none; not that she really expected any after the scene she witnessed in the parking lot.

Groping her way through the darkness, she began to climb the stairs. By the time she reached her bedroom, exhaustion won and she fell across the bed, too tired to remove her clothes, too tired and bewildered to cry. Her house was dark, silent and empty. Just like she felt.

CHAPTER 21

THE JOLT of the speed bump brought Mac to and he raised his head to see the Emergency entrance of Central Hospital. Without looking at the driver he muttered, "Park over there," and pointed to the empty row designated Emergency parking.

The Jeep rolled to a stop in the first slot. "What now?" Emaline asked.

Mac jerked up at the sound of her voice. "What in hell are you doing here? Where's Julia?"

She shrugged. "How should I know?"

He got out of the Jeep, stood for a moment, then turned. "I can't believe I left without her. I hate to ask this, but could you go back and . . . ?"

"I most certainly will not. I'm not your hired hand. Besides, she's not part of this family—yet."

"In case you've forgotten, neither are you," Mac rubbed his eyes, hoping to ease the stabbing pain behind them. "If you won't get Julia, take my Jeep on out to your place. I'll catch a ride with Frank and Dolores and pick it up tomorrow."

He started for the Emergency entrance with Emaline at his heels. "I'm not leaving you like this. I'll drop you off at your place after you're done here."

"Suit yourself."

Frank and Dolores were waiting beside the Suburban and as they fell in step Frank asked, "Where's Julia?"

Dolores pointed at Emaline. "And what's she doing here?"

Mac turned in her direction, then shrugged. "I'm not exactly sure, but we have more important things to do than worry about her."

Dolores nodded. "Of course we do. We've just lost—oh, I can't believe your father is dead." She broke into honking sobs.

"Can't you dam those crocodiles for one minute?" Frank shoved her behind him and turned back to Mac. "What now?"

"The doctor in charge will examine Dad and sign the death certificate," Mac said. "But this time we're having an autopsy."

"What the hell for? The old man suffered a massive coronary."

"Were you there?" Mac asked.

"Well, no. But that's what Sandoval thinks. Isn't he a doctor?"

"No. Bob's the administrator of a mental health facility. He wouldn't know a coronary from a casserole. Besides, he was having a beer with me."

"Yeah," Frank said. "Dad was dead by the time I got to him, and I beat you there by a few minutes."

"Wasn't anybody with him when he died, God rest his poor soul?" Dolores's tear-filled voice floated over Frank's shoulder.

"Shut up." Frank barked.

"Actually, there was someone, Frank." Emaline slid her arm through Mac's. "My father."

Frank glared at her for a long moment, then shook his head. "No way. Dad hated Ed Pierce. Everybody knows that. George Barnes came to find me, and when I got there Bud Pike was cradling Dad's head in his arms. Your dad was nowhere to be seen."

"Frank's right. It was George Barnes I saw running out of the men's room."

"Well, it was my dad who was talking to him when he fell to the floor."

"If what you say is true, why the hell didn't Ed get somebody?" Mac demanded.

Mac saw Emaline bristle; she hated to be challenged. "I'm just repeating what he told me. Daddy told me your father was propped against the wall when he last saw him."

"What?" Mac stopped and grabbed her arm. "Dad was conscious when your father left him?"

"I'm positive."

As soon as they entered Emergency he turned to Frank. "I'm calling Julia. You and Dolores go on down to that far desk and wait for me." He pointed toward the end of the dim hallway, found a pay phone, then dropped a coin in the slot.

"I'll wait with you." Emaline's voice was at his back.

Mac turned. "Damn it, don't you get it? It's over between us. And this is a private conversation. Now, disappear."

After several rings he heard Julia's cheery voice. "Leave a message and I'll get back to you as soon as possible."

Mac waited for the beep, but when he heard it the words wouldn't come. He didn't know where to begin or how to explain his strange behavior. After he learned of his father's death, he hadn't given Julia a thought. Instead he left Radium Springs with a woman Julia knew little or nothing about. How would he ever be able to explain that one?

The sound of a gurney bumping through swinging doors invaded the silence, and Mac peered down the darkened hall. An orderly was wheeling a body toward the morgue. His father. Mac shook his head and blinked until he could see again. There would be plenty of time for that later.

"Havens signed the certificate." Frank's voice came from behind. "Says Doc Jackson will do the autopsy first thing Monday. Now what?"

Mac let out a long breath and shrugged, "I guess we go home. It's too late to make any calls now."

Dolores touched his arm. "Did you reach Julia?"

"No answer. But I plan to run by there right now."

"What about me?"

Mac turned at the sound of Emaline's voice. "Oh Lord, I forgot all about you. Frank, could you and Dolo . . ."

"Not on your life," Dolores growled. "No way that puta is riding with us."

"And I wouldn't share a car with that bitch if you paid me," Emaline retorted. "I'll drop you off and take the Jeep. You can get it later."

"I want to make sure Julia got home safely. If you want to take my Jeep, you can drop me off there."

"Oh, come on, Mac, it's past midnight," Emaline pressed. "If we go all the way to her house, I won't get home before sunup. Besides, she's probably asleep by now."

Emaline was right. It was almost one and he was exhausted after working in Albuquerque until mid-afternoon and racing back to the party. "Okay, okay. Let's get this show on the road."

He turned to his brother. "I'll be at the house first thing tomorrow morning. We'll make the funeral plans."

CHAPTER 22

I T WAS WELL PAST one when Mac left Highway 85 at Shalem Colony Road. He glanced at Emaline and saw she was still awake. She hadn't talked after they left the hospital parking lot, and he was grateful for her silence.

He turned right at his mailbox and bumped down the two-rut road toward the grove of cottonwoods surrounding his home.

"So, this is it?"

"Yes." Mac surveyed the outline of his house and, for the first time since his father's death, experienced a warm rush. After Emaline left him, it was his father who urged him to build.

Mac could still hear that voice, gruff with love. "Get off this land, son. Start over. Go find some acreage and build a place of your own. It'll help you forget her."

He had taken his father's advice and lost himself in the project. First searching for the property, then designing the long, low white stucco building with a wide chimney at each end.

He watched the walls rise to be crowned by a corrugated roof that sloped into low, broad porches that ran the length of the house on both sides. During the day, the deep overhang protected the house from the glare of the New Mexico sun, but at night the large lamps flanking the front door beamed from beneath it, spilling welcome light across the drive.

Mac stopped next to the flagstone walk leading to the entrance.

"Well, here we are."

"It's a great house." Emaline pushed across him to peer out his window.

Mac dodged and shoved the car door open, not wanting a replay of what happened earlier that evening. He hated that he was so vulnerable and that, in spite of how he felt about Julia, Emaline still wielded a certain power over him.

"When did you build it?" Emaline asked. Her shoulder touched his and her musky smell enveloped him.

AT THAT, the years fell away to that first time in the barn when she dragged him toward the ladder to the hayloft saying, "I want to show you something."

Mac's stomach lurched. "Not another chicken snake?" He hated snakes and envied Emaline's fearlessness when it came to dispatching them with a hoe.

"No. Not a snake."

He was halfway up the ladder and could see her waiting at the top, arms akimbo, framed by a halo of barn dust.

Emaline whispered, "It's something wonderful, something secret."

"This better be good. We still have the horses to do."

Just as his hands grasped the top rung, her arms went around his neck while her lips sent messages he had only dreamed about.

She led him to the nearest pile of loose hay, her mouth covering his while her hands searched his body, giving him no time to think, only to react.

Images flashed. Emaline above him. Arousing him. Making him sweat. Making him want to take her. And when he did, she helped him with his first awkward entry.

After it was over, he devoured every part of her body with his eyes, memorizing the rounds of her breasts, the smoky vee between her legs, the dark smudges at her armpits. On impulse he made a bold move and covered the dark center of her breast with his mouth until it stiffened in response. The smell of hay mingled with oats and barley gave way to the taste of Emaline's bare skin as a new scent assailed his nose like freshly turned earth, loamy and sweet.

EVEN NOW he could smell it. Even now, after all those years, that loamy aroma made him remember how she tasted and made him want her.

Mac pushed out of the Jeep and took a deep breath, hoping the sharp night air would clear his head. He cursed himself for wanting Emaline and, in wanting her, betraying Julia. What was wrong with him? His father was dead, his fiancée was God knows where, and all he could think about was bedding Emaline Pierce.

"Are you all right?" Her voice came softly through the darkness.

"I'm worn-out and sad. It's been a long day." He rubbed his face with both hands and nodded toward Emaline in the half-dark. "You better get on your way. I'll drop by and pick up the Jeep tomorrow."

"Fine with me." She got out and walked around to the driver's side. "But how will you get to Hatch?"

She was standing much too close and Mac stepped away. "I'm not thinking straight."

"Of course you're not. You're grieving."

Emaline's arms were around his neck and he felt her breasts pressing against him. He ached to see them—hating himself for wanting to. He didn't love Emaline. That was over. He was going to marry Julia.

Emaline's mouth was on his, her tongue seeking his, and all thoughts of Julia vanished.

Mac unlocked the front door and led Emaline down the wide gallery to the master bedroom.

Now, she lay across him, still moving—still making those familiar tiny noises. She was always insatiable and self-absorbed, milking an extra orgasm or two for herself long after he was spent.

"Give it a rest." His voice cut through the darkness.

Emaline froze and offered a contrite, "Sorry."

Mac didn't answer. There was no strength to answer, no strength to move. Worse still, he didn't want to do anything but lie there.

To have Emaline in his bed brought back memories of a happier time when his father was alive and he and Emaline were sharing the small cottage not far from the main house. For some reason, at that particular moment, the familiar touch of her body gave him the solace he needed.

He was almost asleep when he felt Emaline slowly slide her way upward to nestle against his shoulder. He was too tired to object. Instead, he gathered her to him the way he always did after they made love. Then the room was silent except for their breathing.

CHAPTER 23

BRIGHT SUNLIGHT nudged Julia awake. She opened one eye, rolled to her back and groaned. She was sprawled across the bed on her stomach when sleep finally came and apparently had never moved; her reward—a stiff neck and an aching back.

She staggered to the bathroom, smoothing the wrinkled aqua linen that she chose for the engagement party. A dress carefully selected to match the turquoise of the Navajo ring on her finger.

With that, the evening replayed. Mr. Brantley dead. Mac passing her by, ignoring her and driving away with Emaline Pierce.

Julia told Steve she thought it was over. Then she was in his arms, weeping, glad he was there to comfort her. She didn't expect the kiss or the offer of his handkerchief. Steve's handkerchief, where was it? She peeked around the door and saw it on the floor.

Julia picked it up and brought it to her lips, recalling the gentle touch of his mouth on hers and the smell of Dentyne chewing gum. Dentyne was the first thing she associated with Steve. Was that only a week before?

"This is ridiculous." Her voice startled her back to the reality of the present.

Julia undressed and stepped into the shower, hoping its steamy stream would ease her stiffness and the dull ache rooted in her chest.

Half an hour later, hair still damp, she was wrapped in a cotton robe and hunched over her first mug of coffee when the doorbell rang. She hurried to the entry hall hoping it was Mac, but when she opened the door she saw only Steve's craggy expectant face.

His sable eyes seemed to x-ray her from neck to bare feet before they slowly rose to meet hers. "Am I too early?"

She suppressed an urge to check the knot at her waist and motioned him to follow. "No, it's just that I'm a little late. Coffee? There's a full pot in the kitchen."

"Great. Black's fine." Steve settled his long frame on the stool, took the steaming mug from her and sampled it. "Now, that's coffee." He saluted her with his mug and then concentrated on the contents.

The silence between them seemed more comfortable than awkward, and Julia was satisfied to let it go unbroken. She took a few sips and glanced sideways to study Steve from beneath lowered lashes. His heavy eyebrows matched dark waves that were long for current fashion, and the lines along the sides of his mouth seemed deeper than ever. Still, he was handsome in an offbeat sort of way.

In the harsh morning light, he looked as tired as she felt. He drained his mug. "I didn't sleep a wink. How about you?"

"I got a few, but . . . " She rubbed her neck and frowned. "I must have slept wrong."

"Want me to rub the kinks out?"

Her heart lurched. "No—no. But thanks."

"Well, if you won't put me to work," Steve held out his mug, "I could use another shot of caffeine. It's a long drive back to Albuquerque."

Julia slid off her stool and was almost past him when she felt his arm slide around her waist.

"Talk to me."

She gasped and realized she was trembling, surprised that Steve's touch could affect her so. She rolled out of his grasp and reached for the coffee pot, afraid to face him because her heart was beating much too fast.

"There's nothing to say," she murmured, eyes glued to the black liquid filling his mug.

She crossed the kitchen to empty her cup in the sink, refilled it and turned to face him, hoping she could manage the suddenly awkward situation more easily with some space between them.

"I guess this really isn't a good time." She raised her hand to her damp curls. "I just got out of the shower."

Steve smiled, then took a sip from his mug. "So I see."

Julia, hoping her face wasn't as red as it felt, tried again. "Maybe you should get going. It's a long way."

"Mac hasn't called, has he?"

In spite of the ballooning lump in her throat, she croaked, "It's only nine."

Steve's arms were around her. "I know how hurt you must be." He inhaled. "Mmmm. You smell so good."

"You better go," Julia ducked out of his embrace and headed toward the front door.

Once there, she clasped the doorknob and turned. "Thanks for stopping by. I really appreciate . . ."

Steve's lips were over hers before she could finish the sentence.

The brief and gentle kiss of the night before was forgotten as his mouth engaged hers in a long, searching encounter, entreating her, then commanding her to give in to her own passion.

Her eyes flew open to see Steve staring back. Frightened that she might drown in the intensity she saw, she closed her eyes, but it made no difference. The message he was sending was too powerful to ignore.

She stood locked in the moment, as his body surged against hers and his hands traveled up her back to softly push her breasts against his chest. For some reason, that aroused her more than if he had actually fondled her, and she felt her knees begin to tremble and give way.

Steve broke their kiss with a low moan, "Tell me you want me as much as I want you."

When she didn't respond, he took her left hand in his, studied it for a moment and raised it. "Is this what's stopping you?"

The Navajo ring glinted silver and turquoise in the dim light of the hall, reminding her of Mac's pledge. What was wrong with her? The wedding was a little over a month away but in less than eight hours she had let another man kiss her twice.

"Julia?" Steve gently tilted her chin until their eyes met.

She shook her head. "This is all my fault. I shouldn't have let you kiss me. I have no right. Will you forgive me?"

"You kissed me with as much passion as I kissed you. Why don't you tell me what that means?"

Julia gazed away. "I honestly don't know."

Steve stood for a moment, then reached past her to open the door. "Well, I better get going."

She held out her hand. "Thank you for coming by."

"A handshake? Are you always this formal after arousing a man to the point of distraction?"

Julia's face grew hot with embarrassment as she stammered, "What?"

Steve gave a mocking bow. "It's the Yankee way, right?"

He took her outstretched hand and raised it to his mouth as his eyes locked hers. His lips brushed the edges of her palm, then found the center. There, they lingered to trace the lines as if committing them to memory, in a move that made her knees threaten to buckle for the second time.

Steve released her hand. "I guess this is the best we can do—for now."

Julia found her voice. "Yes. I suppose it is."

"I'll call you."

She nodded and waited until Steve drove away from the curb, shut the door and leaned against it. Her legs were too shaky to carry her any farther.

CHAPTER 24

THE FIRST RING of the phone pitched Mac out of a dreamless sleep into the harsh reality of the day.

Julia. A shiver ran through him at the thought of having to deal with her so soon. What would he say? What could he tell her without lying? And if he told her the truth . . . ?

After a couple of rings he grabbed the receiver and heard Frank's, "It's about time."

"Oh, it's you."

Fingertips feathered up his bare thigh and Mac whirled to see Emaline, eyes shut, wearing a wicked grin. He grunted, then rushed to push her hand away before it reached its destination.

His brother's voice cut in. "When will you be here? We need to make plans."

"Right." Mac squinted at the clock; it was just past nine. "Give me an hour and have Dolores make a big pot of strong coffee. I'm going to need it."

Emaline reached over Mac's shoulder, grabbed the phone to her lips and purred. "Morning, Frank, did you sleep well?"

Mac grabbed the receiver just in time to hear his brother say, "You sonovabitch," before he slammed down the phone.

He collapsed against the pillows. "What in the hell did you do that for? I've got enough trouble as it is."

"Sorry." Emaline lay back, not bothering to cover herself.

Mac shook his head and turned away.

"Not interested? Maybe I can help." Her words were accompanied by the touch of her hand.

He lurched away from her searching fingers to sit on the edge of the bed. "Get dressed. I'm taking you home."

"Not so fast. We have to talk about last night."

"Last night was a mistake."

"It didn't seem that way to me." Emaline slid her arm around his waist. "I got the idea you might have changed your mind."

Mac shook her away and stood. "If she'll have me, I have every intention of marrying Julia in May." With that he headed for the bathroom, pausing to lock the door before turning on the shower.

Mac rolled his throbbing forehead against the cool tile and slogged through the list of his sins while the rest of his body reddened beneath the water's burning assault. He had cheated on his fiancée with a woman he didn't even love. Would Julia ever understand? Would she ever forgive him? After several fruitless minutes he turned off the water, no wiser than before.

Mac was shaved and dressed when the phone rang again. He groaned and unlocked the door hoping to beat Emaline to it, but it was too late, the receiver was to her ear.

"Hello? Doctor Brantley's residence, his lover speaking." Anyone who had ever heard Emaline's voice would immediately recognize her whiskey alto.

Mac wrested the receiver from her hand and stabbed his finger toward her dress, draped over one of the large easy chairs flanking the fireplace. "Hello?"

His answer was the drone of the dial tone.

"Who was it?"

"How would I know?" Emaline said.

"It was Julia, wasn't it?"

"What if it was? The sooner she finds out about us, the better off she'll be."

On her way to retrieve her dress Emaline brushed against Mac, letting her bare body linger against him as her clear-blue eyes challenged his. "She'll get over it."

Mac shoved her away. "I won't. And if there's any repercussion from that cute remark about being my lover, you'll pay."

"We'll see who pays." Emaline picked up her dress, slipped it over her head and let it slide slowly over her body. She turned and gave him an inviting smile. "Enjoying the show?"

"Hardly. I'm just trying to figure out why you came back."

"I came for you."

"Don't give me that. Ed wants Red Stone and thinks this is the only way to get it."

Emaline laughed softly. "I haven't the slightest idea what you're talking about." She picked up the filmy bra and matching bikini, dropped them in her purse and stepped into her shoes. "I'm ready if you are."

CHAPTER 25

JULIA IMMEDIATELY recognized Emaline's voice and slammed the receiver into the cradle.

There was no one to blame but herself. She had let Mac's old flame push her aside and then stood by as Emaline drove his Jeep away from the party. She could have made a move when she arrived at the hospital and saw Emaline slip her arm beneath Mac's jacket. But, instead of taking her rightful place beside her fiancé, she asked Steve to take her home, and once there she let him comfort her—let him kiss her.

And now, this morning, instead of leaping from her bed to rush to Mac's side, she had welcomed Steve into her home, given him coffee and shared a kiss that even now, whenever she thought of his mouth meeting hers and his hands moving over her body, still made her tremble.

One thing was apparent. Her behavior during the past twelve hours was not only puzzling, it frightened her. She could find no reasonable explanation for her actions, and, worse still, she felt no particular desire to explore them.

After Steve left, she had waited until she was dressed to make the call. She dialed, listened to the phone ring and, when Emaline answered, she hung up.

Now, in the silence of her kitchen, Emaline's ". . . his lover speaking" beat against her ears.

Julia muttered, "Coward," grabbed the car keys from the kitchen counter and hurried to the garage.

In minutes she was racing through the sleepy Village of Doña Ana headed toward Shalem Colony Road. She didn't know exactly what she would do when she got to Mac's home; all she knew was that she needed to go.

The empty driveway brought relief. Mac was probably in Hatch going over the funeral details with his brother. Maybe Emaline had taken Mac's Jeep home the night before and was returning it when Julia called. That seemed logical. Maybe she had jumped to the wrong conclusion.

The front door swung into the entry. "Mac?"

When there was no response, Julia made her way along the gallery to the wide opening of the kitchen. She relaxed a little when she saw that the coffee pot still gleamed and there were no dirty cups.

Down the hall, the open bedroom door revealed the clothes Mac had worn to the party piled on the armchair next to the fireplace.

"Mac?" Her voice echoed in the emptiness.

Julia pushed the door open and gasped. The bed was a mess. There was no longer any question about what had happened the night before. Two people shared that bed. Had sex in that bed. The evidence was on the bottom sheet.

She walked to the side she usually occupied, picked up the lipstick-smudged pillow, held it to her nose and whispered, "Shalimar."

The perfume was so distinctive, one never forgot it. Only last night she had smelled that scent as Emaline blocked her way.

Julia sank to the bed, too numb to experience pain—or anger.

"Damn you." Her voice startled her and her eyes flew open to see through the window the grove of cottonwoods sheltering the house from the late morning sun.

Those gnarled sentinels that once seemed so poetic now hovered menacingly above the roof, and the sun that once seemed so benign now beat mercilessly into the barren mesa. Her mother once told her she might as well be living on some alien planet. Maybe she was right.

The sound of the approaching car failed to stir her, nor did the footfall on the tile floor of the gallery; only when Mac sat on the bed beside her and took her hand in his did Julia become aware of his presence.

She heard him say her name, felt his lips brush the back of her hand, then the warmth of his cheek pressing against it.

She heard him ask for forgiveness, heard the pain in his voice, his desperation, his longing—but all she could think of was the Shalimar perfume on the pillow and the stain on the bottom sheet.

His arm circled her waist as his fingers touched beneath her chin. "Please, Julia, look at me."

She shook her head, pushed his hand away and walked to the window.

Mac followed to stand behind her. His arms went around her and she heard him say, "Please try to understand what happened here."

She whirled to face him. "Why did I have to find out about Emaline Pierce from Steve Duke? Why didn't you tell me? I told you everything about my past. Everything."

"I was going to tell you when we were camping, but the storm . . . oh, Julia, I thought I'd lost you."

"You're not making any sense. One minute you say you thought you lost me, the next you're admitting that you slept with Emaline."

"Emaline doesn't mean a thing . . . she hasn't for a long time."

She gave a harsh laugh. "So you slept with her. What lame excuse can you cook up for that?"

He shook his head. "After I lost Dad, everything got confused . . ."

"I know you were upset about your father and I'm truly sorry about that. But, Mac, you walked right by me. You didn't even acknowledge me. You left me behind. Let Emaline drive you to the hospital."

"I tried to phone, but you weren't home."

"There was no message."

"I didn't know how to explain."

"So you brought Emaline back here and made love to her?"

Mac put his hands on her shoulders. "If you'll just let me . . ."

She turned away and heard him let out a long breath before he said, "I won't lie to you."

"If I hadn't come here today, would you have lied?"

"Maybe. I don't know. But I do know that I love you. You're the only one . . ."

"Please. Don't say any more."

Julia stared down at the elegant turquoise ring, the symbol of Mac's pledge, and watched it dissolve in her tears. She struggled to slide it over her knuckle, then slipped it from her finger.

"To hell with you and your damned *Nizhoni*."

Julia threw the ring in the center of the rumpled bedding and walked out of the room.

She stepped into the noonday sun, stumbled past Mac's Jeep and climbed into the Range Rover. Through her tears she could see the front door, still open, still empty.

She drove slowly down the rutted lane leading to Shalem Colony Road, stopped at the gate, then peered into the rearview mirror one last time and saw that the door was closed.

CHAPTER 26

"YOU LOOK AWFUL, but then I suppose that's to be expected." Phyllis Wills held the starched white coat forward so Julia could slip into it and gave her a brief hug. "Poor Mister Brantley, poor Mac, poor you. What a terrible way to end your engagement party."

When the lump in Julia's throat allowed only a feeble croak, her secretary nodded. "Don't waste your voice on me. You have four pages to read."

Phyllis shoved the New Patient file into her hands and gave her a gentle push toward the door. "Better hurry. You're already ten minutes late and you were first on the agenda. But considering what happened Saturday, I'm pretty sure Doctor Max will forgive you."

"I hope so. I could use a break today." Julia hurried down the hall toward the conference room, making every effort to concentrate on the business at hand, hoping she could become involved enough to forget the ache in her heart.

Though she tried to slide into her seat without causing attention, Max Blumfield, Chief of Staff of Piñon Mesa, nodded in Julia's direction. "Just in time, Doctor. I'll fill you in on this week's schedule, later. But before you present the new patient, I know I speak for the rest of us in offering our deepest condolences."

Julia avoided the sympathy she saw in the faces around the table and began to read. "This week's new patient is a twelve-year-old male suffering from Attention Deficit Hyperactivity Disorder accompanied by a traumatic emotional overlay resulting from an unreasonably expectant father . . ."

As soon as the staff meeting ended, Julia was out the door and back in her office, successfully avoiding any contact with the rest of the staff. She wasn't ready for that, yet.

Phyllis glanced up from her typing. "How did it go?"

"Thank heavens the water pitcher was in front of me. I drank half of it." Julia handed her the file. "How much time do I have before my first patient?"

"True to form, Albert Peña's mother canceled. And because she's always late I don't schedule any appointment following his."

"What a relief. I'm going to take some aspirin and lie down; my head is splitting. Would you mind holding my calls?"

Julia swallowed the two white pills chased by a glass of tepid water and sank into the couch, hoping the respite might get her through the rest of the day. At least she was working and her mind would be occupied. Anything that happened on this particular Monday would certainly be better than the bleak Sunday she spent after returning to her lonely townhouse.

Somehow, she had driven home from Mac's house without getting in a wreck. Once there, she stripped, lay facedown on her bed and let her tears ooze into the cool sheet while the scene in Mac's bedroom kept replaying. Her pain. His pain. The ring glinting in the middle of his sullied bed.

Darkness failed to bring the escape Julia sought and, though two aspirin had eased the descending headache, sleep refused to come. For hours she lay in the dark, staring at the glow of the digital clock as each minute slowly flipped past. It was almost four when she finally slept, and two hours later the unwelcome whine of her alarm pitched her into a new day.

Julia was taking several deep relaxing breaths before closing her eyes, when she heard Dolores's voice in the outer office. "I have to see her. Now."

"But Mrs. Brantley, the doctor is . . ."

"I don't give a damn what she is. This is urgent."

Julia gave up and opened the door. "Hello, Dolores. What brings you here?"

Dolores rushed forward and threw her arms around Julia's neck. "I'm going to kill that bastard. How could he?"

"Now, calm down, Dolores. We can talk in here." Julia saw the concern on her secretary's face. "It's all right, Phyllis. A family matter. Will you hold everything for a few minutes, please?"

She shut the door behind her and motioned Dolores to the couch. "Please. Keep your voice down. No one knows."

"Oh, chica, I'm so sorry. After Frank told me what happened, I wanted to come. That bitch. I hate her guts."

"Well, I have to confess, Emaline Pierce's not exactly on the top of my list either."

Dolores pointed at Julia's bare left hand. "You gave the ring back."

"Yes." She squelched the stab in her throat with a couple of swallows as her head began to throb in earnest. If she didn't get Dolores out of her office, she was going to lose it completely. "Well, thanks for coming by. I appreciate your concern."

Dolores ignored the signal. "Don't you love Mac enough to fight for him?"

Julia shook her head. "Right now I'm so hurt and angry I don't know what I'm going to do."

"But you can't give up that easy. Emaline's not after Mac because she loves him. He's always been second best."

"Second best? What do you mean?"

"Frank's the one Emaline really loves, but she'll do anything for her father."

Julia shook her head. "What on earth are you talking about?"

Dolores took a deep breath. "According to Frank, Ed Pierce has been trying to buy Red Stone for years, but Mister Brantley refused to sell it at any price. So the next move was to marry Emaline off to Mac."

Julia remembered the night she first met Mac's family and what he had told her about Red Stone. "You mean Mister Pierce thinks Mac is getting the grove?"

"You got it. But he's in for a big fat surprise because Frank, being the oldest, will inherit his mother's property." Dolores's face creased with delight. "And when we get Red Stone, there'll be no more chiles, no more weather reports, no more long, hot summers."

"But I thought you told me Emaline was in love with Frank."

"Oh, she is, but Frank won't leave me. I have insurance."

"This doesn't make any sense. Emaline and Mac were engaged . . ."

"Frank and Emaline have been lovers for years. Even when she was living with Mac, those two would go at it hot and heavy right under his nose."

Julia felt her jaw go slack. "But Mac must have suspected something."

"Nope. He thought Emaline left him because he went with the Indian Health. But it was just an excuse to end it. That's when she up and went to San Francisco. But her leaving didn't end it with Frank. He goes out there almost every other month."

"Oh, Dolores. I can't believe Frank would . . ."

Dolores snorted. "He thinks he's sooo smart. Tells me he has the gambling itch and has to go to Vegas. But I know what kind of itch he has."

"But maybe he really does go to Las Vegas."

"Don't I wish." The woman paused. "I've never told anybody this, but I've actually seen them going at it."

Julia read the woman's pain and touched her arm. "I'm so sorry."

"Don't be." Dolores blinked rising tears away and gave a harsh laugh. "After I got over the shock, it got to be sort of a game. They'd wait until Mac was off the land and I'd pretend I was leaving, too. Instead, I'd park down the road and sneak back to that little house where Frank and I lived before Mrs. B died. There's a nice-sized room in the attic above the bedroom. A person can hole up there for months as long as they have access to the toilet and kitchen. That's where I hid when I spied on them."

"Why have you stayed with Frank all these years?"

Dolores shrugged. "Beats the hell out of going back to a barrio in Tucson."

"You met Frank in Tucson?"

"He joined the Air Force a couple of years after Mac was born. I was working at the coffee shop in the Davis-Monthan PX. Frank came by for coffee, we fell in lust and he knocked me up. Anyway, the baby was my ticket out of Tucson."

Dolores feathered her hands over her breasts and thick waist. "At first Frank was crazy for me. Couldn't keep his hands off. I used to be beautiful, you know. But then . . ." She touched the scars on her cheeks. "Caught chickenpox from little Allen. It was a real bad case."

"I can barely see them," Julia lied.

"Well, thanks." Dolores slapped her thigh. "Hey. It hasn't been too bad a life outside of the fact that Frank and I hate each other. But I gave him the one thing he always wanted—a son. Allen's the apple of his eye."

Julia nodded. "I could tell."

Dolores's brief respite from anger ended and her eyes narrowed. "Frank's not going to leave me for that whore because of this." She rummaged through her purse, produced a yellowed envelope and waved it in Julia's face. "I found this in Mrs. Brantley's desk drawer the day she died, and with the information that's in this letter I've got Frank right by the balls."

Julia took the envelope and read the bold scrawl. "For Frank Allen Brantley at my death."

"Go ahead. Open it." Dolores bent forward, her eyes flashing her excitement.

"I have no right . . ."

"If I say so, you do. No one knows about this, most especially Frank. Because what's in there is dy-na-mite. And I've kept it hidden all these years."

Julia shook her head. "I can't, Dolores. Especially not the way things stand now. Mac and I may never . . ."

Dolores snatched the envelope back, "Yeah, maybe you're right. This is heavy stuff. No use to burden you with it—yet."

Julia rushed to cover her relief. "Thank you for thinking the letter might help me."

Dolores nodded. "Oh, there's no doubt about that. This letter will destroy Frank and that whore for sure."

Julia thought back to the words the two women had exchanged just outside the rest room at Radium Springs. Dolores's, "I have all the proof I need to make your life as miserable as you've made mine," finally made sense.

Dolores jumped up. "Well, chica, looks like I've done all I can do for you."

Julia rose and extended her hand. "I really appreciate your coming by."

Dolores pumped her hand, then threw her arms around her in a giant bear hug. "We're sisters under the skin, and don't you forget it."

She stepped back and said, "I hope you'll find it in your heart to forgive Mac. He's really a fine guy. Just dumb like most men when it comes to women."

"I can't promise you anything except that I'll be at the funeral to honor Mister Brantley."

"He would like that. I know he would. It's at ten-thirty. Spelling's Mortuary. I'll save you a place next to me. If you're interested, the burial will be at the Hatch Cemetery. Brantley family plot."

At the thought of seeing Mac, Julia's headache jammed into third gear. "No. Please don't. I don't want to make anyone uncomfortable, especially Mac. But I'll definitely be there. I promise."

CHAPTER 27

MAC ROLLED to a sitting position on the living room couch, where he had passed out the night before. A roaring fire and a bottle of Scotch had given him ample excuse not to return to the scene of his crime, which remained in the same state that he and Emaline had left it.

Unfortunately, in the grim early light of a new day there were debts to be paid for his detour into self-pity. The bottle of Scotch was empty, the fire cold, his liver ached and his lead-filled eyes throbbed with each heartbeat.

He slumped over and covered his face with his hands to contemplate the day that stretched bleakly before him. Joyless. Empty. His father gone. Julia gone. Not that he could blame her. He'd played the fool. Maybe lost everything.

The sound of an approaching car broke into his desolation, but the small surge of hope that it might be Julia died when he jumped up to see Frank's red Ford Ranger slam to a stop.

When Mac opened the front door and stepped out onto the porch, Frank paused on the path and grinned. "You look like a bad piece of cow shit."

"Very astute. Want some coffee?"

"Is that all you got?" Frank headed for the kitchen and settled at the breakfast table. "What happened to you yesterday? I thought you were coming to help me make plans."

"Sorry. It was an emergency."

"The Hanta again?"

Mac shook his head. "Don't I wish. Epidemics are a snap compared to a hurt and angry woman. Julia found out about Saturday night."

Frank opened his mouth to say something, then seemed to change his mind. "Got a beer?"

Mac checked the time. It was just past seven. "Isn't it a little early?"

"Not for me. I'm still playing nursemaid to those G-D chiles. Been up since four. Guess you didn't hear we were supposed to have a front come through at dawn. They were predicting hail but the damn thing occluded. So, hell, yes, it's the middle of the day for me."

Mac couldn't help but laugh through his headache. "Hey, who goes by the clock? I'm so hungover it could still be yesterday." He set a longneck on the table, poured himself a mug of stale, reheated coffee, and took the opposite chair.

Frank opened the newspaper and pointed to their father's picture. "I brought this over so you could see Dad's obit."

Mac scanned the laudatory article and put the paper to one side. "He deserved as much. So, the funeral's tomorrow?"

"I saw no reason to wait. Might as well get it over with." His brother held out the empty bottle. "Boy, that sure hit the spot. How 'bout the other wing?"

After Mac deposited a second bottle on the table, Frank took a long draught and said, "Was she worth it?"

"That's none of your business."

"Oh, but it is." Frank sat back and fixed his colorless eyes on him.

Mac bristled. "Why are you so damn interested in what happened Saturday night?" When he saw his brother's eyes cut away, he felt compelled to cover his sudden rush of guilt. "Good Lord, Frank. Emaline and I were engaged to be married. We lived together almost a year. Saturday night was just a . . ."

Frank held up his hand. "I know exactly what it was. But I don't think you do."

"A mistake. That's what."

"Not on Emaline's part. That bastard Pierce made her come home. Asked her to make another stab at getting you back."

"Why would he do that?"

"For some reason Ed seems to think Red Stone will go to you."

Mac hoped his tone remained even. "But, he's mistaken."

"You're dead right about that. Once Red Stone is mine, I'll be rid of the Square B and those G-D chiles." Frank shuddered. "You can't believe how long I've waited to get that monkey off my back. Just the sight of storm clouds on the horizon or the sound of thunder made my guts wrench. But now, Mama's little cash cow down in Mesilla will free me at last. Soon as the will's read, I'm divorcing Dolores and heading west."

Mac almost spilled his coffee. Frank had never complained about the long hours, or the crop failures, or the weather. Instead, he played the faithful servant, helping the elder Brantley make their name synonymous with the finest chiles in New Mexico.

"You? Leave the Valley?"

"I can't wait. You can do what you want with the goddamn chiles. Sell 'em. Plow 'em under. Hell, throw a bash and burn 'em."

"Guess I've never thought much about how you felt, Frank. I wish you'd told me."

"I did what any good son would do. I loved Dad and he depended on me. I couldn't let him down. Just like you couldn't. He was proud of us both."

Mac nodded and took a gulp of coffee in a vain attempt to wash away the grief that blocked his response.

Frank's voice broke the silence. "Now, about Emaline."

Mac rubbed his aching eyes with the heels of both hands. "Why do you keep bringing Emaline into this? It was a mistake."

"You never did get it, did you?"

"Get what?" Mac paused, stopped by the strange expression on his brother's face.

Frank hunched forward. "Emaline Pierce has belonged to me since the morning of her fourteenth birthday. I took her then, and for the next four years I took her whenever and wherever I felt like it."

Mac's mind raced back to that first day in the hayloft and forward through the years. Frank and Emaline? When had they found the time? Emaline was always on the school bus when he got on and she always got off at his stop. They would do their homework, then ride or, after that hot day in the hayloft, head for the cot in the tack room.

"I don't get it. When did you . . . ?"

Frank grinned. "It wasn't easy, but I managed."

"You bastard. She was just a kid."

Frank threw back his head and laughed. "Kid? Emaline was never a kid. Why, she was the one who made the first moves on me, throwing her shoulders back so I could see the tits she had grown over the summer."

"You knew better than that. You were thirty years old—twice her age. Don't try to tell me she took advantage of you."

"Well, that's what I'm telling you. That heifer was hot."

Frank must have read Mac's disgust because he slumped back in his chair, shook his head and said in a low voice, "I swear to you, I didn't take her cherry. But I didn't find out until years later who did." His eyes grew icy, and when he spoke his words rasped through the silence. "Would you believe it? Her father."

"Ed Pierce?"

Frank nodded. "It went on until Emaline was about four. That's when Palatia caught him. I'm surprised he's alive today."

Mac nodded. There had been something old about Emaline, even in the beginning. She always made the first move when it concerned sex and continued to be the initiator throughout their relationship.

Saturday night had been no different. In her usual fashion, Emaline had taken charge. For a few hours she enabled him to forget the pain of his loss. But if her goal was to recapture what they once shared she failed. Instead, she had finally set him free.

Mac took a sip of suddenly rancid coffee. "She didn't stop with you, Frank. The day after her birthday she initiated me."

It was Frank's turn to look stunned. "But Emaline told me it didn't happen with you until the summer she graduated."

"She lied."

Frank stared at Mac for what seemed like ages, then squared his shoulders. "So she lied. It doesn't matter about you or all the other men she's been with. I still want her."

CHAPTER 28

PHYLLIS MOVED from behind her desk to take Mac's hand. "Again, let me say how sorry I am about your dad."

"Thanks, Phyllis. I have to admit it was quite a shock. I should have been more concerned about his health, but he seemed so indestructible."

She nodded. "I know. None of us wants to admit our parents are getting on. Shall I tell her you're here?"

"Not yet. I need your help."

Before he left for Hatch, Mac picked up the telephone and secured a three o'clock appointment with Julia, asking that Phyllis keep his visit a surprise. At first he planned to keep his mission a secret but finally decided to widen the gap that already existed between Julia and himself by explaining his predicament.

"Julia returned my ring yesterday. It's pretty bad between us. Not her fault. Something I did. I'm here to try to make amends."

"Oh, dear."

"Please, let her be the one to tell you. The only reason I'm bringing this up is because I have to leave for Albuquerque after the funeral. Indian Health wanted me there yesterday, but when I told them about Dad they gave me a few days to handle things. I just need someone to know where I am in case anything . . ."

"Same phone and all?" The woman was suddenly all business, and when Mac moved toward the door she raised her hand, saying more formally than he would have liked, "Doctor Fairchild may be sleeping.

Told me she hardly slept a wink over the weekend. Now, I know why. Poor thing."

Mac cracked the door and stepped inside to see Julia curled on the couch with her right arm covering her eyes to shield them from the light and her left hand, palm open, hanging over the edge of the cushion.

His first instinct was to kiss her awake, but she was no longer his. Instead, he settled in the leather chair next to the couch, his aching eyes consuming every part of Julia, wanting to touch her, knowing he shouldn't.

After a few tortured moments, he took her hand in his and whispered, "Hey there, Red."

He watched Julia's eyes come into focus and her surprise when she realized who it was. She yanked her hand away and sat up.

"How did you get in here?"

"I made an appointment with Phyllis this morning."

"She didn't say anything."

"I asked her not to."

Julia stood and quickly crossed the room to sit behind her desk. Mac followed to stand in front of it. "We have to talk."

He watched her run her hands through her short copper curls, a gesture she made whenever she was flustered. "There's nothing more to say."

"But there is. I found out something that might make a difference." He sat down across the effective barrier of the large desk, wishing Julia had remained on the couch. She would have been more accessible there. He needed to touch her, put his arms around her, kiss her, but he guessed she had moved to protect herself from her own vulnerability, or at least he hoped so.

"Frank came by the house early this morning to tell me he's going to divorce Dolores." Mac read the interest in Julia's face and relaxed a little. "He wants to marry Emaline."

"I see."

"You don't seem too surprised."

"Dolores was here this morning. She told me about Frank and Emaline, but, after what happened Saturday night, that left me even more confused."

"Well, you can count me as the biggest dumbbell in Doña Ana County; I just found out the truth about them this morning."

Mac related the sordid history of Emaline and the Brantley brothers, ending with, "There's one thing you should know about Emaline that might explain all this."

"Don't you dare defend her."

"I'm not, but Frank told me this morning that Emaline was sexually abused by her father when she was small."

Julia's eyes widened, then grew hard. "Ed Pierce should be hung for that."

"I agree, but surely you can see why her behavior's been so skewed."

Julia nodded. "As a clinician I can understand. But that doesn't account for your actions."

Mac hunched into his shoulders as the steel band around his head ratcheted another notch. "I can't explain my behavior, clinically or otherwise, except that it was stupid and hurtful."

He counted a few ceiling squares before offering a lame buffer to his cause. "Frank says he wants Emaline no matter what."

Julia's face filled with disgust. "Then that makes him as sick as she is."

"I suppose you could say that."

Julia stared at him for what seemed like an age. "And what about you?"

"I told you, Emaline doesn't mean a thing to me and hasn't for a long time. If Frank wants her, he's welcome to her."

At that, he saw her eyes soften. "Poor Dolores. I hope Frank doesn't think he's fooling anybody. She's known about them for years."

"She has?"

"She told me she's seen Frank and Emaline together—many times."

"The only reason Emaline made a play for me was because of . . ."

Julia beat him to it. "Red Stone."

Mac felt a small push of hope. "You believe me?"

"The whole mess is too weird not to believe. Besides, Dolores said the same thing, except she thinks Frank will inherit the grove."

"It's possible Dad could have changed his mind. Anyway, we'll find out tomorrow. The will is being read after the funeral."

Julia rose from her chair and turned to gaze out the window. "Do you know anything about a letter to Frank from your mother?"

Mac hardly heard her question. He saw the chance to get around the barrier and moved quickly to her side. Once there, he felt the old familiar sexual charge flash between them as Julia whirled to face him.

"Don't do this to me," she begged.

Mac moved slightly away but stood his ground, noticing Julia's breathing was picking up and a fine veil of moisture was forming on her upper lip.

"You mentioned a letter?"

She tore her eyes from his and went on. "Dolores has a letter addressed to Frank. She told me she found it in your mother's desk the day after she died. She told me the letter was—'dynamite.'"

"I don't give a damn about that. I just want—" Mac touched Julia's cheek with the back of his hand.

She flinched. "Don't."

He ignored her protest by tracing the line of her jaw to her ear, then downward to the silky nape of her neck.

She shivered but kept talking, though her voice wasn't quite as forceful as it had been. "Dolores wanted me to read it but I told her that things between us were uncertain and I didn't want to be privy to such . . ."

Mac leaned slowly forward to invade the little space between them and, as his mouth met Julia's, he felt her lips tremble and soften in response.

"Stop it."

The force of her hands slamming against his chest made him stagger backward, allowing her enough room to brush past him and put the desk between them again.

"You have no right to do that."

Her eyes filled and Mac silently cursed the anguish he saw in them and the stupid, pointless evening with Emaline that put it there. "I would give anything to undo what happened."

He took a step toward her but stopped as Julia, face crumbling, glanced frantically toward the door.

"Okay, I'll go. But I need you, Julia. I want us to get married just like we planned."

"Married? After what happened Saturday, I would be insane to ever trust you again."

Mac held up his hand to deflect her words. "Don't say it's over. Give me a chance to . . ."

"Get out." Her ragged voice cut into his plea.

He walked to the door and paused before he opened it. Julia was turned away from him but he could see her body lurch with each silent sob.

Mac's words strained across the room in thin, husky rasps. "I love you, Julia. I've never loved you more."

He let himself out and walked quickly past Phyllis Wills, afraid she might stop him. Afraid of what she might see if she did.

CHAPTER 29

THE PARKING LOT at Spelling's Mortuary on Griggs Street in Las Cruces was crammed with cars by the time Julia arrived, so she opted for a space in the Safeway lot behind the building. From there she could see the threads of people coming from all directions, some walking alone while others came in clutches of two or more.

Julia peeked in the rearview mirror to see a pale reflection featuring eyes bloodshot from too many tears and too little sleep underlined by distinct purple smudges. She made a small attempt to liven her face by adding more lipstick, but the addition only made her more of a washout.

The soft chime of the carillon called her from the car, and she hurried toward the building. Most of the other mourners were clumped at the main entrance exchanging small talk. Wanting to avoid as many inquiring eyes as she could, she decided to enter through the side door.

She was just picking up the pen to sign the guest book when a hand covered hers and Steve Duke pressed against her. "I've missed you."

At his touch, Julia tried to ignore the thrill that coursed through her. "It's only been two days."

"You're wrong. It's been forty-nine and a half very long hours."

"Really?" Julia felt her face grow warm and she stammered, "It was nice of you to come down for the funeral."

"I won't lie. The funeral's just an excuse to see you."

"I won't lie either. I'm glad you're here."

Steve's hand surrounded hers and Julia heard him whisper, "Are you free this afternoon?"

At that, the memory of that Sunday kiss returned and the muted sympathies of the people standing in the receiving hall drowned in the rapid beat of her heart.

Julia nodded. "I canceled everything." Steve's face lit up. "I knew that long haul from Albuquerque would be worth it."

"Worth what?" Mac demanded behind them.

Steve extended his hand. "My condolences, Mac. Your dad was a fine man."

Mac's brief handshake was an obviously strained courtesy. "Thanks." He turned to Julia. "I hope you'll be joining the family."

Julia reached for Steve's hand before she spoke. "I'm afraid not. I'm sitting with Steve."

Mac's eyes widened, then he glanced down at her hand clasping Steve's. When he looked up she saw the pain in his eyes. "As you wish. Thank you both for coming."

Julia stared down, embarrassed by her unnecessary cruelty, and when Mac turned away she released Steve's hand. She had meant to hurt Mac, but instead of the expected pleasure, she was forced to swallow around the growing boulder in her throat.

"What was that all about?" Steve asked.

She was ashamed of her unexpected tears. "It's over. But I told you last Saturday night that it would be."

Steve reached for her left hand and gave a low whistle. "If I say I'm sorry, I'll be lying."

She yanked her hand from his. "So don't say anything."

Julia followed Steve into an empty pew in the back of the chapel and knelt to pray. It was a habit she couldn't ignore, a part of her Episcopalian upbringing.

At first no words came, until finally a feeble petition for Mac's father formed and she slid back into the hard wooden pew to watch the chapel fill.

Though there were rows of people between, Julia could see Mac seated in the front pew. Next to him, she saw Frank's silver mane and

Dolores's black crown, echoed by Allen's shiny pompadour. A quick scan of the rest of the congregation produced the Sandovals, but after a second close inspection Julia realized all three Pierces were missing.

When the service ended, Julia saw Mac touch the side of his father's casket and lower his head. Her eyes filled at his sorrow and she bowed her own to hide her unbidden and sudden empathy for the man she once was positive would be her husband.

Steve pressed a neatly folded handkerchief into her hand and was just draping his arm protectively across her shoulder when the funeral recession music filled the room.

Julia dabbed her eyes and stood, breaking contact with him, and when he tried to put his arm around her waist she took a step away and shoved his handkerchief at him.

She watched the casket roll by, but avoided any eye contact with the family. She couldn't bear to see Mac's face or Dolores's black question marks. Even then, she couldn't stop the stinging tears and hoped they would be read as grief for Mac's father, not for her broken heart.

As soon as the rest of the people began to stir Julia abandoned Steve, slipping through the chapel doors and down the wide reception hall to the side exit. Once outside, she pushed toward the Safeway parking lot, wanting to escape, hoping the pain of seeing Mac would dissolve with distance.

She was almost to her Range Rover when Steve grabbed her arm. "Hey, wait a minute. What's your hurry?"

Julia ignored his question and kept walking.

"Aren't we going to have lunch?"

"I have to get back to Piñon Mesa."

"What for? I thought you canceled your appointments for the rest of the day."

"I have to get away from here."

Steve stepped in stride beside her and grabbed her arm. "Of course you do. But you have to eat something. At least, you should."

She couldn't help but smile through her tears. "Who do you think you are, a doctor?"

"That's what they tell me up in Albuquerque." He pointed toward the Organ Mountains. "There's a dive called Don's up at San Augustin Pass; food's next to deplorable, but you can see the whole valley. How about it?"

Julia shook her head. "I'll make a terrible lunch partner."

"Let me be the judge of that. Come on. It's a beautiful day and the drive will do you good."

CHAPTER 30

"INTO YOUR HANDS, oh merciful Savior, we commend your servant, Mackenzie Luke Brantley . . ." Mac raised his bowed head to scan the crush of people standing on the other side of his father's grave one last time, then gave up. Julia wasn't coming.

"I'm sitting with Steve." Her words and her hand clasping Duke's had gnawed at Mac throughout the service at Spelling's and even now continued their ferocious attack.

It was plain Julia made an obvious move to hurt him and he couldn't blame her for that—he had hurt her in the worst possible way.

What bothered Mac most was his longtime rival and how quickly he had insinuated himself into Julia's life.

Though Julia mentioned that Steve Duke was her attending physician in Albuquerque, Mac had been unpleasantly surprised to see him at Radium Springs. Did Julia invite him? No, she wouldn't have. It was the Sandovals' party. Steve was their longtime friend. It was Steve who recommended Bob for his job at Piñon Mesa.

Mac shut his eyes as the minister's voice droned above him. He wanted to think about his father, but all he could see was Julia moving into Duke's outstretched arms as the band struck up a slow dance. He had intended to cut back in, but Emaline walked into his arms and the evening went to hell.

He'd have to do something about Steve Duke and quick. With that bastard hanging around Julia, he wouldn't stand a chance at reclaiming her.

"Oh, God." His anguish found a voice.

Frank clutched his arm. "You okay?"

Mac nodded and the vise released. He saw that Frank's eyes were as dry as his. Brantley men never cried in public.

He glanced past Frank to see Dolores sobbing. Let Dolores do the wailing for the family. She needed the practice. She would have plenty more crying to do after the will was read and Frank delivered his news.

"Your turn." Frank's jab jolted Mac back to the task before him and he took the small spade filled with dirt from his brother's outstretched hand.

Sometime during his musings his father's casket had been lowered and when he saw Frank's sprinkle of dirt on the lid of the simple bronze box, his heart wrenched.

His dirt hit the casket just as the minister said, "Go in peace," then he was shaking outstretched hands and mouthing "thank you" to those offering condolences.

Both Bob and Myrtle Sandoval clutched Mac's hand. "If there's anything we can do . . ."

"Not a thing, thanks, but I hope you'll come on out to the Square B and share some of Cuca's nachos and a drink."

Bob's face relaxed. "Is that where Julia went? When I didn't see her I . . ."

Frank's curt, "Let's get outta here," saved Mac and he broke away, saying, "See you two out there, okay?"

"You bet." Bob nodded and steered Myrtle toward the gravel path.

The two men followed the couple down the cedar-lined path to the cemetery exit and headed toward the truck.

Frank waited until the Sandovals' car passed, then muttered, "Glad that's over," and hauled himself into the pickup.

Mac climbed in beside him, leaned back and closed his eyes as the vision of Julia seated next to the man he detested most burned clear in his mind.

Frank's next question didn't help. "I saw Julia in the back of the chapel sitting next to Steve Duke. What gives?"

"Damned if I know. Where was Emaline?"

"Headed back to San Francisco. They can't do a closing without her. She'll be back day after tomorrow and stay through the weekend."

Frank shot him a knowing leer. "Can't seem to keep her hands off me."

Mac rolled his eyes. Only a few days before, Emaline hadn't been able to keep her hands off him. "You really going to leave the Valley?"

"You got it. I'm moving to San Francisco as soon as I can get the ball rolling, you know, the divorce."

"Julia tells me Dolores knows about you two."

The color left Frank's face. "She knows?"

"Seems she has for a long time. Dolores showed Julia an envelope addressed to you from Mama that was to be opened at her death and told her there was dynamite in that letter."

"Dynamite?"

"That's the word she used."

The two spent the rest of the trip in grim silence. By the time they reached the hacienda, the parking area was already jammed with cars and others lined the drive.

Frank inched past the cars parked along the edge of the road and headed for a vacant spot near the closest barn. "Never known a friend of Dad's to turn down free drinks and food."

He surveyed the dusty field and stepped down. "Go on in. I want to check the chiles. If we don't get rain soon, we'll have to irrigate."

"Don't be too long. People will want to see you."

He started for the long line of people at the front door and paused, realizing he needed a few minutes to collect himself before he could face anyone.

The verandah was empty. Mac veered toward it, hoping for a brief respite from his grief, but the fragrant honey of just-blooming wisteria did nothing but add to his misery.

His mother had often taken tea with him beneath that scented arbor, and Mac ached for her touch and to hear her soft laughter once again. She would have known what to do—would have given him sound advice. If she were alive, he wouldn't be in such a mess. She hated Emaline.

Voices on the other side of the door cut him loose from the poignant memory, and he hurried away from the hacienda toward the large cluster of pampas grass and the fish pond his mother built when he was six. Though the gazebo was no longer there, Mac knew he would find the refuge of a comfortable bench behind the protection of the high grass.

Reflections of the noon sun danced between the bright green pads and pale-pink lilies that floated above the hazy glints of goldfish darting below.

Images from his childhood came flooding back—his father, his mother, the happier times.

He sank to the bench and let his grief take over, relieved that no one would be able to see him. He was a grown man, almost forty, much too old to be discovered bawling like some baby.

Slamming doors and friendly calls cut through the pampas to remind Mac of his mission and pull him toward the hacienda. He entered through the kitchen to find the house filled with Brantley friends clutching a drink in one hand and one of Cuca's nachos in the other. After exchanging a few pleasantries with those who stopped him, he headed for the front door, where Dolores stood talking with the family attorney.

She pointed the lawyer toward the bar and waved Mac over. When he reached her, she demanded, "Why wasn't Julia at the cemetery?"

"Your guess is as good as mine."

Mac started to move away, but Dolores caught his arm. "What was she doing sitting with Steve Duke?"

"You know just as much as I do, Dolores. Will you excuse me?"

Mac pushed her hand away and headed for the bar, suddenly in need of a drink. He didn't want to think about Julia and that bastard. She had every reason to be furious with him, but was she mad enough for a payback with Duke? He had seen her car leave Spelling's with Duke right behind her. Where did they go? Back to her place? It killed him to think that at this very moment Julia might be wrapped in Duke's sympathetic arms.

Myrtle Sandoval blocked his path. "Gotcha. Now, you come over here and tell me what's going on."

"What's going on is I'm getting a drink; what can I get for you?"

Myrtle hooked her arm through his. "You know I don't drink during the day, but help yourself. Just know I'm not letting you slip away without an explanation."

She accompanied him to the bar and waited while he tossed down one Scotch and retrieved another. When he turned, he saw the concern in her eyes.

"Is it that bad?"

Mac nodded. "Do you mind stepping out onto the verandah? I don't want anyone to hear."

Myrtle trotted behind him through the door. "I don't know if I want to hear."

Once Mac was sure they were alone, he delivered the news. "Julia returned my ring."

"What on earth? That girl's nuts about you. She's lost her mind."

"I wish it were that simple, Myrt, but I did something unforgivable and she has every reason to break it off."

Myrtle was silent for a moment. "I won't ask what, but I have a pretty good idea. I saw Emaline drive you away from the party."

"Yeah. I wasn't thinking very straight that night."

"Did you know that Steve Duke drove Julia home after you and Emaline left?"

Myrtle might as well have picked up a gun and shot him. Julia didn't mention that Steve had taken her home. But by the time they met Sunday, there were more important issues at stake. Did Steve stay in Las Cruces until the funeral? Mac shook his head. No, he had mentioned something about it being well worth the trip. It made no difference, at that moment he would gladly choke the life out of the sonovabitch.

Myrtle patted his arm. "I didn't think you knew. But if you did what I think you did . . ." A clap of thunder interrupted the end of her sentence.

They both turned to the north, and Myrtle gasped, "Oh Lord, that's an awful black cloud."

Mac rushed for the door. "There's hail in that cloud; I've got to find Frank."

CHAPTER 31

THE DRIVE across the mesa filled with bright desert blooms was the perfect medicine for Julia's depression. To her surprise, Steve possessed a sharp wit and a genuine sense of humor, and his Emergency Room tales were so fascinating that for a while she was able to forget about Mac and Emaline.

"Well, here we are."

Julia squinted into the bright sunlight to see dust swirling lazy circles across the barren parking lot and a faded blue door swinging idly on its hinges marking the entrance. True to Steve's description, Don's looked more like a run-down gas station than a thriving restaurant.

Steve noticed her dismay. "Don't let the place put you off. We're here for the food and the view."

They walked into darkness. When her eyes adjusted, Julia saw tables covered in faded red-checked oilcloth with green, half-burned candles leaning at odd angles. Worse still, the room was empty except for a couple of drinkers straddling stools at the far end of the bar.

"Hey, Steve." A blonde waitress peered through the cracked kitchen door and waved.

Steve waved back and pointed toward a half-open sliding glass door. "We're going out on the porch. A couple of Dos Equis and two of Don's famous burritos, okay?"

"Make yourself to home. I'll be right out." The waitress disappeared and yelled the order.

Julia followed him to the deck overlooking the valley. Far below and in the distance it appeared as a greening strip on either side of the

Rio Grande. To the north were the Doña Ana Mountains that greeted Julia every morning she awakened, but from this height they resembled a cluster of low sienna mounds. To the south the mountain behind the campus of New Mexico State, fondly referred to as "A" Mountain, seemed almost flat.

"I can't believe it." Julia waved her hand across the vista. "The view is breathtaking. Why isn't this place jammed?"

Steve led her to a table at the railing. "It is on weekends."

"Do you come here often?"

He nodded. "Anytime I'm in Las Cruces. Don's an old high school buddy. We played first-string basketball together."

Julia sat just in time to dodge a plate laden with a burrito smothered in chili and cheese that landed in front of her.

"Don makes the weirdest burrito west of the Pecos, but don't let the goo put you off. One taste and I'll guarantee you won't be able to stop." Steve took a long swig of beer and dove into his meal.

Steve was right. Between the creamy, zesty bites Julia studied the man across the table. He was intriguing. And his mouth—she felt herself flush, embarrassed by the heat that came at the memory of Steve's kiss and the powerful attraction he held for her.

She sensed his stare and decided to take a bold approach. "So, why aren't you married?"

Steve's eyes hardened for just an instant, then he gave an uncomfortable laugh. "I never expected you to ask that."

"Surely, there have been other women in your life. Haven't you been in love with a few? Even serious with one or two?"

"No tales to tell here." He drained the rest of his beer and motioned to the waitress for another before he countered, "What about you? I mean, anybody before Mac?"

"Yes. Someone much older. It didn't work out. Guess I'm not so lucky when it comes to romance."

"Don't be so hard on yourself." Steve put his hand over hers. "Isn't it better you found out what kind of guy Mac is before you married?"

When she didn't answer, Steve turned toward the panoramic scene, seemingly lost in his own thoughts.

Lulled by the food and beer and the hum of conversation behind her, Julia shut her eyes and sat back in her chair to soak up the warm afternoon sun. She was attracted to Steve. Even now she could taste his mouth on hers and the sudden rush of her heart echoed the impact of the memory.

Steve's voice broke into her fantasy. "Daydreaming?"

Julia's eyes flew open. Did he see something in her face? Was it flushed? She cleared her throat. "There's nothing left to daydream about."

The dull ache, diminished by the food and Steve's humor, returned. Julia turned north to see the sky crammed with angry, roiling clouds. "That's a surprise. I didn't hear anything about rain."

Steve jumped to his feet. "That's a hell of a storm. We better get going before it hits. I've got to be in Albuquerque for the seven a.m. shift."

CHAPTER 32

IT WAS FIVE O'CLOCK, but the sky was still dark with clouds and thunder rolled in the distance.

"That was one hell of a storm," Mac mumbled and drained the rest of his drink. He was slumped in one of the pair of brown leather lounge chairs that had graced the hacienda library for as long as he could remember.

Frank Brantley sat across from him—one eye swollen shut and turning an ugly purple, the other half-open and bloodshot. His funeral suit bore the loamy spatters of New Mexico mud as did his boots. Yes, Mac's big brother was definitely drunk.

Mac supposed he was just as bad. At least his boots seemed to be in the same condition. He had raced after Frank, made it to the barn, then watched the hail pound the nearest field of chiles into sad, limp clumps.

His brother shouted curses at the storm, wildly flailing his arms at the heavens, until a golf-ball chunk of hail felled him and Mac dragged him to safety.

When the hail subsided, the two trudged through the rain to a half-emptied house, bid the last of the mourners goodbye, then watched the cars stream down the road.

Mac gave Frank a half-salute. "Well, guess I should hit the road."

"No way, Bro. At least not until we knock back a few in honor of Dad." Frank motioned him toward the study. That had been almost two hours before and now they both were loaded.

The bad news was he wasn't as wasted as Frank. He wanted to be. The ache for Julia demanded it.

"Are you drunk, yet?" Frank slurred. "Well, I am. I'm drunk as a skunk." He chuckled to himself. "Whole damn crop's gone except for that piece on the other side of the river."

Mac tried to nod in agreement, but his head refused to obey. "Yeah, that's what I heard."

"Damn hail's a killer. But I won't have to worry about replanting. Won't need to. Won't ever need to again."

Frank leaned forward until he almost lost his balance. "Hey. Did you hear that? No more fucking chiles. Just Red Stone and Emaline." He pointed toward the bar. "How 'bout getting another bottle and let's celebrate?"

"I'd like that but I can't drink another drop. Besides, I was supposed to be on the way to Chaco Point long before now."

"Chaco Point?" Frank tried to focus his eyes, but failed. "Hantavirus?"

"New case. New location. Very puzzling."

"What about the will?"

"Read it without me."

"Nah. We'll wait. How long?"

"No more than a few days. At best a week. I'll know more once I get there."

Frank emptied his glass. "Nothing's going to happen to the damn will. Nothing can change."

Mac shut his eyes, afraid Frank might read the truth in them. But maybe his father had changed the will. Maybe Frank would get Red Stone, after all. It didn't matter to him. Still, better to let sleeping dogs lie.

He hunched forward and suppressed a hiccup. "Well, I better get going." But when he tried to stand, his legs refused to hold him and he fell back in the chair.

"Guess I'm not going anywhere tonight."

There was no response. Frank had passed out.

CHAPTER 33

JULIA STOOD in the dimly lit entry locked in Steve's arms, barely aware of the rush of cool, damp air sliding around them through the open front door. She heard the pelt of the rain on the porch, heard the thunder crash after each flash of lightning, heard her heart pounding against her ribs. She knew she was in over her head, but she couldn't make herself pull away from the compelling draw of Steve's lips.

The trip down the mountain had been filled with tension, not because of the blinding rain, but from the palpable lust they shared.

At a stoplight on the high mesa, Steve took her in his arms. The moment their lips touched was still etched in her mind: the rough-smooth texture of his mouth, the way he coaxed her tongue to meet his, the urgency of their kiss.

An impatient honk from the car behind them broke them apart, but that one kiss was enough to leave Julia aching for more.

Lightning stabs followed by sharp cracks of thunder chased them up the walk. Even at their fast pace they were soaked by the time they reached the porch.

Julia searched the depths of her purse. "I can't—ah, voila." She waved them in Steve's face, then dropped them. "Sorry about that. Guess they have a life of their own."

They both laughed as Steve retrieved them and unlocked the door.

Once inside he asked if he could kiss her, and she answered by raising her mouth to meet his.

This first kiss was a surprisingly tender contrast to the one at the stoplight, and Julia felt him tremble as his tongue barely touched hers in gentle invitation.

After a few moments, Steve drew away to plumb the depths of her eyes with such hunger that she could no longer stand the separation.

When her arms circled his neck, he groaned as his mouth took hers and he crushed her to him, leaving her breathless and aroused.

Julia knew she should step out of his embrace, tell him to leave— but she didn't. Instead she let him trace her waist, her hips, then slide his hands to cup beneath her rear and clasp her to him.

As soon as she realized Steve was as excited as she was, she pushed out of his grasp. When she spoke, her voice held little command. "You'd better go."

Steve's eyes narrowed and, though it was brief, the look she saw made her try levity to break the tension. "There must be something about this hallway . . ."

Steve laughed and his eyes softened as he reached for her hand. "Must be. I'm sorry. I just can't help myself when you're so close."

He backed against the door, shutting it with his weight, drawing her to him so that her head rested on his chest and she could hear the ragged beat of his heart.

Julia leaned into him, her arms dangling at her side too heavy to lift. In truth, her whole body was weighted with longing. She needed to be careful. One wrong move and she would spin out of control.

As promised, Steve made no further moves. Instead, he held her loosely in his arms, resting his head lightly on hers as their passion faded along with the distant thunder.

When he finally spoke, the words resonated through his chest. "I'm in love with you."

Julia didn't answer; she couldn't say "love" and mean it the way she knew he did.

Steve put his hands on her upper arms and moved her away. "Did you hear me?"

Julia nodded.

"What are you going to do about it?"

She barely heard her own voice. "I don't know."

"I want you, Julia."

"It's too soon. I need time to work this through."

Steve studied her for a long moment. "Yes. Maybe it is." His arms went around her. "I'm on duty all next week and because I can't change the schedule I'll have to give you some space—but not for long."

His lips burned into her forehead and he turned to open the door. "I'll be in touch."

"I'd like that."

"You can count on it." He smiled and shut the door behind him.

Julia let out her breath and rested her throbbing head against the cool wood. She hardly knew the man, yet the chemistry between them was too powerful for her to ignore. A lot of it was probably rebound and her anger at Mac, but Steve had been there for her at Radium Springs and had given his sympathetic support since then. What was it about him that attracted her so? Animal magnetism? The fire she detected beneath his smooth exterior? His mouth against hers?

She knew she was vulnerable. Mac had hurt her and Steve was the perfect payback, but that was the reaction of an adolescent. Was that it? Or was she acting out from some past need she hadn't addressed? What if Steve hadn't put the brakes on his desire? Would she have been able to stop him? Worse still, would she have wanted to?

Julia moaned into the silence. "I can't believe I'm doing this. It's destructive behavior. What's wrong with me? I must be losing my mind."

CHAPTER 34

THE INTERCOM on Julia's desk clicked. "Doctor Fairchild? Will you please pick up the telephone?"

Julia hesitated. She had made it through the week including a weekend that seemed to last a month without leaning on family or friends.

Steve called every morning, either waking her or catching her after her run across the high mesa. He would ask how she was and if she were thinking of him, then say he loved her. Though the question hung in the air, he didn't press for any answers.

The previous Friday Steve suggested he come down, but she held him off.

He laughed. "Scared of me?"

Julia laughed, too. "Not you. Me."

There were no calls from Mac, but she didn't expect any. After her angry reaction to his visit to Piñon Mesa and her behavior at the funeral, it was unlikely that he would even try.

That left only the women in Julia's life. Avoiding her mother had been easy; Lucia was still in England and blissfully unaware of Julia's turmoil. It wasn't that she didn't want her mother to know, but it meant she would have to admit to yet another failed relationship.

Dolores called once, babbled her concern and hung up. But Myrtle was more difficult to hold at bay. She left daily messages until that past Friday, then finally, "I know you're hurting and I'm here if you need me."

Julia picked up the receiver. "Yes?"

"Frank Brantley is here to see you."

Julia couldn't believe her ears. What on earth would Frank Brantley have to say to her?

When she didn't answer, Phyllis added, "You have some time."

From the muffled sound of her voice Julia could tell that Phyllis was probably turned away from Frank and speaking behind a cupped hand.

"Oh, all right. Send him in."

She rose as the door opened to reveal Mac's brother. He appeared surprisingly chipper considering the loss of his father and the recent devastation of his chile crop.

"Have a seat." Julia motioned to the chair in front of her desk and sat as soon as he did.

"Thank you for seeing me, Julia. I know it must be difficult for you."

Julia ignored his tendered kindness. "You have only a few minutes. Better get on with it."

Frank's eyes flattened as his lips spread in a thin smile. "I didn't cheat on you, Julia, so don't get high-handed with me."

She clenched her teeth to keep herself from feeding the fight and spread her hands in mock placation. "Sorry. How may I help you?"

"Have you spoken to Mac?"

Her heart quickened at her ex-fiancé's name. "No, not since the funeral."

"He's been up at Chaco Point. He left the morning after the funeral. He'll be gone a week but I haven't heard from him. Must be in the Four Corners. No phone."

"So?"

"Well, I'm certain that's why you haven't heard from him."

Julia tapped her pencil against the desk in staccato. "I don't expect to hear from Mac. Ever. It's over between us."

"No, it isn't. You're still in love with him. You're just hurt over what happened with Emaline."

She bridled at his smugness. "I didn't know you were a mind reader."

"Oh, I've been known to do a little from time to time, but you're an easy read." He paused, and when she gave no response he asked, "What's with you and Steve Duke?"

That was a shocker. How would Frank know about Steve? Julia

hoped she didn't betray her surprise at his question and kept her voice even when she replied, "Steve is just a friend."

"Knowing the good Doctor Duke as I do, you can bank that he'll try to be more than a friend. He has a reputation to uphold."

He studied her for a moment and raised his hand in caution. "Better watch out for Steve, he's always been jealous of Mac. He could be trouble."

Julia decided that was enough and stood. "Is this the reason you're here?"

Frank shook his head. "No. I have more important things to discuss. First, Mac tells me you know about Emaline and me."

Julia settled into her chair. "That's right."

"Emaline slept with Mac only because her father was pushing her to."

Julia couldn't keep the sarcasm out of her voice. "Gee, that solves everything, doesn't it? For someone who's supposed to be a real estate mogul, she certainly seems to buckle under whenever the great Ed Pierce speaks. Doesn't that bother you?"

Frank snorted, "You're the shrink, what do you think?"

Julia sat back in her chair. "Mac told me about the sexual abuse. Thank heavens Palatia found out."

"Emaline barely remembers what happened. She was just four."

"You'd be surprised what children recall. But that certainly explains Emaline's behavior through the years. Her use of sex to exercise control is classic."

He shrugged. "Whatever."

"Emaline needs professional counseling, Frank, or she'll continue to act out with any man she needs to control. You don't want to deal with that, do you?"

He flashed a brief smirk, but his eyes remained cold and flat. "Since I have knowingly shared her with my brother and several other men for twenty-some-odd years, I think I can manage anything she might hand me. Emaline and I have no secrets."

"How lucky for you."

"Enough about Emaline; I came to plead Mac's case."

Julia couldn't conceal her surprise. "Oh?"

"If I can handle that night, can't you?"

Before she could answer, Frank went on. "What happened didn't mean a thing to Mac. It was just reflex—old times—you know? It has nothing to do with his love for you."

Julia shook her head, unable to comprehend Frank's rationalization. "You Brantley men are the strangest people."

"No stranger than most men. I believe you shrinks call it compartmentalization."

Frank settled back and stared at her for a moment. "The resemblance is amazing—you know—to my mother. I can see what drew Mac to you in the first place."

Julia pictured the portrait of Selma Brantley hanging over the fireplace at the hacienda. "She was a beautiful woman. Mac loved her very much."

"Yeah. He and my father worshipped her. I did, too, until Dolores came into the picture. My mother never forgave me for bringing a pregnant Mexican home."

Julia heard the same venom in Frank's voice as the night they had met and realized he bore no love for his wife. Since he brought Dolores into the conversation, she decided to ask, "Just what do you plan to do about Dolores?"

Frank steepled his hands. "No one is going to keep Emaline and me apart. Certainly not that bitch."

Dolores's words echoed in Julia's mind. "Frank's not going to leave me for that whore because of this." Then she had waved the yellowed envelope. "With the information in this letter, I've got him right by the balls."

Julia hesitated, not sure whether she should bring up the letter. She decided to let it ride. That letter was none of her business, now. Instead she said, "Good luck."

"Thanks. I know it's hard for you to say that." He stood. "Well, that's about it. I just wanted you to know the facts."

Julia gave a derisive sniff. "Those may be the facts as you see them, but they just don't quite add up for me."

His eyes flashed. "Don't be a damn fool, woman. You and Mac are so right for each other . . ."

He leaned over the desk as sorrow replaced anger and his voice softened with entreaty. "As far as I'm concerned, even though Mac and I have our differences there's no finer man I know. He would die for me and die for you, too.

"Far as I can tell he's never felt this way about any woman. Not even Emaline. So give it some thought before you crucify my brother for one error in judgment."

He walked to the door and turned. "Don't blow it, Julia. It's all up to you."

CHAPTER 35

F RANK'S PLEA dogged Julia for the next two days, but the pride in those window-pane eyes when he spoke of Mac was burned in her memory. It was the only tender emotion she had observed in this angry and sarcastic man, but there was no doubt Frank loved his brother.

She woke Thursday morning so wrung out and disgruntled, not even an extended jog could shake her depression. After a long shower Julia was hunched over her coffee, staring at the television, when the telephone rang.

She hesitated, then jammed the receiver to her ear. "Doctor Fairchild."

Steve's low voice greeted her. "It's been over two weeks since I held you in my arms. Miss me?"

For the first time since he began calling, Julia had to admit she did. "Yes, I've missed you. Happy now?"

"Knocked outta my socks. Cancel your late appointments. I'm coming south."

Julia's depression fell away. "Today? What wonderful news. When will you be here?"

"Mid-afternoon. I'm taking you to White Sands for a picnic."

"Terrific. On Thursdays my last appointment's at three. Why don't you pick me up at the hospital about four?"

Once she arrived at Piñon Mesa the day deteriorated. Her first patient ran out of the office and disrupted a small play group of hyperactive children, sending them in all directions. By the time Julia and

Phyllis, with the help of two orderlies from the hospital wing, got the situation under control, she was running almost an hour behind schedule.

Julia saw clients through lunch, then grabbed a doughnut to go with her umpteenth cup of coffee. By the time Steve arrived at Piñon Mesa to pick her up, she was strung out on caffeine and a sugar high.

An hour later, Steve's Ford crested San Augustin Pass and hurtled down the back side of the Organ Mountains toward the wide plain bound by the Jarilla Mountains in the far distance.

"White Sands is about a half-hour from here." Steve glanced in the backseat. "And I have wine, steaks, water-soaked corn in the husk and salad. So settle back and relax. Everything's under control."

"If you don't mind, I think I'll grab a catnap. It's been a long day." Julia put her head back and shut her eyes, grateful for the few minutes she would have to rest before they got to their destination.

At the change in engine pitch, she opened her eyes to see that they were traveling between high gypsum dunes that in shadow turned to cool blues outlined in blazing white.

Suddenly homesick for the East, she murmured, "It reminds me of snow."

Steve turned off the narrow road into an empty parking lot and gave her an impish grin. "It's not quite snow, but we're going sledding just the same."

"Sledding? Here?" Julia laughed.

"You got it." Steve opened the trunk and produced two pieces of heavy corrugated cardboard. "Sand sleds. But first, we have to set up camp."

In no time, Steve laid out an old Army blanket and several large square pillows before a rock-rimmed fire pit. Next came a grill, an ice chest and a picnic hamper. He set the fire and motioned Julia to join him. "To the slopes."

Getting to the crest of the dunes was a struggle, but the trip to the bottom was exhilarating.

When Julia began to climb the same dune, Steve pointed toward a cool blue unsullied stretch. "Never the same dune. Let's go for the next one."

Soon the campsite and the car disappeared as they worked their way toward the setting sun. Julia was about to cry "Uncle" when Steve turned and yelled, "Time to backtrack. We don't want to get caught in the dark."

Thirty minutes later, as the sun slid behind the mountains, Steve pointed toward the parking lot and his car. "Last one back is a rotten egg." He pitched his sled on a last run toward the campsite.

"Hey, wait for me." Halfway down Julia lost her hold on the board and rolled into Steve's open arms.

"Gotcha, now." He grabbed her to him. They clung together laughing until Julia noticed a stray lock of hair on Steve's forehead and brushed it away.

Steve took her hand and brought it to his mouth, his eyes betraying a sadness she had never seen before, then lay back, drawing her to lie in the cool sand next to him.

Julia let his desire surround her until she could hear only the wind sloughing across the sands to mingle with their breathing.

Though she could no longer ignore Steve's obvious hunger and her own arousal, in the back of her mind she heard Frank's warning but shook it away. Didn't Steve just say he was crazy about her? Wasn't he there for her when Mac abandoned her? Wasn't he at her side the next day to offer comfort? That counted for a lot, but was it enough to begin another relationship and so soon?

When Steve moved against her in that ancient invitation, Julia jerked out of his embrace. "Please. Stop. Please, Steve. I mean it."

He pushed away, eyes averted, and took several deep breaths. "Okay. King's X for now." He stood. "Hungry?"

Julia nodded, relieved that the dangerous moment between them was past. "Not just hungry. I'm starved."

"Let's get back to the campsite. I'll crack some wine and light the fire."

JULIA UNLOCKED her front door, stepped inside the dark entry, and turned into Steve's arms.

His voice floated above her, filling the darkness. "I want you." His mouth met hers with a kiss so deep it took her breath away.

Steve swept her in his arms and covered the stairs with such speed and ease it was as if he held a feather. Julia knew exactly where he was taking her, but she was too lost in her own need to protest. Once upstairs, he lowered her to the bed and lay beside her.

"Say you want me."

Julia had made that decision long before they put out the campfire. They were laughing at some gory Emergency Room story Steve was telling when he stopped in mid-sentence to stare at her with such hunger that she felt herself blush.

She supposed Steve finished the story, but his eyes told her everything she wanted to know.

Julia rolled to face him, then whispered, "Oh, yes, I want you," and found his lips to seal the bargain.

CHAPTER 36

MAC BENT OVER the dying woman to place the stethoscope on the far side of her left lung. The sounds he heard weren't good.

"Rest easy, Ann. I'll have the nurse give you something for the pain."

As he turned to go, a bony hand grabbed his wrist as the woman rasped, "How long?"

He peered into the Indian's lined face. Her dark eyes dulled with fever begged for the truth.

"Not long. Be patient." Mac placed his hand on her burning forehead and watched her face relax at his touch, then he made his way into the hall to see Sylvia Chee standing at the nurses' station.

It suddenly struck Mac how very attractive she was; tall and slender with warm almond-shaped chocolate eyes. They had worked side by side since he had come to Indian Health, but until now he had been oblivious to this part of her.

She gave a sympathetic nod. "It's almost over, isn't it?"

"Poor woman." Mac put the chart back in the rack. "I'm sure she'd rather die in her hogan. She's worried about what will happen to her spirit. If she weren't so sick, I'd take her home."

Sylvia shook her head. "Isn't stalking the Hantavirus enough? Why take this death watch on? You need some sleep."

"That's Joe Pinto's mother in there. After what Joe did for me, it's the least I can do."

"You're more of an Indian than I am, Mac Brantley. Are you sure you weren't adopted?"

He grabbed for her hand. "Maybe I was Indian in a past life. How about a cup of coffee?"

Once they were settled at a table in the cafeteria, Sylvia asked, "How's life?"

Mac shook his head. "A mess."

"You haven't called your lady?"

"What would I say? I made a mistake. Acted the fool. What excuse do I have?"

"Oh, for Pete's sake, don't be such a coward. Call her. Tell her you love her. Women are suckers for a good line." Sylvia drained her coffee and stood. "And, if she's stupid enough to turn you down, you know my number."

Mac watched Chee glide out of the cafeteria and looked at his watch. Almost nine. Maybe he would try to call Julia, but only after he checked on Joe Pinto's mother.

Mac, Joe Pinto and Joe's eldest son, Bill, watched Ann Pinto die. Her labored breaths filled the room followed by lengthening pauses, though earlier in the evening she had mumbled lost words and at times seemed to be humming some ancient shaman's song.

Joe's son asked, "How much longer?"

"Can't say, really," Mac said. "Maybe minutes, maybe hours. I didn't think she'd last this long."

"Dad?" Bill Pinto motioned his father into the hall and, after a few minutes, Joe returned alone.

"Big trial tomorrow. He has to prepare. But, I understand." He nodded toward his mother. "Bill is her favorite grandchild. She sold the last of her silver jewelry to pay for his first year in Law School. She's mighty proud of him."

"Does he like the DA's job?"

Joe nodded. "He's just an assistant but maybe someday . . ."

Ann Pinto's death rattle interrupted her son's words. He rushed to her side and fell to his knees.

Mac slipped from the room then pushed himself toward the nurses' station. "She's gone."

He motioned for the chart. "Let me sign off, make a long-distance call and direct me to the nearest cot."

CHAPTER 37

JULIA STOOD in the bathroom, straining to hear the rev of Steve's motor above the rush of the shower. When it faded, she stepped into the steam-filled stall and took a deep breath, letting the moisture fill her lungs as her body went limp with relief.

The moment she said yes Julia realized she made a mistake, but it was too late to stop him—she had rolled the dice.

Steve didn't seem to be in a hurry. He was probably waiting for her to make the next move, but she couldn't.

Then the phone on the bedside table rang, throwing them apart.

Steve pointed at the insistent intruder. "Do you need to get that?"

Julia heard concern and a professional tone to his question. Anyone practicing medicine knew what a call that time of night could mean.

She thought for a minute, tempted to use the phone call as a way to wiggle out of her commitment. "I don't have any tough cases right now. If it's my service, they'll leave a message."

Then they sat on the bed—Steve on one side, Julia on the other—and waited.

The ringing ended, then after a brief pause began again.

Again Steve pointed to the telephone. "Better grab it, Julia. It might be important."

Before she could bring the receiver to her ear Mac began talking. "Don't hang up. I need to see you. Your turf, your terms. I'll be back in Las Cruces tomorrow or the next day for sure. At least think about it, will you?"

She placed the receiver back in its cradle. "I guess you recognized the voice."

He nodded. "I know it like my own."

The silence that followed played over them like ice.

Finally, Steve stood. "Guess I'd better get on my way."

Julia followed him to the top of the stairs as a wave of guilt rolled through her. She needed to say something, but all that came out was a lame, "Thanks for this afternoon."

He stopped midway down the stairs and turned. "Sorry it ended so soon."

Julia hesitated; it would have been so easy to say she felt the same way, but she decided not to. She had come so close. Too close.

When she didn't reply, Steve went on to the door. "I'll just let myself out, okay?"

JULIA SOAPED and scrubbed her body from head to foot, not once but twice, as if that alone would atone for her stupid mistake. When the hot water finally lost its sear, she dried herself and crawled into the comfort of a long T-shirt to finish the rest of her bedtime routine. Her final act was to reach for the wheel of birth control pills, a step so ingrained she didn't give it a second thought.

Julia peered into the mirror. Guilty as though she had completed the act. She wanted Steve—wanted him badly enough to let him take her to bed.

But now, it was over. Definitely and finally over. She would end the relationship before another opportunity presented itself. That would be easy. Steve was in Albuquerque and she was over three hours away in Las Cruces. Time would pass. Memories would fade. After a while everything would be forgotten.

CHAPTER 38

STEVE TOOK the pint of Jack Daniels from the bellman's outstretched hand, palmed him a few bills and closed the door. He splashed two fingers of the dark liquid into the glass he had copped from the bathroom and walked to look north out of the window. From his room on the fourth floor of the Hilton he could almost see Julia's house.

He shook his head, still unable to believe Mac's incredible timing, but even if Julia had fallen into his arms after the call, he seriously doubted that the erotic draw they both felt in the hallway downstairs would have been the same.

Why was it so different with Julia? He took any woman he wanted: married, unmarried, young, or pleasingly older. He courted them, bedded them, serviced them until he grew tired and left them. He had never let himself become emotionally involved with any of those women, not even Palatia. She was more like a mother to him. The mother he had never known.

But this time it was different. After that March afternoon in the ER, when he drowned in the deeps of those tawny eyes, his life changed. Maybe it was because he had never met anyone like Julia.

She was from a world he didn't know. He had never been east of the Mississippi, and though he had read *The Great Gatsby* he could barely picture a life that revolved around summer sunset sails and the winter dazzle of a new snowfall in Manhattan.

To him Julia seemed fragile, elegant and—as the fiancée of his arch rival—unobtainable. But he wanted her. Maybe his competition with

Mac upped the stakes a little, but for the first time in his life Steve Duke knew he was in love.

He had planned to befriend Julia, take his time, let the relationship develop, but Mac handed her over, devastated and in need of comfort, thrusting fate gloriously and finally on his side. Even so, it became an exercise in restraint to bide his time until Julia gave in to her own obvious desire.

And this evening, when she was locked in his arms in the darkness of the entry hall, to his delight Steve realized that Julia had changed her mind. Once upstairs, he fought the urge to take her quickly. He held himself back and waited for her to take the lead.

When she said that she wanted him, his heart practically jumped from his body, and for a moment he felt like he did the first time he had sex—afraid of what might or might not happen—but when she opened her arms and folded him to her and he felt the fire in her lips— felt her heart lunging.

Then the phone.

"Damn." Steve downed the fiery liquid and returned to the dresser to pour another. He'd call her. See if he could go back.

No. It was much too late for that. Besides, he couldn't take the chance that she might refuse. The only way to make it up was in person—in bed.

Would Julia give him another chance? If she did, she would be his. He was sure of that.

Steve drained the glass and turned to stare into the mirror as frustration crowded his face. It was still early and he was wide awake, suffering from an unrequited libido.

He splashed more whiskey in his glass, picked up the phone and dialed.

At the sound of Palatia's voice he said, "I know it's been a long time, but I need you. Can you get away?"

At her response Steve felt the first stirring of desire and as it grew, his smile widened and he relaxed against the dresser. "I'm at the Hilton. Four-oh-two. Hurry."

CHAPTER 39

B Y SOME MIRACLE Mac slept until the following noon. When he finally awakened, he didn't know where he was, but as the sounds outside the dark room fell into place, he knew he was at Chaco Point and that Ann Pinto was dead.

He took a quick shower and donned his rumpled clothes, counting on a starched white coat for cover-up.

A cup of cafeteria coffee jolted him out of his stupor enough to head him toward the bank of pay phones in the hall and dial Piñon Mesa.

"Phyllis, this is Mac Brantley."

A chilly voice came back.

"Is she free? Just for a few minutes . . . please?"

The phone clicked and the hold beep chirped in his ear for what seemed like an eternity.

"Yes?"

Julia's curt tone didn't give Mac much hope, but he plowed forward. "Did you get my message?"

"Yes. I don't have much time. What do you want?"

"I just wanted to hear your voice, is that a crime?"

"Well, now you have. If that's all . . ."

"Don't hang up. Please." Mac heard his desperation, but he didn't care. "I'm still at Chaco Point but I'll be back in Las Cruces by the first of the week if everything goes well up here. Could I see you?"

After a long pause she said, "Nothing's changed as far as I'm concerned. But just for the record, did you send Frank to plead your case?"

"What?"

"He came here to see me last week."

Mac's eyebrows shot up. His brother pleading his case? That was a new one. "You're kidding."

Her voice softened. "I didn't think you sent him, but I needed to ask."

Mac pushed his case. "Will you see me?"

"It won't do any good."

"How do you know?"

Julia's failure to respond hurt him, but it wasn't as painful as the sound of the dial tone that followed.

He hung up and turned to see Sylvia Chee.

"Any luck?"

"What?" Mac shook his head. "No. I'm afraid not."

"Sorry." She patted his arm and smiled. "Hey. Don't forget. My offer still stands."

Before Mac could answer, Sylvia had turned to consult with a nurse.

CHAPTER 40

JULIA'S EXTRA-LONG Monday morning jog did little to erase her growing guilt over what had almost happened the Thursday before.

Somehow she pushed herself through a short Friday schedule and her hostile conversation with Mac, then escaped to Ruidoso for the weekend. She spent most of the day at the race track, but once she was in bed her aborted sexual encounter with Steve replayed.

Each time Julia thought about it, she blushed. Not the pleasant rush from a happy memory, but the discomfort caused by a terrible faux pas. She hated to admit that lust had gotten the best of her. Even though the phone call from Mac saved her, as far as she was concerned she was now no better than he.

She rolled into the Piñon Mesa parking lot just as Bob Sandoval was getting out of his car. He waved and pointed to his watch and hurried inside, leaving Julia to bear the added guilt of avoiding Myrtle since the party.

She had written the proper thank-you to send along with a bouquet of spring flowers, but couldn't bring herself to pick up the telephone and call her best friend. Though she missed Myrtle's chirpy "okey-dokey," talking to her would mean rehashing the events following the engagement party and questions about Steve.

Julia pushed herself out of the Range Rover and trudged toward her office. The usual Monday staff meeting lay ahead, but today she was listening. For the first time in months there was no new patient to present.

Following the meeting Julia occupied herself with her patients for the rest of the morning and was just about to head for the cafeteria when Phyllis buzzed her.

"El Paso calling."

Julia picked up the receiver and let Jorge Perez-Gasca's deep voice wash over her like a soothing benediction.

"PG. How nice to hear your voice. How are you?" She hadn't seen her birth-father since early January and was embarrassed at how remiss she had been.

His bass interrupted her. "More important, my dear one, how are you?"

"Busy. Tired. I've missed you."

"And I, you. That is why I called. I have business in Las Cruces this afternoon. Would you have some time for me about four?"

"Of course. Do you mind meeting at my house? We'll have some privacy there."

"Splendid. Until then."

Julia hung up and swiveled to gaze across the broad blooming mesa. A year had passed since she and her birth-father connected, and though she had known Perez-Gasca for only that short time, a strong bond had been established.

Their first meeting was in a private room at Café Quentero in El Paso. Their subsequent evenings together would last exactly two hours and a half and followed a prescribed ritual.

After ordering broiled quail and champagne, Perez-Gasca would discuss politics, the arts and business in general, then would carefully quiz Julia about her latest activities.

When the quail arrived, he would pick over his while she ate hers. But promptly at seven-thirty, at no matter what stage they were in their meal, Perez-Gasca would look at his watch and excuse himself with, "Dinner at eight." He would give her hugs and kisses, say his good-byes and disappear, leaving her to finish her dinner or dessert alone.

Though he never failed to ask about her mother, Perez-Gasca hardly mentioned his family except in the most general terms. From what Julia could glean, he had fathered five sons ranging from early forties to late twenties. Four had married and produced ten grandchildren. Other than that he gave little information except to voice concern over his eldest son, his namesake, who was still a bachelor.

To her delight, Julia discovered that she was Perez-Gasca's only daughter. But sadly, she knew her existence would always remain a secret. Her birth-father never apologized for excluding her. He simply said that telling the family would be an inconvenience.

Perez-Gasca had visited her home only once, shortly after they met. Julia remembered how pleased he was with her choice of the beige stucco two-story condo and its attached garden, where a showy red bougainvillea cascaded over a high privacy wall.

The Mexican tile floors were accented by two Zapotec rugs defining a sitting area composed of the same comfortable down-filled couches she had chosen for her suite in Sutton Place. Perez-Gasca complimented her on her "exquisite" taste, and later, when she took him to Piñon Mesa, he told her how proud he was of all her accomplishments.

At those thoughts, Julia found herself eagerly counting the minutes until they would meet.

She rounded the curve to see the white Lincoln Continental parked in her driveway with Jorge Perez-Gasca leaning against the fender—tan as ever, silver mane in place and impeccably attired in navy pinstripe. Even at seventy-plus, he still commanded.

"Julia, my dear." Her father's face filled with concern and his hand was on her shoulder before she could turn off the motor. "What's the matter? Not your mother, is it? Is she all right?"

"Oh, Mother's fine. She's in England with my stepfather."

"But something distresses you." Perez-Gasca opened the door and extended his hand. "If it is not your mother, then it must be your man."

Julia let him help her from the car and fold her in his arms. But instead of the soothing result she expected, tears she was sure she no longer could produce pushed into her eyes.

Perez-Gasca put her at arm's length. "Tears?"

Julia blinked them away. "Do you mind if we go inside?"

When they were settled next to each other on the sofa in front of the kiva fireplace, he took her hand in his. "Now, tell me, what makes you so sad?"

Julia told her story, carefully omitting any reference to Steve, while

Perez-Gasca gave her his full attention and made all the appropriate sympathetic sounds.

When she finally gave in to her pain, he embraced her and let her cry it out against his shoulder.

"*Pobrecita*. I am sorry you have to bear this unhappiness, but I am also sad for Mac."

Julia pulled back. "How can you say you're sorry for Mac? He's the one who hurt me."

Perez-Gasca shook his head. "I know, I know. But even after what happened, I would guess he is still very much in love with you."

"Those were his exact words. But I don't understand."

"No, I am sure you don't. But, Julia, darling, haven't you ever been tempted, just a little?"

Julia blushed at the too-recent memory of Steve's body covering hers and how lucky she was that Mac had called.

Perez-Gasca smiled. "Is it possible that you might be a little human, too?"

She shrugged, too embarrassed to give voice to her own near-slip.

As the afternoon faded to dusk, Perez-Gasca pleaded Mac's case and ended with, "If you love him, you will have to find a way to forgive him."

Julia knew she was treading on dangerous ground, but she couldn't help herself. "Did the Señora forgive you for sleeping with my mother?"

Perez-Gasca turned his kind, brown eyes to hers. "The Señora knows nothing of my peccadilloes and, though I am not very proud to admit it, there have been several. But Julia, despite everything, I love my wife."

"But what about my mother?"

He shook his head. "Your mother was a beautiful but fleeting moment in my past. Or so I thought, until I discovered much too late in life that I was blessed with a daughter. At that news my heart filled with so much love I thought it would burst."

Julia saw the sorrow in her father's eyes and felt tears at the back of her own. "I'm so sorry."

Perez-Gasca kissed her forehead and gently smoothed his thumbs across her eyebrows. "I suspect you still see everything in black and white. But that is not real life. The older you become, the more you will find most of what we experience is captured in tones of gray. That is why we must exercise compassion and understanding for one another."

"Like the Señora?"

"Yes, like my Natalia."

"So, you think I should forgive him?"

"Can you?"

"He swears the woman means nothing to him."

Perez-Gasca beamed and patted her hand. "Do I detect a crack in your Puritan armor?"

"Yes—no—I don't know."

"Do give it some thought. Forgiveness is a balm for the soul." He glanced at his watch and rose. "I must be going. I am expected."

"I know. Dinner at eight." She stood and put her arms around his neck.

He hugged her hard and placed a second kiss on her forehead. "I beg you, give your next move careful thought. Pride is a lonely companion."

"I'll try." Julia walked him to the car and leaned in the window for a goodbye kiss. "When can we meet again?"

Perez-Gasca took out the thin leather-bound calendar he always carried and, after a brief run-through, he said, "I will have to get back with you on that; my schedule is very full."

"I'll wait for your call." Julia stepped back as the Lincoln purred to life, rolled slowly down the drive, then stopped.

Perez-Gasca poked his head out the window. "Know that I love you and will always be there for you."

Julia waved until the car turned at the end of the street.

Once inside, she climbed the stairs and walked to the guest bedroom. Through the window she could see a tiny sliver of the Rio Grande reflecting the pale-mauve afterglow. Mac was there. Alone as she was. She slowly rubbed the bare finger of her left hand and, for the first time since she had flung the Navajo ring onto his bed, Julia regretted that she had been so impetuous.

CHAPTER 41

THE FOLLOWING morning Mac opened the front door to his house and stretched his arms wide as he inhaled the cool desert air. The pre-dawn sky was still deep blue, promising a fine spring day marred only by the loss of his father and the mess he'd made of his love life.

Three hours later, refreshed from a shower and a change of clothing, Mac was just squeezing his Jeep into the only slot left in the small parking lot of the law firm when Dolores, glowering and red-faced, banged on the window.

"I have something to show you."

"Good morning to you too, Dolores." Mac nudged the door into her hip and she stepped back.

"For you, maybe, but not for your brother."

Mac ignored the warning prickle at the base of his skull. "Can't this wait? We're almost late."

"Did you hear me?" Dolores raised her voice. "He's going to pay."

"Pay for what?"

"He wants a d-i-v-o-r-c-e to marry that whore. But he won't. He can't. Not when he reads this." She shoved a yellowing envelope at him. "I've got him by the balls, the bastard."

Mac saw his mother's writing and shuddered, then pushed the envelope back into his sister-in-law's bright-red taloned hand. "Why don't you hold on to that until after the will is read? Who knows? Things might turn out differently."

Her anger faded to curiosity. "You know something I don't?"

"Life is full of surprises."

Dolores stuffed the envelope into her large purse. "Oh, hell, I've waited this long. What's another hour or two?"

Minutes later, Mac was staring at the attorney, who, seemingly unaware of a large black fly dive-bombing his balding pate, was running a well-manicured index finger down each page. When he reached the bottom of a page, he would tap it exactly three times, then carefully place it facedown on the gleaming surface of his desk.

After the seventh page, Mac turned to see Dolores and Allen shifting fitfully in their chairs while Frank sat, hands clasping one knee to hold his tan ostrich-skin boot on top of the other knee, his pale eyes glued to the moving manicured finger.

Allen shot a geeky smirk at Mac, then crossed his eyes. Mac winked and grinned back, but a surge of pity caught in his throat. Poor Allen would be the sure loser in all of this. In a few minutes, he would be cut loose or bound forever in his parents' struggle.

The attorney's voice broke the silence. "First, let me again offer my condolences. Mackenzie Brantley was a fine man. The Valley will miss him."

At those words, Mac choked back a wave of unbearable grief. His father had been in the ground three weeks, but the pain of his loss remained sharp and deep.

The attorney stood the will on end, then on both sides to be sure the pages were properly aligned. "Let's get this show started."

His voice dropped an octave into lawyer-drone. "I, Mackenzie Luke Brantley, of Doña Ana County, New Mexico, being of sound mind and disposing memory, do hereby publish and declare . . ."

The attorney read through the boilerplate and took a deep breath as all four Brantleys came to attention. The blow was delivered much too soon. Instead of naming Frank as first inheritor, his father slammed them with the hard copy.

As each word fell, Mac was barely able to catch a breath since the air in the room became too thick to inhale.

Frank's question was barely audible. "Will you read that paragraph again?"

The lawyer's head jerked up. "Certainly, Frank. Article Three,

Paragraph A: If my son, Mackenzie Luke Brantley, Junior, survives me, I devise and bequeath all of my interest in that real property and improvements thereon bounded on the north by the lands of Emilio Gutierrez, on the east by State Road twenty-eight, on the south by the Doña Ana main canal, and on the west by the Rio Grande, as recorded in the Courthouse of Doña Ana County, New Mexico. If Mackenzie Luke Brantley, Junior, does not survive me, I bequeath this property to New Mexico State University. If, however, Mackenzie Luke Brantley, Junior, is married to or ever becomes married to Emaline Palatia Pierce, the land will immediately revert to New Mexico State University."

In the next instant Frank towered above Mac, hands so tightly balled that his knuckles glared white through his skin, his face so clumped with rage that the vein in his forehead pulsed with each throb of his heart.

He stuck an accusing finger in Mac's face. "Did you know about this?"

There it was. The question Mac had hoped he would never have to answer. For a moment he considered lying, but too many people knew the truth. "Yes."

"You sonovabitch. I'm gonna kill you." Before anyone could move, Frank's hands were around Mac's neck.

Through the buzzy haze, silhouettes moved and Dolores's voice filtered through his pulsing ears. "Have you gone loco? That's your brother."

Frank's grip relaxed and Mac saw Dolores and Allen holding one of his brother's arms while the lawyer gripped the other.

"Get a hold of yourself, Frank. Are you all right, Mac?"

Mac nodded and rubbed his neck, afraid that if he spoke he might break down.

Instead, it was Frank who began to heave, his harsh sobs filling the room with pain.

At that, the attorney headed for the door to the outer office. "I'll be right back."

Mac supposed it was the attorney's way of allowing the family some privacy. He glanced over at his brother and was relieved to see

Frank regaining some semblance of composure. He let out a long breath and relaxed, sure the worst was over.

But it wasn't.

Dolores's singsongy voice cut the air. "Too bad, Frankie, no Red Stone, no whore."

She made the mistake of bending forward just far enough for Frank's open hand to smack the side of her cheek and knock her off the chair.

Allen jumped to her aid, yelling, "Hit Ma again and you'll be history." He struggled his mother back into her chair, then slumped into his own to glower at his father.

Dolores slowly rubbed the red welt on her face for a few minutes, then turned glittering obsidian eyes on her husband and purred. "I'm so sorry, darling, did I somehow offend you?"

Frank shook his head and began mumbling something under his breath. Whatever it was it caused Dolores to flush.

When she stood and pulled the letter from her purse, Mac raised his hand. "Not here, Dolores."

"I can't think of a better place," she crooned and placed the letter gently on Frank's knee. "For you, *mi amor.*"

Frank read the envelope. "This is my mother's handwriting. It's addressed to me. Where did you get this?"

"I found it some time ago. Sorry. It's a wee bit late."

When she turned and started toward the door Allen called, "But, Ma, what about the rest of the will?" His question went unanswered. His mother slammed the door behind her.

Frank ripped open the envelope and began to read, then turned a sickly green as his hands began to twitch. Finally, he threw the paper to the floor, gave a lost, low moan and, knocking his chair on its side, raced from the room.

Both Mac and Allen dove for the paper, but the up-ended chair gave Mac the edge he needed. He grabbed the paper. "Sit down, Allen."

Allen glared across the overturned chair. "That belongs to my father."

"That's right and if and when he wants you to see it, you will. Until then it remains in my safekeeping."

The lawyer's return ended any further discussion.

The rest of the will was pretty much as Mac expected. Frank got the chile and the hacienda. Dolores got twenty-five thousand dollars to "take that trip to Paris." For her years of devotion and "fine chiles rellenos" Cuca received the same. Allen's money was left in trust "for educational purposes only."

When he heard that, Allen muttered, "Fuckin' old cheap-ass fart."

Once they were in the parking lot, the boy shoved his copy of the will in his back jeans pocket and hauled into his truck. "Guess I won't be seeing much of you anymore."

Before Mac could reply, his nephew gunned the truck into the street and screeched away, leaving a fine layer of dust to settle around him.

Only nine-forty. In less than an hour he'd lost what was left of his family. He shrugged away his desolation and crawled into the Jeep.

Once there, he removed his mother's letter from his pocket, intending to place it in the envelope with Frank's copy of the will, but temptation won. He unfolded the paper to see his mother's familiar hand.

My beloved son, if you are reading this, I am gone and now you must know the truth. Please try to understand my selfish reasons for keeping this a secret until my death, and if your father is alive, I beg you not to blame him. Only out of his deep and abiding love for me did he agree to go along with my wishes. He cherished me through the years, doing the best he could to make up for a tragic incident that happened early in my life. The only good thing that came from this horror is that you were born.

I guess the only way to tell you is to be straight about it. When I was seventeen, Ed Pierce got drunk and forced himself on me. I tried to fight, but he was too strong and, in taking my virginity, he made me pregnant.

If it weren't for your father and his loving kindness, I would have taken my life at the shame of it all. I tried to make up for that by being the best wife and mother I could. I hope you believe that.

You might come from Ed Pierce's seed, my darling, but you were raised a Brantley and you will always be a Brantley. The only reason I'm telling you now, is that I cannot meet my Maker without letting you know who your real father is.

I love you, son. I always have. Please try to understand and forgive.

Mother

Mac pushed back against the headrest. None of what he read made any sense. Frank—Ed Pierce's son? Emaline's half-brother? No wonder Frank was retching as he ran from the office.

He read his mother's letter again and put it back in his pocket. There was only one thing he knew to do.

CHAPTER 42

JULIA SHUT the door behind the last client of the morning, returned to her desk and, glad for a few added minutes of peace, leaned back and closed her eyes hoping she could grab a few moments of shut-eye.

The intercom buzz startled Julia awake. She reached for the telephone then hesitated. Her mother was due back from England any day.

When the buzzer sounded again, she picked up the receiver. "Yes?"

Phyllis's reply came in a muted voice. "Mac is here."

Julia's heart flipped and raced through her chest. She held the receiver away and took several deep breaths before she felt calm enough to say, "Please send him in—and, Phyllis, if Albert Peña darkens that door on time, take drastic measures."

Julia quickly removed her white coat, but when she stood to hang it on the nearby hook, her legs were trembling so, they balked. At her second attempt, some power other than her own kicked in, and by the time Mac opened the door she was on her feet.

What Julia saw shocked her. Mac seemed to have aged overnight. His hair was disheveled and there was little color in his haggard face, but it was the pain in his eyes that drew her toward him and into his arms.

When he clutched her to him, a raspy moan came from deep in his lungs. "If you had turned me away, I don't know what I would have done."

For several minutes neither spoke, then Mac stepped away. "It's been a helluva morning."

Julia motioned toward the couch and he collapsed into the soft cushions, bringing her with him.

She took Mac's hand and held it tight as he covered the meeting at the law office and his brother's reaction to the loss of Red Stone.

Frank's assault was no surprise to Julia. She often saw that anger smoldering at the back of his icy eyes. "I'm sure he'll forgive and forget all about this. Give him time."

Mac shook his head. "You didn't see his face. He meant every word. And if that weren't bad enough, once they got him under control Dolores began mouthing off about Emaline and Red Stone, and Frank clipped her a good one. That did it. Before I could stop her, Dolores took out that abominable letter, gave it to Frank and walked out."

"It was just a question of time before she unloaded that letter, you knew that."

"I guess. But she could have waited until they were back in Hatch before she dropped the bomb."

"Was it that bad?"

Mac nodded. "Worse than you could imagine. Frank started reading and then he bolted."

He slid the letter from his pocket. "When he dropped this, I beat Allen to it. No need for the boy to know about this. Here. Read it."

Julia shuddered and shook her head.

He pushed it into her hand. "You have to. Please."

As she read, everything fell into place. Frank's see-through eyes raking over her that first night at the hacienda. Emaline staring up at her through those pale mirrors at Radium Springs. Something had clicked in the back of her mind even then, and now she knew why. Both had inherited Ed Pierce's colorless blue eyes. Ed Pierce was Frank's natural father.

She felt a curl of nausea at the base of her throat. The fact that Mac and Frank had shared the same woman for so many years was deplorable, but this was worse—this was incest.

"Poor Frank." Julia handed Mac the letter. "What a mess."

"It's worse than that. I'm scared of what Frank might do now that he knows." Mac put the letter back in his pocket and drew Julia to him. "I had to be with you."

"I'm glad." She rested her head against his chest, realizing how very much she had missed him.

CHAPTER 43

HALF AN HOUR later Mac parked beside Dolores's Suburban, headed for the side verandah and into the empty library.

He listened a moment for any movement in the other part of the house, and when he heard none he went to the desk, opened the center drawer and deposited a manila envelope with Frank's copy of the will and Selma Brantley's letter sealed inside.

"Oh. It's you." Dolores's strangled voice cut through the emptiness. "What are you doing here?"

Mac spun around to see his sister-in-law listing to one side of the wide doorway, her face tear-stained and mascara smudged in wide circles around her eyes.

"Never mind what I'm doing here. What are you blubbering about? I thought you'd be dancing in the streets."

"Well, I'm not. I'm miserable. What kind of life do I have to look forward to now?" Her face scrunched and she covered it with the dish towel she was holding.

Mac settled into the chair that had once belonged to his father. "Shouldn't you have thought about that before?"

After a few shuddering burbles, her reply came in a muffled wail. "But I couldn't stand it any longer. All those years right under my nose." She raised her smudged face. "And, I might add, under yours too."

At that, Mac gave into his anger. "No matter what happened between Frank and Emaline, that letter has ruined at least two lives.

You might as well have taken a gun and shot them both."

Dolores's only reply was a muted sob, as her free hand groped for the back of the couch.

Mac sniffed his disgust, walked over to the bar and poured himself a Scotch. "Want a drink?"

"A little vodka."

"You've already downed more than a little." He filled a tumbler, shoved it into her hand and watched her sag onto the couch.

"I guess Frank hasn't been here."

She shook her head, took a large gulp of the clear liquid and resumed her weeping.

"What about Allen?"

"No."

"Did you check for any messages?"

Her response was unintelligible, but she was shaking her head again, so Mac walked to the desk. Nothing.

"Where's Cuca?"

Another shrug. After more odd mumbling between sniffles, Mac realized Dolores had lapsed into Spanish.

From what he could make out between her sobs, it seemed that Cuca had left right after the funeral to go back to Mexico.

"I wouldn't blame her if she left for good. You always treated her like dirt."

Another shrug.

"Don't worry. I'm sure she'll be back. She's faithful as a dog. It's probably just another one of her pilgrimages."

Mac watched his sister-in-law's shoulders rise with each sob as he splashed a little more Scotch into his glass and downed it.

"I'm going over to the Pierces'. Frank just might be there, heaven help him. If you hear anything, call Julia and leave a message."

Dolores's head jerked out of the towel. "Julia?"

"Yeah, Julia. We're back on speaking terms. At least one good thing happened today."

His sister-in-law's face brightened for a second and she said, "I'm glad," before she lowered her head to continue where she left off.

CHAPTER 44

THERE WAS ONLY one car parked in the Pierce driveway. From the Texas plate and the Alamo Rental sticker Mac guessed it was Emaline's.

He rang the bell, waited an appropriate time, then remembered Palatia Pierce never locked her doors and turned the knob.

When the door swung inward he yelled, "Hello? Anybody here?"

When there was no answer, Mac searched the living and dining rooms, then continued down the hall to Ed Pierce's office. He heard wheezing on the other side of the door and, assuming the older man was asleep, shoved it open to see Ed Pierce collapsed over his desk in a dark pool of blood.

Mac's first thought was that the shooter must have been his brother, and sent up thanks that Ed was still alive. Attempted manslaughter was bad, but not as bad as murder.

As far as Mac was concerned Pierce deserved to die a horrible death for raping his mother, but he stanched the urge to turn and walk away, shoved his hatred aside and became the doctor he was supposed to be.

"Ed? Can you hear me?" When there was no response, Mac circled to the back of the chair. The exit wound was in the fleshy part of the side of Ed's neck. He palpated the right carotid artery and was surprised to find a steadier pulse than he had anticipated.

"Ed? It's Mac Brantley." There was a small snort, a gurgle, then a long silence before the labored breathing resumed.

After making as close an examination as he could without moving the man, Mac grabbed the phone and dialed the hospital. "This is Doctor Mac Brantley. I'm at Ed Pierce's place just south of Hatch off Highway one-eight-five. Mister Pierce has sustained a gunshot wound. I don't have my medical bag, so I can't give aid. Please send an ambulance."

When Mac slammed down the phone, he was greeted with an eerie silence. Ed had stopped breathing.

He jumped to stand behind him, placed both hands low on the man's back and slowly pushed. "Breathe, damn you."

Another gurgle and snort preceded the return of Ed's breathing but the widening stain on the desk signaled an added loss of blood.

At that, Mac ran to the hall and, after opening several doors, found the linen closet and grabbed as many towels as he could hold.

Though less than a minute passed before he returned, he saw that Ed was losing more blood with each breath. There was no more time to waste.

"Ed? I have to find the entry wound; you're losing too much blood. This will hurt like hell, but I have to do it."

Mac hooked his arms beneath his enemy, lifted him to a sitting position, then searched for the wound. There was a gaping hole in Ed's trachea but it seemed as if the bullet had entered the front of the neck at an odd angle, just missing the right carotid artery and the spinal cervix. With luck and no more blood loss, Ed would probably survive.

Mac slapped several towels over the wound with his free hand, put two more towels on the desk to soak up the lost blood and, after placing the last towel over that, lowered Ed back to his original position. He felt for the pulse again and found it diminished. Not a positive sign, but the breathing seemed less labored and the gurgling had stopped.

A car door slammed and Mac whirled to peer out the window. It was Palatia Pierce, carrying what seemed like a sack of groceries. He looked at his watch. Twelve-twenty-seven. Only thirty minutes since he'd left the Square B.

He placed his ear against Ed's back. Though the breathing was uneven, there was no rale and the heartbeat seemed steady. He lifted one shoulder. No new blood. The man seemed stable enough to leave unattended for a few minutes.

Mac arrived in the kitchen in time to see Palatia depositing the sack on the kitchen counter. "Hello, Palatia."

She jumped, gave a small scream and turned. When she saw who it was, some color returned to her face. "Oh, Mac. You gave me quite a start. What are you doing here?"

Mac decided not to blurt the news about Ed right away; he needed some time to figure out the best way to tell Palatia that her husband was seriously wounded.

"Looking for Frank."

He saw her eyes flicker resentment. "He was here earlier, but he left."

"Alone? What about Emaline?"

Palatia pushed back against the counter and gave him a veiled stare. "What about her?"

Mac noticed that her knuckles were white from gripping the edge of the countertop and that her body was ramrod straight. Something was definitely amiss, but there was no time to pursue the issue.

At the distant sound of a siren, Mac put his hand on Palatia's chilly arm. "I don't mean to alarm you unnecessarily, but there's been an accident. Ed's been shot."

Palatia sagged against him and whispered, "Oh Lord. He's dead."

"That'll be the ambulance."

"They're coming for his body?"

"Ed's still alive. I didn't mean to imply that he was . . ."

Before Mac could finish, Palatia's face flooded with fear. "Did he say anything? I have to see him."

Mac put out a restraining hand, but Palatia avoided him and lurched down the hall toward Ed's office.

He managed to grab her arm before she got to the door. "Don't go in there."

"If he's alive, I have to be with him. Let me go." She tried to shake off his grip.

Mac held tight. "Ed shouldn't be touched or unduly excited. The best thing you can do is show the men where to bring the gurney. Can you do that?"

When she didn't answer, he shook her. "Can you do that, Palatia?"

She nodded. There were no tears in her eyes, only a smoldering, sullen expression.

Mac waited until Palatia had disappeared into the front hall, then hurried to Ed's side. His vitals were stable. The bastard would probably live to be a hundred.

The gurney rolled in, followed by a frantic Palatia, who grabbed Mac's arm. "You have to come to the hospital. You can't leave me alone."

He shook his head. "Tom Havens is Ed's doctor; let him . . ."

Palatia's panicky eyes stopped him; this was no time to reason with a borderline hysteric. He'd have to put his search for Frank on the back burner, and after Ed was safely settled he would call Julia to fill her in.

CHAPTER 45

THE FOLLOWING MORNING Mac's was the first message Julia heard. "Ed Pierce died yesterday evening without ever regaining consciousness."

All thoughts of sleep slipped away as Julia dialed his number.

"Was it a clot?"

"They don't know, but Tom Havens assures me there will be an autopsy."

"Was anyone with him?"

"Palatia came back in the room for a second visit. Wasn't in there for more than a few minutes when all the alarms went crazy. Pierce's heart was flatlined by the time the Code Blue team got to him. They tried to jump-start him several times but got no response.

"The poor woman was so agitated that they wanted to sedate her, but she refused. Havens took her home and offered to stay but she assured him she would be okay."

He let out a deep sigh. "It's all my fault. I should have stayed with him."

"Don't beat up on yourself. You stayed until Tom got to the hospital. Ed was his patient."

"But I'm still responsible." Mac paused. "I know this is short notice, but would you run up to Hatch with me? I really should see how Palatia's doing and it would be nice to have backup."

AN HOUR later Mac wheeled into the Pierce driveway. There were two cars parked in front. One of the cars belonged to Steve Duke.

Julia's heart began to hammer. Seeing Steve again was the last thing she needed. Especially since she hadn't been able to put him out of her thoughts no matter how hard she had tried. It was too late to make up an excuse and to stay in the car. Mac had already opened her door.

"That's Palatia's car; she was driving it yesterday. Emaline's rental is gone."

He checked the second license plate. "It's an Albuquerque prefix. I'll bet that's why the line was busy. Palatia must have taken it off the hook."

When the message registered, Julia felt an uncontrollable sting of jealousy. "Are you saying what I think you're saying?"

Mac chuckled and gave her a knowing leer. "Steve and Palatia go back a long, long way. In fact, there were rumors about them during our senior year in high school."

Julia drowned in her resentment. She remembered asking him about the other women in his life when they were having lunch at Don's the day of Mac's father's funeral, but when Steve had said, "No tales to tell there," she let it go.

Palatia answered the door, a silk robe clutched to her body, her hair draped softly over her shoulders. She wasn't pleased to see them.

Mac glanced at his watch. "I'm sorry to disturb you, Palatia. When I tried to call, your line was busy, so I thought you were up."

"I didn't sleep too well last night. Losing Ed has been such a shock, and I'm worried about Emaline. God knows where she is."

Julia spoke up. "Our coming here unannounced was thoughtless and inconsiderate. We'll come back another time."

Palatia's displeasure melted. "I'm sure you must have a good reason." She widened the door. "Come on in and have a seat. I'll make coffee."

Julia watched the woman glide down the hall toward the kitchen

and realized how beautiful and youthful she was. It wasn't at all difficult to imagine that Palatia and Steve could be lovers.

She and Mac moved into the living room, chose a comfortable
couch covered with grey suede cloth and settled into square pillows
made from small Navajo rugs. The morning sun filtering through the
shutters accented the deep red-and-grey Navajo rugs gracing wide-
planked wooden floors.

Facing the couch were two deep armchairs upholstered in oxblood
leather, flanking a massive Spanish trunk.

Julia was impressed. "This is a lovely room."

Mac nodded. "Palatia always was artistic. Now that Ed's dead,
she'll be a very wealthy widow."

Palatia returned with a tray of cups and a coffee pot. She had
changed into jeans and a bright yellow silk blouse, and her hair was
neatly restrained by a silver-and-turquoise clasp at the nape of her
neck.

She poured coffee all around, then settled into one of the side
chairs at the end of the coffee table.

Before anyone could speak, a door opened followed by the sound
of bare feet padding down the hallway.

In a tone betraying an intimacy that couldn't be ignored, Palatia
said, "Steve drove down late last night." Then she called out, "Steve?
Be sure you're decent. Mac and Julia are here."

Julia jerked her head toward the wide, cased opening. How could
she face Steve now that she knew about him and Palatia? Her first
impulse was to head for the front door, but if she bolted she knew Mac
would question her act once they left the house.

She was saved when the footsteps stopped, backtracked down the
hall and a door softly clicked shut.

Julia felt eyes boring into her back, but when she turned, Palatia
quickly lowered hers and took a sip from her cup. "Now, what may I
do for you?"

Mac's answer was hardly what Julia expected. "I need to locate
Frank immediately, and I figured you wouldn't have let your daughter
out of this house without leaving a forwarding address."

Palatia stared at Mac for a long while. Finally she asked, "Why do you need Frank?"

"There's still much to settle in our father's estate. Even though I have Red Stone, the chile farms belong to Frank and the hail storm destroyed most of our crop. Something has to be done. Soon. Or it will be too late."

When Palatia remained silent, Mac continued. "If you're worried that I'll tell the authorities where they are, don't be. I want Frank and Emaline as safe as you do."

"Authorities? Why would you tell the police anything? It was suicide. Frank and Emaline have nothing to worry about. They were long gone before Ed shot himself."

"Well then, I don't see any problem with your giving me the number. Do you?"

Palatia lowered her head for a moment, then rose and walked to a small writing desk in an alcove off the living room. When she returned, she handed Mac a folded piece of paper. "You should be able to reach Frank at that number in a couple of days."

CHAPTER 46

MAC MANEUVERED his Jeep into an empty slot at Sam's Super Sonic Drive-In and pushed the intercom. "Two double hamburgers all-the-way, two orders of fries and two chocolate shakes with whipped cream topping."

He grinned at Julia. "We haven't done this in a long time."

"Not since February."

"Right. We were on our way back from Alamogordo to our place . . ." He paused and turned to gaze through the windshield.

Julia's heart tugged. "Wasn't that a lovely day? You attended that Hantavirus briefing at Holloman Air Force Base and I did the town."

"Yeah." Mac smiled. "It was a terrific day."

Julia took the only opportunity Mac had given her since their breakup to make a move. "I can tell you in minute detail what happened after we pigged out here."

His eyes crinkled at the edges. "When your zipper stuck and . . ."

The clank of the tray on the window ended the moment.

Mac handed Julia her burger and drink and both spent the next minutes inhaling their greasy indulgences.

After he paid the waitress, Mac rolled up the window and started the motor. "That sure hit the spot."

"Sheer decadence." Julia patted her stomach.

She waited for the uptake, but all she got was the rev of the motor as Mac backed away from the Super Sonic. "I'll have you home in no time. Hang on."

Julia turned away to stanch budding tears. She had given Mac every possible indication that she was ready to forgive him, and he was ignoring her. Why was he behaving this way? He was the one who broke the trust.

By the time the Jeep stopped in her driveway, Julia's mind was made up. She hopped out and walked around to the driver's side. "We have to talk."

She didn't wait for him to answer, but as she turned for the front door she heard the motor die and the car door open. By the time she unlocked the double bolt, she felt the warmth of Mac's body before his voice sounded softly at her back. "You're right, we do have to talk."

Once inside, Julia headed for the kitchen and called back. "I'll nuke some coffee. Have a seat."

She pointed Mac toward a small kitchen table next to the window facing the patio and shoved the scalding mug in his hand.

"To begin with," she announced, "we both are to speak the truth. I'm not into games."

"You're right; this is no game."

Julia tried to read the message in that but Mac's eyes, usually the color of the sky, darkened and receded beneath his brow, giving his face a different cast.

She suppressed a small wave of panic at the thought that she might be pushing him into a corner, but knew it was too late to retreat. She plunged on. "I don't understand what's happening between us."

"What seems to be the problem?"

Was he joking? Again Julia tried to read Mac's mood and failed. Though his eyes hadn't left her face from the moment they sat, she felt as if she were sitting across from a stranger.

"You say you love me, but . . ." She paused, hoping he would pick up the beat. Still no response. This was maddening. Finally, exasperation beat out prudence. "Bottom line, Mac, I need to know where you stand in this relationship."

When he finally spoke, his voice was deep and carried a different cadence.

"Did I ever mention Sylvia Chee to you? She was the doctor in attendance when they took me to Chaco Point and you to Albuquerque. She's a Navajo. Yale undergrad and medical. Brilliant. A keen internist. Could have the world, but she chose to return to her people. You would like her."

At the mention of another woman, Julia trembled inside. Had Mac found someone else already?

"I only mention Sylvia because the other day she accused me of being Indian."

Julia shook her head in disbelief. "What does that have to do with us?"

For the first time since she had begun the conversation, Julia saw a small smile creep across Mac's lips. "Everything, as far as I'm concerned. Beginning with the moment I first saw you. Some cultures call it fate, others, kismet or karma. That Christmas afternoon something drew me out of the house and away from the promise of Cuca's sopaipillas. I meant to turn south toward Las Cruces and the Sandovals' cocktail party, but when I reached the interstate I turned north. Something made me turn north to find you."

"Oh, Mac." Julia shut her eyes to see his red Jeep retreat from the overlook at Elephant Butte on her first lonely Christmas in New Mexico.

His next words were barely audible. "I knew you loved me the day we flew into the Mescalero Apache Reservation. I knew it because you gave yourself to me that night—freely and willingly. At that moment we were *Nizhoni.*"

"Walking in beauty." How wonderful that evening had been. "Why can't we be *Nizhoni* again?"

Mac shook his head and let out a heavy sigh. "Perhaps we can, but you have to agree, things have changed between us since then. I messed up with Emaline and that sent you in another direction. It's more than obvious to me that Steve Duke has managed to snag a piece of your heart."

Julia shifted uneasily in her seat, wondering how much Mac knew or at least suspected. She didn't want to tell him about Steve, but she had promised to speak the truth, no matter what.

Then she heard him say, "So, in answer to your question, I know I love you, but before we can go on, you need to decide where your heart belongs."

Julia wanted to will away the memory of Steve's mouth commanding hers, but the imprint of his lips still burned. Why couldn't she get him out of her mind?

Mac's chair scraped against the tiles and she raised her eyes to see him standing above her. "I thought that was the case."

"You're overreacting. Reading too much into . . ." Her voice sounded much too feeble to be convincing.

"Into what?"

"It's not what you think. Believe me."

"How do you know what I think?" Mac ruffled her hair with his hand. "I'll call you tomorrow, okay?"

She nodded and he was gone.

CHAPTER 47

JULIA SHIFTED her position on the hard chair. Her coffee was cold, the sun was set, but Mac's parting words, "You need to decide where your heart belongs," still remained fresh in her mind.

Where did her heart belong? She was in love with Mac. What was not to love about him? Even thoughts of his night with Emaline no longer seemed to rankle as much as they once did. But if that were true, why was she so obsessed with Steve?

The sound of the telephone cut through the early evening darkness to drag Julia from the breakfast table and her dilemma. "Doctor Fairchild."

"Chica?" Dolores's voice was slurred and muffled. "That you?"

"Dolores? What's the matter?"

"Nothing. Nothing. Just wanted to say goodbye. You're a great gal, you know. Too good for those damn Brantleys. You hear me? Too good."

Dolores was drunk, but what was this "goodbye"? Julia spoke as calmly as she could manage. "Dolores, where are you?"

There was a long silence followed by a muted, "The Square B. Where else? I'm queen of the Brantley hacienda. That's what Frank used to call me—in the beginning. Ohhhhh, Lordy, I'm not drunk enough, yet."

Julia's mind raced. Was she dealing with a possible suicide?

"You know, we haven't visited since before Mister Brantley's funeral. Why don't I come out?"

"No. No. I just need another bottle of vodka, that's all."

"I'll pick some up on the way. How does that sound?"

Her answer was the clatter of the receiver as it hit the floor.

"Dolores? Can you hear me? Please answer me. Dolores."

Julia frantically depressed the hook to break the connection and call Mac. When she couldn't get a dial tone, she realized she was being held hostage. Dolores had made the call; Dolores would have to end it.

THE DETOUR off the interstate through Doña Ana cost valuable time, but Julia knew Mac would have his medical bag and a key to the hacienda.

She saw his Jeep parked at his front door and felt much better. At least he was home. She leaped from her car, ran to the front door and tried it. Locked.

"Mac?" Julia pounded on the unforgiving wood with her bare fists. "Please open the door. It's an emergency."

Pressing her ear to the door, Julia prayed for the sound of his footsteps, but after a few seconds of silence, she abandoned that plan and ran across the grass to Mac's bedroom window.

To her dismay the curtains were drawn.

"Mac? It's Julia." She banged on the window with what strength was left, her hands aching, her heart hammering. "If you're in there, please open the window. I need your help."

She heard stirring, then a bleary-eyed Mac peered through the curtain and cranked open the casement.

Before he could speak, she blurted, "Dolores is drunk and threatening suicide. I'm going on ahead in case the front door to the hacienda is unlocked. Hurry and don't forget your bag."

She gunned the Range Rover back down the lane and turned north on Highway 85, checking her rearview mirror until she saw headlights coming out of Shalem County Road and knew Mac was behind her.

By the time Julia parked next to the Suburban in front of the hacienda, more than half an hour had passed. Precious minutes had been lost by stopping at Mac's, but there was no other answer. Was it too late?

She tried the front door. Unlocked.

She stepped into the wide central hall, walked a few steps and called out, "Dolores?"

A moan was followed by a brittle clatter.

In the dim light Julia saw an empty vodka bottle roll through Dolores's bedroom door to clink against the far wall of the hallway.

Julia ran the last few steps to see Dolores lying faceup on the bed, her naked body partially covered by a sheet, her left wrist dangling over the edge of the mattress, spurting blood in dreadful cadence to each heartbeat.

Julia kicked a small paring knife away to reach the woman's side. "Dolores? Can you hear me?"

When Dolores didn't answer, Julia yanked her belt from her blue jeans and cinched it around Dolores's forearm. That done, she grabbed for the right arm and smiled. The wrist was still intact.

She heard footsteps as Mac called out, "Julia?"

"In here. Hurry."

She felt Mac beside her. "I'll take it now."

Julia moved away, then retrieved the phone receiver from the floor and placed it in the cradle.

Mac firmly slapped Dolores on both cheeks. "Wake up, Dolores. Do you hear me?"

Dolores's eyes fluttered open. "Oooh. Stop that, it hurts."

"You damned fool. Thank God you called Julia or you might be dead."

She lifted her uncut wrist. "I was going to slit the other one and get in the tub, but I got too drunk."

"Thank heaven for small favors," Mac said. "You did a good enough job to need stitches."

He fished in his bag, found a roll of gauze and began to bind her wrist. "If you wanted to die, why didn't you poison yourself? You've got a whole hothouse full of the damned stuff."

Dolores tried to focus on Mac. "You always thought I poisoned your mama, didn't you?"

Julia's heart tugged at the pathetic expression on the pock-marked face, and she placed a consoling hand on the woman's clammy forehead. "Save your strength, chica, we have to get you to the hospital."

Dolores grabbed Mac's hand with her good one. "No, no, I have to tell you what happened with Mrs. B. Please."

"You don't have to . . ."

"It was the Belladonna."

Mac straightened. "You gave my mother Bella-donna?"

She nodded. "It was for her colic. Sure it's poisonous in big doses, but just a little relaxes the stomach. I'd been giving it to her for years. I swear I was careful. I only put one drop on her tongue when she couldn't stand the pain anymore."

Mac tried to pull his hand from hers, but Dolores hung on. "Those damn Nu Mex Sixes. You know once your ma started, she couldn't stop."

He nodded his agreement. "That's true enough."

"Besides," Dolores whined. "I couldn't have done it, anyway. The night she died, Frank and I were in Juarez."

At the mention of his brother's name, Mac came to attention. "Speaking of Frank, have you heard from him?"

"After what I did?" Dolores let go her death grip and collapsed into the pillows. "My life is over."

"Don't be ridiculous," Julia said. "Losing Frank's not worth taking your life. Think of poor Allen."

A tear escaped the edge of one of Dolores's eyes and disappeared into her raven hair. "My baby's all grown up. He doesn't need me."

"Allen needs you more than ever."

"Julia's right." Mac finished the crude tourniquet and stepped back. "Besides, you two have a chile pepper farm to run."

"But I have to finish about Mrs. B." Dolores sobbed. "She knew I kept the dropper bottle on a high shelf in the hothouse. I told her it was dangerous, but she must've been in so much pain, she took too much. Say you believe me."

Mac covered her hand with his. "Of course, I believe you. Now, let Julia help you dress."

Dolores's eyes clamped shut as she sank back. "I don't want to go anyplace. Can't I just stay here?"

"Sorry. The wound is too deep and you need a tetanus shot." Mac turned to Julia. "I'll phone in while you help her dress."

IT WAS almost ten by the time Mac settled Dolores for an overnight stay at Central Hospital and joined Julia for a sandwich in the cafeteria. His haggard face was witness to his exhaustion, and it was obvious that not even the third cup of black coffee he was downing would give him a second wind.

Julia drained her cup. "It's been a long day. What now?"

He groaned and stretched. "How about twenty-four hours of uninterrupted sleep?"

"Great idea. But what about Frank and Emaline?"

"I can't do anything about them tonight."

Julia reached across the table to touch Mac's hand. "You're beat."

"You're right. It's all I can do to hold my eyes open."

"If that's the case, you shouldn't be driving. I'll be glad to take you home and we can come back for your Jeep first thing in the morning."

Mac studied her for a long moment. "Thanks, but I can make that drive in my sleep. Old intern trick."

Julia realized that Mac was standing his ground and bristled. "Fine, drive yourself, but don't blame me if you end up in some damned irrigation ditch. It'll serve you right."

He grabbed her hand before she could rise. "Don't be angry. I'm just trying to do what's best for us."

"Suit yourself, you stubborn . . ."

Sudden tears jammed her eyes and she searched her purse for her keys.

Mac stood. If he saw her distress, he didn't acknowledge it. "Let's get out of here before I requisition this table and use it for a bed."

CHAPTER 48

IT WAS WELL after nine the following morning when Lucia Fairchild's cheery chirp raced across the ozone to pierce Julia's gloom. After the two women exchanged their usual greetings and discussed Lucia's trip to England, there was a long pause.

Julia knew her mother expected an update on the wedding, but she couldn't quite bring herself to reveal her tenuous relationship with Mac, or her senseless preoccupation with Steve.

The bleep of an incoming call saved Julia and, abandoning her protesting mother, she depressed the hook.

Mac wasted no time on pleasantries. "The police just called. They want me at the hospital, a.s.a.p. Would you mind meeting me there?"

Half an hour later, Julia parked in the physician's lot next to Steve Duke's sedan. After taking several deep breaths to quell the butterflies fluttering against the sides of her stomach, she walked slowly toward the hospital entrance.

A short, stocky man Julia recognized as a detective with the Las Cruces Police was standing next to Mac near the hall leading to the morgue.

"Julia, this is Detective Manny Garcia, famous for his prowess on the basketball court."

Mac drew her to him. "Meet Julia Fairchild, a clinical psychologist at Piñon Mesa."

Manny gave her a brief nod, then said, "Maybe you two can help me clear up a few holes in Palatia's story."

"Palatia's here?" Mac asked.

The detective pointed toward the dimly lit corridor. "I got her and Duke down there. By the way, do you have any idea why he's in town?"

Before either could reply, Manny's heavy eyebrows arched, then he gave Mac a knowing wink. "Still at it, you think?"

Mac shrugged. "Who knows? It's been years. How can we help?"

"The attending nurse swears Ed regained consciousness but wasn't making much sense. Palatia says he never opened his eyes. What do you know?"

Julia touched Mac's arm. "Here comes Steve."

He arrived, face tight. "What in hell are you doing here, Brantley?"

"I was the one who found Ed. What's up?"

"How should I know?" Steve said. "We've only been here a few minutes."

Julia left the huddle to settle beside Palatia, who clutched a handkerchief embroidered with a large "D." It matched the one Steve loaned her the night of the party—the one she'd neatly pressed and tucked in the back of her lingerie drawer.

She buried her unreasonable rush of resentment. "How are you?"

"Could be better. I've known Manny since he was in kindergarten, but he's almost acting like I'm a criminal."

At the sound of the men's approaching footsteps, Palatia gave a tremulous smile. "Hello, Mac."

Mac started toward them, but Garcia grabbed his arm and pushed open the swinging door. "You can chat later; you're needed in here."

When Steve followed, the detective put up his hand. "Not you, Duke, just the attending physician."

Palatia put up her hand. "Wait a minute. Mac isn't—wasn't Ed's doctor; Tom Havens was."

"Havens is already in there." Manny pointed to the closing door. "He's the one who asked for Mac."

Steve settled on the other side of Palatia, who buried her face in his handkerchief. He slid one arm around her shaking shoulders. "It's going to be all right."

His words were for Palatia but his eyes never left Julia's. As her heart began to climb toward her throat, she broke from his gaze.

Hating that he was able to affect her so and realizing she needed to get out of there before she made a fool of herself, Julia stood. "I'm going to visit a friend. If Mac comes out before I get back . . ."

Steve's eyes dulled. "Yeah. We'll tell him to wait here."

Minutes later, Julia leaned over the patient information desk. "Dolores Brantley?"

The volunteer consulted the computer. "Room one-oh-three."

She hurried down the hall, then peeked into the small private room to see Dolores dressed and hunched forward in the straight chair beside her bed.

"Good morning."

Dolores glared. "What's good about it? I have a king-sized hangover and I'm starving. Did Mac sign me out?"

"I don't know. We came in separate cars."

Julia settled in the only other chair available in the cramped quarters. "Mac's in the morgue. Ed Pierce's autopsy. Since he was the one who found him . . ."

"Ed's dead?" Dolores crossed herself, muttered some incantation beneath her breath, then gasped. "Do you think Frank did it?"

"I can't say. We know Frank went to see Ed and the two exchanged words. But, according to Palatia, Ed tried to commit suicide after Frank and Emaline left the house."

At the mention of Emaline, Dolores paled. "He was with her?"

Before Julia could respond, the door flew open. "Ma. Thank God you're okay."

A pale Allen Brantley brushed past Julia to embrace his mother, then knelt at her side. "I went home. Saw the blood. Oh, Ma."

He flashed a welcoming smile at Julia. "I found the note Mac left and came as fast as I could. I'm so sorry. Will you forgive me?"

"For what? You didn't do anything, mijo." Dolores grabbed Allen to her as tears filled her eyes. "Besides, I'm perfect now that you're here."

CHAPTER 49

JULIA WAVED to Dolores over Allen's shoulder and left the tender reunion to hurry toward the morgue. She was nearing the end of the corridor when Steve appeared out of nowhere, yanked her into an unoccupied room and shut the door behind them.

"I need to explain about Palatia."

"What makes you think . . . ?" Julia's voice caught in her throat, then she forced the words. "What makes you think I care?"

She knew she should leave, find Mac, but couldn't take the first step. Being with Steve was like taking an aphrodisiac. Instead, she moaned, then moved to meet his lips and found herself returning his kisses as voraciously as he took them.

Steve broke their kiss. "I know you love me." Dark eyes searched hers as his fingers mined her upper arms. "Say it."

Julia shook her head. "I can't."

She tried to avoid Steve's mouth but he was too powerful, and she was too aroused.

At the sound of voices in the corridor outside, Steve pressed her against the wall as the door cracked slightly. The bustle from the hall invaded, then receded as the door slowly closed, leaving the room quiet except for their heavy breathing.

His voice came low and pleading. "You have to understand about Palatia. She's like a mother—a mentor. She encouraged me to become what I am. Gave me money. Moral support." He paused. "And love."

At that, Julia regained some of her sensibility and renewed her struggle. "Let me go, damn it."

His grip was like a vise. "Not until you hear it all."

"I don't want to . . ."

Steve paid no attention to her protest. "Mac and I have always been less than friendly rivals. It started in high school when I lost captain of the basketball team to him, then he edged me out as Editor-in-Chief of the *Bull Dog* and beat me for a basketball scholarship at the university. If that weren't enough, there was always Emaline.

"I had a crush on her since the sixth grade and thought there was a good chance to date her during our senior year. She and Mac were always fighting and breaking up, so when I heard they were on the outs, I dropped by with a bouquet of flowers. Before I asked her, Emaline laughed in my face, threw the flowers on the floor and ran out, leaving her mother and me standing alone in the kitchen.

"Palatia could see I was hurt and came to comfort me. I don't exactly recall when the comfort changed to something more, but before—we did—anything—she told me she had barred Ed Pierce from her bed when Emaline was four. From that day on, Palatia was there for me. And now, I guess you could say I'm paying my debts."

"By sleeping with her?" Her anger renewed, Julia stiffened and tried a third time for freedom.

Steve groaned and released her. "She was frightened and lonely last night. I heard her crying and went to her room to be sure she was all right."

He let out a long breath and turned away to stare out the window into the parking lot. When he spoke again, his voice was barely audible. "And I stayed."

"And yet, you say you love me?"

Steve faced her. "I won't try to justify what Palatia and I have together. She would do anything for me and I would do the same for her."

He took Julia in his arms. "Believe me, I've never felt this way about another woman. I've never asked anyone to marry me."

She shook her head, hating that she was so confused. She loved Mac, didn't she? But if she did, why was she standing inches away from a man she desperately hoped would kiss her again?

It seemed he could read her mind and at the touch of Steve's mouth, Julia leaned into his kiss, letting his passion consume her. When she realized he was slowly edging her toward the empty hospital bed, she used every last bit of will to push him away. "Please. We have to stop. Someone might come in."

Steve stepped back, eyes yearning. "You're right. We'll both be missed, but I promise you one thing, I intend to make you mine."

He smoothed her lips with his thumb, then kissed her softly on her forehead. "Guess I was pretty rough on you. You'd better freshen up. I'll go first."

Julia repaired her makeup with trembling fingers, then checked the corridor before she eased through the door. She circled the main lobby and stopped at the small gift shop, giving her heartbeat time to return to normal before making her way back to the morgue.

Relieved to see that the bench once occupied by Palatia and Steve was now empty, she opened one of the morgue doors just enough to hear Mac say, "If that's it, I'll be on my way."

She sat just as the door swung wide and Mac, with apology on his face, came out. "Sorry it took so long."

"No problem. I went to visit Dolores, who's champing at the bit to get sprung. But, she's not alone. Allen's with her."

"That's good news. I was afraid he might have left the Square B for good. As for Dolores, she won't have to wait a minute longer. I've already stopped by the nurses' station and signed her release."

They were halfway down the hall when curiosity won and Julia asked, "What happened back there?"

"Doc's preliminary exam ruled out suicide," Mac said. "From the angle of entry, there's no way in hell Pierce could have shot himself. Doc confirms that there were no powder burns on Pierce's hand or around the entry site. And, just as I thought, there were no major organs involved."

"But, if the wound wasn't the cause of death, where does that leave it?"

"We won't know until Doc completes the autopsy, but here's news—Palatia was alone with Ed when he went Code Blue, and he was flat when the team got there. They worked on him a good while, but it was no use."

"Too bad."

"Manny took Steve and Palatia down to headquarters."

"Oh, no," Julia gasped. "Did he arrest Palatia?"

Before Mac could answer, a nurse stopped them. "Thank heavens I caught you, Doctor Brantley. Manny Garcia's on the telephone. He wants to see you at headquarters right away."

CHAPTER 50

THE POLICE DEPARTMENT, done in the same Pueblo style as the stately whitewashed Doña Ana County Courthouse, was nestled among the rest of the municipal buildings. But the bow to New Mexico's Indian heritage stopped once Mac and Julia entered the controlled access doors. Inside was all business. Dispatchers manned switchboards and a senior officer presided over an elevated station desk.

Julia quickly scanned the waiting room and was relieved to see no sign of Steve or Palatia. A run-in so soon after their meeting might prove disastrous. She was here with Mac. To support him if necessary.

Mac stepped to the desk. "Manny Garcia? He sent for me."

"You Brantley?"

When Mac nodded, he jerked his thumb toward a hall leading off the lobby. "Fourth door on the right."

Garcia welcomed them to his cubicle, pointed them to a wooden bench, then sat on the top of his desk. He stared at Mac for a long time before he said, "Why didn't you tell me?"

"Tell you what?"

"That Frank shot Ed Pierce."

Julia saw Mac's eyes narrow for the barest instant, but when he spoke his tone was even. "That's news to me."

Manny snorted. "Aw, c'mon, Mac, don't bullshit me. Palatia says she told you about Frank the day you found Ed slumped over his desk in a pool of blood. The two men fought, Frank shot him, then hauled ass."

Julia couldn't help but break in. "That's a lie."

The detective's coal-black eyes shifted to her. "Really?"

"Yes, really. Palatia told Mac she threw the gun away on the mesa to save Ed's good name—and—" Julia stopped. The story sounded as flimsy as it did the first time she heard it.

Garcia laughed softly. "That's a good one."

Julia shut her mouth and glared at him.

Mac strained forward. "That's exactly what Palatia told me, Manny, I swear."

Garcia grabbed a small tape recorder, set it on the edge of his desk next to him. "This is not official, just saves me time later. Okay?"

Mac waited until Manny activated the tape then went through the details of how he had found Ed Pierce, heard a car drive up, then seen Palatia carry a sack of groceries into the kitchen. He remembered how tense Palatia seemed and how strangely she behaved when she learned Ed was still alive.

"You're telling me the woman left her husband for dead, drove out on the mesa to dispose of the gun and went grocery shopping?"

Mac nodded. "If Frank did shoot Ed, why didn't Palatia report it right away?"

"I asked her the same thing," Manny said. "She says Frank threatened to kill Emaline if she made the call and that he kidnapped Emaline for protection."

Mac laughed. "I think it would be more believable if Palatia told you Emaline held Frank hostage. Don't you?"

The detective gave a snorty chortle. "Knowing Emaline the way we do, hell, yes. What's your story?"

"I think Frank and Emaline have run off together. They've been lovers for years."

Garcia's jaw dropped. "Get outta here. Weren't you and Emaline engaged or something? I seem to remember hearing something like that while I was in the Marines, stationed at Quantico."

"We lived together for almost a year, then she left me."

"And you knew nothing about her and your own brother? Man, that's awful."

Mac shrugged. "All past history."

"Maybe. But it sure is relevant." Manny made a few scribbles on a blank sheet of paper, then shoved it away. "Especially since Palatia's thrown the blame in Frank's direction and, in doing so, implicated you as an accessory. She says you know where he is and that you're lying to protect him."

Julia jumped to her feet. "Now, that is a lie. I was there—with Mac—at Palatia's when she handed him the paper with Frank's phone number on it. I saw her write it down with my own eyes. Show him."

Mac pulled her down beside him. "I don't have it. I copied the number in my address book and threw the paper in the kitchen trash."

"Oh, Mac."

Manny came off the desk. "But you have the number?"

Mac nodded. "Yes, but so does Palatia."

"I don't care who has it. I need that number."

Mac raised his hand. "No need to rush. They won't be at that number for a few days."

Manny's heavy brows shot north. "So, you do know where they are?"

"The number Palatia gave me has a San Francisco area code. Probably Emaline's condominium. But I'm willing to bet Palatia's talked to her daughter a time or two in the last couple of days. Why don't you subpoena her phone records?"

The detective grinned, fished for a sheet on his desk and held it up. "Way ahead of you." He ran his finger down the list. "Here we go. Tuesday, April eleven. There were two person-to-person calls made to Pavilion Hospital in Albuquerque. One at eleven-twenty a.m. lasted eight minutes. A second at seven-thirteen p.m. lasted three. But at one a.m. on April twelve, someone from Palatia's number called Cabo San Lucas. It lasted twenty-two minutes."

At the mention of Pavilion, Julia came to attention. She tried to recall what Steve had told her about Palatia. "When she discovered that Ed had been shot, she called me." Yes, that accounted for the first call. But the second? Around seven? That was about the time Ed flatlined. Why didn't Steve mention that call?

JULIA WAITED until they reached the parking lot to say, "What now?"

Mac shrugged. "I don't have a clue. But the gauntlet's down. Palatia's done a masterful job of putting the blame on Frank and incriminating me."

"I can't believe Manny Garcia bought it."

Mac raised a cautionary hand. "But we don't know that Palatia's lying. It's entirely possible Frank might have shot Ed especially after finding out he was his father. The only thing is, if that were true, why didn't Palatia call the police and an ambulance? And why didn't she keep the gun as evidence?"

"Maybe she's protecting Emaline," Julia said. "A mother would do that."

It was almost four. By the time Julia got home it would be seven in New York. Her promise to call her mother right back the night before had given way to her concern over Dolores. Now it was time to pay the piper.

She waited until Mac was settled on the passenger side. "It's been a long day. I'll drop you by the hospital so you can pick up the Jeep."

"Sorry. Guess we should have brought both cars."

Wasn't he going to say something—do something—to give her an opening to invite him to come home with her? She needed to be with him—validate their love so they could begin again. But on the brief ride back to the hospital, Mac was silent.

Julia parked several spaces away from the Jeep, then got out to stand next to him, a smile pasted over her pain.

Mac reached to touch her shoulder. "About tomorrow."

She didn't let him finish. "Don't worry about the weekend. I have a lot of unfinished business to clear up."

"Oh?" Mac's eyes darkened. It was the same expression she had seen as he sat across from her in her kitchen the afternoon before. Did he think she was seeing Steve? Wasn't she?

She raced to cover the flash of guilt. "My mother is back from

England. She was on the line when Dolores called. I need to tell her we've postponed the wedding."

At those words, his eyes returned to their familiar sky-blue. "That won't take all day, will it?"

"No. But, it was your suggestion that I take some time to work a few things through."

"Hoist on my own petard. Call me at least, will you?" He planted a quick kiss on her forehead and turned toward his Jeep.

Julia watched him move away, his steps sure, as if he didn't have a care in the world. She wanted to run after him—beg him to marry her without delay—protect her from Steve—or was it from herself?

CHAPTER 51

THE FOLLOWING MONDAY, Ed Pierce was buried.

Late that afternoon Manny Garcia called Mac to report that his surveillance team had seen only Palatia and the minister in attendance.

"Any word on my brother?"

"Nope, but I've sent a private investigator down to Cabo."

"Why send a PI? Can't you go yourself?"

"Not officially."

"Well, keep me posted." Mac hung up and turned to see Julia climb the steps to the side verandah and sink into the soft padding of the lawn chair next to Dolores.

Seeing her after a two-day hiatus made his heart lurch. He never thought he could miss her any more than he had when he was in Chaco Point, but he did.

He spent Saturday morning clearing out any possible reminders of his misspent evening with Emaline, and in the end tossed out all the bed linens and towels. That afternoon he went to Sears, returning home laden with packages that included a new comforter with matching throw pillows. Even with that, the evening had stretched endlessly on.

He made several trips to the telephone, but each time turned away. He had told Julia to make the call. He would leave it at that.

Sunday was no better. Mac was so bored that he offered to accompany Dolores and Allen to church, then took them to the Easter buffet at the Hilton. He spent the afternoon walking the field next to the barns that Allen chose to replant. That had taken up the balance of the day, but once the sun set Mac could stand it no longer.

He dialed Julia's number and cursed beneath his breath when her answering service kicked in. Where was she?

"Hey, Julia, seems like two years instead of two days. Who says I'm so smart? But I have really good news. Cuca's back and the kitchen's been liberated from Dolores. Is that enough to tempt you to Hatch for dinner tomorrow?"

Now, she was there and suddenly it no longer mattered how she felt about Steve. All Mac knew was that he needed to have her lips against his.

Julia's voice filtered across the verandah into the library, drawing him to the door and onto the porch. He made a shushing motion to Allen, who was seated on the low wall swinging one booted leg back and forth, then bent to kiss the top of Julia's head.

"I've missed you."

Julia smiled. "Me, too."

Dolores snorted from the depths of her chair. "Will you two cut the sweet talk and get me a drink? I bet Julia could use one, too."

"Sure." Mac wheeled toward the door. "Guess we could all do with one. Beer, Allen?"

"No thanks, Mac, maybe later. I have to make a quick check on the chile seeds."

Mac paused. A different Allen sat on that wall. Frank's disappearance had changed the boy from adolescent to adult practically overnight.

"Wine?"

"Sure." Julia struggled out of the deep cushions. "I'll come help."

Mac poured Dolores's vodka over ice. "How's your mother?"

"Fine, I guess."

"And the wedding postponement?"

That brought a long quivering breath and a small, "She's thrilled."

A shiver slithered down Mac's spine. Julia hadn't said much about how her mother felt about the marriage. Not that he asked. But somehow, without Julia having to say it, he knew Lucia Fairchild's initial approval of him had soured.

He raised his eyes to see that Julia's were filled with distress and decided not to comment. She was here; that's all that mattered.

He splashed some Scotch on the rocks for himself. "What's your pleasure?"

Julia stepped toward him and raised an affectionate hand to his cheek. "I don't care. Red. White. Whatever is open."

Before she could move, he took advantage of her close proximity to harvest one deep kiss after another.

There was no protest, only her body against his and her mouth softly pliant beneath his. For the first time in weeks, things seemed almost right again.

Dolores's shout broke into their passion. "Need any help in there?"

"Damn," Mac said, then yelled, "hold your horses, woman, we're on our way."

He handed the two drinks to Julia, but before she turned to go he extracted another kiss and whispered, "Come home with me tonight."

Julia hesitated. "Let's see how the evening goes. Okay?"

What was holding her back? Only a few days before Julia had questioned his reluctance to be intimate. Now, after the two-day break, it seemed the shoe was on the other foot. And where was she when he had called? With Steve? The next thought was too terrible to consider.

Mac pushed away his torturing demons and kissed her softly. "You're the boss. Go on out, I'll bring the wine and a proper glass. Maybe the nachos are ready."

The three finished their drinks and nachos as the light faded from a purple sky, then joined Allen at the table for Cuca's Monday night special of stacked red enchiladas topped with cheese and the customary fried egg.

The Brantleys' dinner conversation focused on the revised planting schedule. To Mac's surprise, when Allen presented a detailed master plan covering the following weeks, it seemed almost as if Frank were in the room.

A sudden ache filled his chest. He swallowed several times to loosen its grip and sent up a small prayer that soon Frank would be seated in his usual spot at the table.

Allen's voice jolted him from his sorrow. "So, even though we've lost six weeks, the river chiles will hold us until we can harvest in mid September. How does that sound to you, Mac?"

Before Mac could respond, the clang of the front door knocker echoed through the house.

Cuca spun through the swinging door and slid past the silent diners into the hallway as each turned toward the wide opening, straining to hear the muted conversation.

The front door slammed and heavier footsteps followed light until Cuca appeared with Manny Garcia behind her.

"Sorry to intrude, people, but I've got news."

Mac half-stood and pointed to the empty chair next to Allen. "Have a seat, Manny. Care for a glass of wine?"

Manny shook his head. "No thanks. I'm here on official business."

His statement was met with silence. Dolores abruptly shoved her chair away from the table and stood. "I think Allen and I will make a last trip to the barn before it gets too dark. Will you excuse us?"

Allen jumped up. "Right. The barn."

Dolores gave the detective a pleading look. "You don't need us, do you?"

Garcia smiled. "As a matter of fact, I was just about to ask you to leave the room. If I need you, I know where I can find you."

Mac waited until he heard the front door shut. "Thanks for letting them off the hook."

"No need to involve them at this point." The detective lowered his voice. "Got some bad news. Frank was the first customer of the day at the bar in the old Hatch Hotel the morning of Ed's murder. Downed six quick shots. Told the bartender he was out to kill Pierce. Sorry."

Mac bristled at that. "Now, wait just a minute. So Frank was a little drunk when he got to Pierce's. That doesn't mean he pulled the trigger."

Julia spoke up. "And what about Emaline? If she cared so much about her father, why didn't she show for the funeral?"

Garcia nodded. "Good point. And I'm not saying she's entirely out of the loop, nor is her mother. Palatia's story doesn't add up at all if what Mac told me is true."

Mac relaxed a little. At least they hadn't nailed his brother completely to the wall. "All I know is what Palatia told me that first night."

"And you have no reason to lie. But why would Emaline want to kill her father? They always seemed to be real close."

"Shock. Anger. Betrayal."

"Good motives, but what's the trigger? Before you answer . . ." Manny held up his hand and produced a tape recorder. "If you don't mind. It's for my benefit."

Mac nodded and waited until the detective activated his machine.

"I'm pretty sure Emaline found out my brother Frank is Ed Pierce's illegitimate son. That bastard raped my mother."

Manny jerked forward. "You're shittin' me, man."

"I wish I were. When grandfather Allen's brother died suddenly, leaving Red Stone Grove to him, he pulled up stakes and headed for Las Cruces, bringing my grandmother and their only child, my mother, with him.

"The family was just outside Marfa, Texas, when they were hit head-on by a beer truck. Wiped out both my grandparents.

"Some nice people brought Mama on to Las Cruces, got her a room at the old Amador Hotel and introduced her to Dad, who was just putting out his shingle. He helped her settle her estate and I guess they fell in love in the process."

"I didn't know your dad was a lawyer," Manny said.

"Well, he wasn't for very long. My grandfather Brantley died unexpectedly shortly after Dad and Mama got married. Since Dad was the only child, he took over the Square B and the chiles."

"So, how does Ed Pierce figure into this?"

"About five years before my mama arrived, Ed Pierce moved to Las Cruces from Georgia. There was money—inherited, I suppose. He began buying all the pecan groves he could except for the prize stand, which my mother inherited. Of course she knew nothing about pecans; she was barely seventeen.

"The story my dad told was that Ed was sure a grieving young woman would be an easy target for a sale and managed to get an introduction to my mother at a Sunday School picnic. He tried to court her, but she told him she was in love with Dad. That accounted for the animosity the two men bore for each other. At least we boys thought so, until last Tuesday."

Manny let out a low whistle. "Some tale. But are you sure about all this?"

"I've seen the proof. My mother wrote Frank a letter to be given to him when she died."

"But she died years ago. When did you see it?"

"The same day Frank found out. The day Dad's will was read."

"This doesn't look good. The fact that Pierce was shot the day Frank found out the truth about his parentage points the finger at him. Besides, what motive could Emaline possibly have?"

"How would you react if you found out you've been having an ongoing love affair with your own half-brother?"

Garcia sat back in his chair and stared at the ceiling for a few moments before he spoke. "I used to wonder what could drive a person to kill—exactly what it took to shove him over the edge. Most people think it's because of something big, but it's my guess that it's an accumulation of little things over time or something unimportant to the overall situation but still significant enough to make the big difference."

The room remained silent until Manny finally sighed. "So much for philosophy. I think I'll have that drink now, if you don't mind. Vodka neat. Doesn't stay on the breath."

Mac stood and started for the library but barely made the doorway when Manny called after him. "I'd be real grateful if you could produce that letter." Then he grinned. "I'd sure hate to have to cite you for obstruction."

"No problem. I know exactly where I put it. Be right back with your drink."

After several minutes Mac appeared with the vodka. The expression on his face told all. "It's gone."

The three hurried to the library with Mac in the lead followed by the detective. "Are you sure you know where you put it?"

"Of course, I'm sure." Mac rushed across the room to the desk strewn with papers. "I've been through every drawer. It isn't here."

Julia stepped as close to Mac as she could and murmured, "Maybe Dolores . . . ?"

Mac shook his head then straightened. "Julia's right. I might have inadvertently stuck the envelope in the wrong file. No reason to panic. It'll turn up."

Manny settled in one of the deep leather chairs and took a swig of the vodka. "I need that letter, Mac."

"Not to change the subject," Julia said, "but did you contact the Las Cruces Airport?"

"Way ahead of you, there. Butte Air is the only service. We went over all their manifests for Tuesday, the eleventh. No Emaline Pierce, no Frank Brantley. In fact I recognized the names of most of the passengers. Besides that, most everybody in Las Cruces knows Emaline Pierce, 'cause she ain't no dog."

Julia colored at Manny's unthinking remark, but that didn't stop her. "What about that call from Cabo?"

"Palatia told me she returned a call from a boat chartering company lining up some fishing days for Duke's vacation next month. And Steve backed her up."

"At one in the morning?"

"Maybe they keep strange hours south of the border."

"Maybe Palatia couldn't sleep. Grief does that." Julia thought a moment. "Could they have chartered a plane? Maybe that's why Palatia left her husband in that condition—to get Emaline and Frank out of the country before the police got into it."

Manny knit his brows. "Could be. Could be. I'll call the charters first thing tomorrow."

"If Frank and Emaline are in Cabo, a call that time of night would make sense."

Mac held up his hand. "But Palatia told me they left together. Didn't you find Frank's truck at the airport?"

"It didn't turn up on the first sweep." Manny downed his drink and stood. "Well, I'll be getting along. I've got my work cut out for me. Yours is to keep on searching for that document."

Mac and Julia stood on the wide front steps until the detective's taillights faded.

She slipped her arm through his. "The stars are going to fall right on top of us."

Mac took her in his arms. "I need you, Julia. Come home with me tonight."

When Julia didn't answer, Mac stepped away. "Why are you hesitating?" His voice was harsh in the silence of the evening. "Is it Steve?"

"Steve means nothing to me. You know that." Her voice betrayed her.

Mac tried to see what was in her eyes, but Julia moved back into his arms. "It's just that I want everything to be right."

"But I thought it was. Don't you want to be with me?"

"Not at your place . . . I can't." She hesitated, then sighed into his chest, "It's that bed."

"The bed? My bed? You never complained before." Then Mac remembered the lipstick on the pillow and the scent of Shalimar pervading his bedroom that sad Sunday afternoon and realized that Julia would never be comfortable in that bed.

CHAPTER 52

THOUGH THE HOURS at Piñon Mesa consumed a major portion of Julia's time, she often found herself thinking about Steve. It was as if he had dropped off the face of the earth. There were no calls, no messages on her answering machine, nothing. For a man who was supposedly so smitten, she found his behavior strange and disturbing.

At Mac's request, when the day ended she would hurry to Hatch to have dinner at the hacienda, since he felt it necessary to be there during the replanting as a backup for Allen. By some miracle the boy was able to recruit enough men to do the planting and, though it was late in the season, the Square B hummed with activity.

The Thursday after the chile seeds were finally in, the two of them took their drinks and slipped away from the hacienda to the fish pond Selma Brantley built.

Mac steered Julia toward the large bench protected by the feathery plumes of pampas grass and once they were settled he slid a paper from his shirt pocket.

"I haven't been able to get what you told me the other evening out of my mind. So, I've been doing a little thinking about the house."

He unfolded it to reveal a rough sketched plan that extended the wide gallery through the present bedroom, then angled toward the river to end in a series of other rooms.

Mac traced his finger over a large square. "This will be the master suite, with a bath and closets on either side. And the bedroom will open onto a large deck overlooking the river. The other bedrooms," he paused, then smiled. "We can probably figure out a use for them later."

"Oh, Mac." Julia found his lips, thrilled he still wanted a future with her. He would give her love. Children. Security. What more could she ask? Wasn't that what she wanted?

The sensuous pleasure of his mouth meeting hers deepened as the pace accelerated.

After a time, he broke the kiss to find the sweet spot at the base of her throat. As his mouth began its search, Julia froze. She knew what he wanted. Knew she would be vulnerable to his next moves.

Mac must have felt her stiffen because he stopped, gave her some space. "Sorry."

"Don't be—it's just that—I'm a little undone."

"Undone? By what?"

She raised her lips to touch his in soft entreaty. "It's just that I never thought about having sex on a bench."

He laughed. "Not even if I offer to let you take the top?"

Julia laughed too, relieved that the tension between them could still be so easily broken. Mac was a fine man. He would be a perfect partner—a great father.

She gave him a small wink. "We can discuss who gets to be where later."

"Is that a promise?"

"You bet."

Mac drew her to him. "I want you."

Julia peered into the dark water where pale pink lilies floated above goldfish tailing languidly below, then into Mac's pleading eyes. Why couldn't she tell him what he wanted to hear?

Instead she countered, "Shouldn't our first priority be finding Frank?"

Mac groaned and refolded the paper. "You're right, but Lord knows how long that will take. I haven't heard a word from Manny since Monday."

"Did you ask Dolores about Selma's letter?"

"She claims she knows nothing about it. But thinking back on it, she saw me put the envelope in the center desk drawer. She was drunk, but maybe not that far gone."

He folded her into the warmth of his shoulder. "I don't want to talk about that now."

"Neither do I."

"Hey, Mac?" Allen's voice carried across the broad lawn to interrupt. "Phone. It's Detective Garcia."

Mac pulled away with a rueful smile. "Even Garcia's conspiring against our being together."

He loped across the grass with Julia not far behind, but by the time she reached the library he was coming out the door.

"Manny wants me at the station. There's been a break. Will you come, too?"

Julia nodded. "I'll follow you in my car."

She started for the library door with Mac close at her heels, muttering, "First it was me and now it's you. Will we ever get back in sync?"

THE DETECTIVE greeted them with, "Do I have something to show you."

He produced a manila envelope and tilted it so that five glossy eight-by-ten photos slid into his hand, went through them, chose two and re-packaged the rest.

Manny slapped one on the desk. "Take a gander at this."

Though the telephoto was grainy, Julia immediately recognized the woman stretched out on the chaise in front of a sliding glass door. The reflection behind mirrored a beach with breaking surf. "It's Emaline."

"Uh-huh. But you'll never guess in a million years who she's with." Manny produced the second photo with a grand flourish.

Julia gasped as heat flooded her cheeks. Sitting on the end of Emaline's chaise was none other than Steve Duke.

Mac's voice loomed from behind. "My God, that's Duke. Where in hell is Frank?"

"Still no word," Manny said. "And I don't want to alarm you, but in the light of this new development, seems like your brother's been the victim of a double cross."

Mac settled on the long bench against the wall. "Oh, Lord. You don't think they killed him, do you?"

Manny stood. "Don't even think that. Frank isn't in Cabo. That's for sure. But he could be holed up someplace trying to figure things out."

"But what is Duke doing down there? How's he involved?"

"Steve was in this office with Palatia," Julia said. "Manny interviewed them just before he saw us."

The detective rifled through the file, found a sheet and ran his finger down the page. "There was another call to Cabo made at—yes, here it is. At one-ten. Not an hour after Palatia and Steve left my office. Lasted six minutes. Duke had plenty of time to get to El Paso to catch the three o'clock America West to Phoenix and the connecting flight into Los Cabos. And that's exactly what he did. Damned fool. He didn't even bother to cover his tracks."

Julia turned away. Steve wasn't at Ed's funeral because he followed Emaline to Cabo. How could she be so stupid? Not only was Steve feeding her a bunch of garbage, but Palatia as well.

She turned to Manny, "What about the charters?"

"You were right on the button. The Tuesday Ed Pierce was shot, Air Charter flew a Ms. Smith to Phoenix. Wheels were up at twelve-oh-one p.m. But the interesting part is, the arrangements were made long-distance by an aviation service in Albuquerque. I'd be willing to bet the request for the charter was received after that eleven-twenty call to Duke."

Mac stood and came to the desk. "After reading my mother's letter, Frank might have changed his mind about the divorce. Maybe he dumped Emaline."

"Could be. But Frank'll probably turn up one way or another. You can count on that." Garcia raised his eyebrow at Mac and leered. "But, now that we know about the Widow Pierce and Duke, I wonder . . ."

"Palatia may be your ace in the hole," Mac said. "There's nothing like a woman scorned."

Manny shoved the photographs back in the envelope. "Are you

two up for a meeting with the Widow Pierce tomorrow morning? She's coming in at nine with her attorney to make a formal statement."

Mac nodded. "I'll be here. But I thought she did that last Friday."

"That was off the record."

Julia shook her head. "Count me out. I have to work. Besides, what good would it do to include me?"

"To observe Palatia's reaction to the pictures," Manny said. "It won't take long. Couldn't you give us an hour?"

"I'll make a few calls when I get home this evening, but I'm not promising anything."

Mac shepherded Julia out of the station and into the night. "We missed dinner. How about buzzing by the Super Sonic?"

She stifled a yawn. "I think I'll pass, if you don't mind. I need to get some sleep."

Mac took her in his arms. "How about some company?"

Julia shook her head. It wasn't fatigue that stemmed her desire. It was her confusion over Steve. "Please, Mac, not tonight. Forgive me, will you?"

"You're making this awful tough."

"I don't mean to. It's just that I've been running on empty for so long."

TWO HOURS later Julia stared into black, but all she could see was the eight-by-ten glossy of Steve and Emaline. Her reaction to the photograph had thrown her for a loop.

As ridiculous as it seemed, she was curdled with jealousy. It was brutally clear she was more than just infatuated with Steve.

She rolled over, dragging her pillow with her, desperately seeking needed sleep. Instead, she replayed the evening of the engagement party when Steve took her in his arms to comfort her. He hinted then he was in love with her, just after that first fleeting kiss—a gentle introduction to their meeting the following morning when his kisses left her weak-kneed and confused.

Julia moaned into the darkness. She was hopelessly drawn to a man whose passion for her had seemed genuine until a few days before, when she learned of his longtime affair with Palatia.

Even then, despite the fact Steve gave no excuse for his relationship with the older woman, the heat between them was still palpable and she had drowned in his kisses.

But now, Steve's obvious liaison with Emaline was too much to bear. What kind of man was he? How could she possibly allow herself to care for him? And why couldn't she put him out of her mind and get on with her life?

CHAPTER 53

WHEN JULIA ENTERED Manny Garcia's office, Palatia Pierce's eyes widened. "First you spring Mac on me, and now this. What's she doing here?"

Manny pointed Julia to the only empty chair in the tight circle in front of his desk. "I asked Doctor Fairchild to join us in a professional capacity."

Palatia spun to the man on her right. "Professional? We don't need a shrink. Do we?"

The man seemed vaguely familiar; then it hit Julia—he was a prominent El Paso attorney. She waited for him to object to her presence and was surprised when he spoke in a plummy drawl, "I have no objection. I know of Doctor Fairchild by her beauty and reputation, but I don't think she knows me."

The detective waved a hand in the man's direction. "Doctor Fairchild, this is George Dumas, representing Mrs. Pierce."

The man nodded. "It's a pleasure."

Garcia settled behind his desk. "Before we begin with the formal part of our meeting, I have some good news. Especially for you, Mrs. Pierce."

All four bent forward as if drawn by a common thread.

Palatia's voice was strained. "You've found Emaline?"

Manny glanced at Mac. "Yes."

Though the woman remained quiet, she was gripping the arms of her chair so hard her knuckles were white from the strain.

The detective pressed on. "Could you tell us what happened to Frank Brantley?"

Dumas put his hand over Palatia's. "Mrs. Pierce will not answer that question."

Manny hunched his shoulders and shook his head. "Mister Dumas, this is still informal. Everything is off the record."

Dumas puffed into his legal mode. "When one is summoned to the Las Cruces Police Department, nothing is off the record."

"Fine by me." The detective opened a drawer, took out the manila envelope containing the damning evidence and a file folder, then placed them on the desk before him.

"Now, Mrs. Pierce, as you know we subpoenaed your long-distance phone records and have ascertained that you made several calls on the day your husband was shot." He slid a sheet out of the file. "Let's see. There was a call to Pavilion Hospital in Albuquerque at eleven-twenty a.m. Lasted eight minutes. Would you like to tell me about that call?"

Dumas cut in, "She doesn't have to answer that."

Palatia patted the attorney's arm. "It's all right, George, he has the record in front of him. Yes, I called my friend Doctor Steven Duke. It's been some time since I've seen him and I wanted to chat."

Manny stood. "Chat? Your husband is bleeding to death and you're calling to chat?"

"Now, now, Detective," Dumas wagged his finger.

Mac turned to Palatia. "But you told me Frank arrived at the house sometime between ten-thirty and eleven."

Her brows arched in surprise. "I did?"

"And I got to your place a little before noon." He paused before continuing. "I had already called for an ambulance by the time you drove up. That was about twelve-thirty."

"Groceries?" Palatia rolled her eyes to the ceiling. "Do you really think I'd leave my husband shot and dying and go grocery shopping?"

Mac's tone remained neutral but his fingers bit into Julia's hand. "Are you saying you were already in the house when I got there?"

"Why would I lie?" She shrugged at the detective, then turned to Mac. "I distinctly remember telling you that Frank came to the house a little before noon. That he'd been drinking and he and Ed were screaming and yelling at each other for some time before I heard the shot."

Mac's jaw dropped. "But that doesn't make any sense. If you heard the shot, why would you leave? And what about your pitching the gun on the mesa?"

Palatia laughed. "Oh, Mac, have you been eating some of those funny little mushrooms?"

Manny jumped in before Mac could retort. "Where was Emaline during the fight?"

Palatia shrugged. "In her room, I guess."

"Seems mighty strange she didn't hear the commotion and come to find out what was going on," Garcia said softly.

He reached for the file and extracted another sheet. After running his finger through several paragraphs he looked up. "Says here Pierce was pronounced dead at three-oh-four p.m. The report states only the time he expired. Hell, as far as anyone knows, Ed could've been shot at nine that morning."

Dumas swelled and leaned forward. "Are you asking my client if her husband was shot at nine?"

Palatia shook her head. "I'm telling the truth, George, I'm not afraid. He wasn't shot at nine. Frank shot him a little before noon. I was there. I should know what time my husband was shot."

Manny pounced. "Why didn't you call the police and an ambulance?"

Dumas put his hand over Palatia's. "Don't say any more. You're not on trial here."

"Yet." The detective retrieved the first sheet. "You made a second call to Doctor Duke at that same number around seven that evening. That call lasted only three minutes."

Palatia nodded as she took a freshly pressed handkerchief from her purse and brought it to cover her eyes. "Yes, that's right. I called to tell Steve that Ed was dead and asked if he could come down so I wouldn't be alone. As you know, Manny, Steve and I are longtime friends."

Manny gave her a small smirk. "And did Doctor Duke come to Las Cruces?"

Palatia shook her head but kept it lowered. "Not until late that night. He couldn't get away." She paused and let out a shuddering breath. "It was the worst night of my life."

Julia couldn't believe how well the woman was playing her part.

"Then, could you tell me please, Mrs. Pierce," Manny scanned the sheet, "why you made the twenty-two-minute call to Cabo San Lucas at one a.m. on that terrible night?"

Dumas jumped in. "That's it. No more. You just crossed the line, Detective. Mrs. Pierce will not answer that question."

Garcia placed the two sheets of paper back in the file, then picked up the manila envelope. "Guess it's show time."

The detective poured out the eight-by-ten black-and-white glossies, put them in some sort of order and placed them in a row facing the circle of chairs.

Palatia gasped, then jumped up to stand over the five incriminating pictures.

When Julia joined her, she struggled to suppress her own shock. The two glossies she had seen the night before were only the prelude. The final three seemed to have been shot several minutes apart and showed Steve leaning over Emaline, followed by a picture showing her in his arms. In the final shot he lifted Emaline and was carrying her through the sliding glass door into the hotel room.

The moan started deep in Palatia's throat and rose to be stifled by her fist covering her mouth. When she lurched forward, Julia helped the trembling woman into her chair.

Neither George Dumas nor Mac, who were still standing and staring at the pictures, seemed to be aware of Palatia's plight. Only Manny Garcia's raven eyes followed the woman's retreat.

His voice cut through the charged silence of the room. "Pardon me, Mrs. Pierce, but do you wish to make a statement?"

Julia felt Palatia tense beneath her touch and take a deep breath. But, when the woman straightened and raised her eyes to meet the detective's, there was no emotion in them and her voice was low and even. "Yes."

As Garcia scrambled to activate the tape, everyone else quickly found their place and waited to hear what she would say.

CHAPTER 54

ALLEN BRANTLEY set the tray on the oilcloth-covered table and looked around. The cottage, unused since his uncle Mac moved out, reeked with the must of heat and closed windows.

He knew this house well, having spent his early years here until his grandmother's sudden death. Overnight he was installed in a monk-like room next to his father and grandfather while his mother moved into his grandmother's room. That's when things started to go sour.

"Dad? I've got your food." He heard springs creak, then feet hit the floor.

The narrow stairs behind a closed door groaned and the door flew open. "Gotta pee first. Hope that coffee's lava-hot. Damn, my head aches."

Frank Brantley, hair mussed and unshaven, clad only in his shorts, lurched toward the small bathroom to relieve himself.

That done, he lumbered back and grabbed Allen in a hug that took his breath away. "I love you, Son. Don't you ever forget it."

"Me too, Dad." Allen hugged back as hard as he was able. "Ma says the eggs won't hold long but the chile should take care of that."

"That bitch is full of surprises. Who'd a thought she would cook for me after all that's happened? Not poison are they?"

Allen laughed. "I watched every move she made. You're safe." He busied himself with setting up the food Dolores had prepared after Cuca left to clean Mac's house.

"Thank the Lord that woman was smart enough to retrieve Mama's letter before Garcia came out."

"What are you going to do, Dad?"

"Lay low until I can get more facts." Frank scraped the last of the eggs into his mouth. "Mmmm." He gave a satisfied burp. "Doro's better at huevos than Cuca ever was—but nobody can beat Cuca at the chiles rellenos."

Allen smiled to himself at the use of his mother's nickname. His father used it often when he was a small child, but as time passed "Doro" was replaced by "bitch" or worse.

He settled in the chair across from his father. "Mac's down at headquarters. He called Ma this morning to tell her Manny Garcia's got Mrs. Pierce down there for questioning."

"Talk about bitches, that Pierce woman takes the cake." Frank took a gulp of coffee, shuddered as the hot liquid hit his gullet. "How am I going to defend myself against her word? Who's going to believe that bastard Pierce was still alive and well when I adiosed?"

"Maybe it's time to let Mac in on things."

"Maybe. But, he and I didn't part real friendly." Frank drained his mug and started on the beans and tortillas. "I need to talk to your ma about our next move. See if you can get her down here without causing too much fuss."

Allen rose. "Nobody's on the Square B but us. Cuca's cleaning Mac's house."

"That's right. Chile seeds are in. Crew's gone." Frank stood. "I'll shower and clean up. Give me about thirty minutes and bring her over, okay?"

"Why don't you come on up to the house? It's just Ma and me."

Frank shook his head. "I don't think that's such a hot idea. Anyone could drop by." He piled the dishes on the tray and shoved them toward Allen. "Better get going."

WHEN ALLEN returned to the house, he put the tray on the kitchen counter and, after a brief search, found his mother in the greenhouse. "Dad wants to see you."

Dolores put down the flat of seedlings and turned. "Did you tell him where Mac is this morning?"

"Yeah. I also told him maybe it was time to let Uncle Mac in on his whereabouts."

Her reproach bore through him. "I told Frank that very thing last Saturday, when you two finally let me in on the truth."

"Don't get on that again, Ma. You were in the hospital when I got back home Friday."

"And I might not have been in the hospital if you hadn't left me all by myself without a clue as to where you were."

Allen rolled his eyes heavenward, regretting that he hadn't kept on going west after his four-day spree in Juarez.

AFTER HIS grandfather's will was read, Allen had driven around Las Cruces for what seemed like hours until hunger headed him for Sam's Super Sonic. Three double hamburgers and two shakes later he felt like a new man and decided a trip to Juarez was exactly what he needed. Besides, he was legal in Mexico. Across the border, information was seldom required as long as you produced the money, and he was flush.

Tuesday melted into Friday, leaving him broke, hungover and in probable need of a penicillin shot, but once his head cleared, Allen had made up his mind. He would return to the Square B, pack up and get out of the Valley for good.

His intentions were short-lived. When he reached the drive to the hacienda and saw the Suburban in the distance, Allen knew he couldn't leave; his mother needed him.

He slowed as he approached the parking area, then veered down the side road past the rotting chiles to the barns. He was unable to face his mother, yet. Not the tears. Not the booze. She was probably still in the bag and had been since she dropped the letter in his dad's lap.

Allen parked in the shade of the barn, stepped down from the cab of his truck, and walked into the cool darkness.

A soft nicker drew him to the nearest stall and his horse Mondo. "Hey, boy. Miss me?" He slid his arms around the horse's warm, slick neck and buried his nose in the redolence of Mondo's mane.

"This week has been the shits, man. Dad ran off with some dame.

Uncle Mac got the pecan grove, and I got a trust fund for my college education. Ain't that just ducky?"

A familiar voice had drifted from the hayloft above. "Don't be such a goddam candy ass, boy. It's a damn site better'n what your grandpa left me."

Allen started at the unexpected noise, then broke out in goose bumps. "D-d-d-ad? Is that you?"

"Sure is. In the flesh. Do you have a key to the house? If you do, go get me another bottle from the bar. I'm not drunk enough, yet."

Allen scrambled up the ladder. In the dim light he saw his father sprawled across a block of hay bales. "What are you doing up here? I thought you ran off with—"

Frank waved an empty bottle at him. "Well, you thought wrong. That's all over. I've come home to claim my kingdom, such as it is. Got here just past midnight, so I slept in the cottage. Where's everybody?"

"Cuca went back to Mexico for a while. I guess Ma's in the house."

"No, she isn't. I banged on all the doors this morning hoping to find another bottle. House is locked up tight as a drum and all the curtains are closed. Do you think she headed for Tucson or something?"

"Not Tucson, for sure. Ma told me she'd go to hell before she'd go back there. Her car's here. Are you sure she's not . . . ?"

"I tell you, Son, she isn't in that house and I have to say I was relieved I didn't have to face her sober. Lucky I keep an extra bottle in the toolbox on my truck."

Frank pitched the empty in the air, watched it arc into the darkness, and when it thudded on the soft ground below, he motioned for his son to join him. "Come give your poor old dad a hug."

Allen did as he was asked, ignoring the scratch of his father's beard and the fetid stench of whisky-breath, to settle on the hay beside him. "Where have you been?"

Frank raised up on one elbow. "I made a beeline from the law office to the bar in the Hatch Hotel, downed a number of shots for some Dutch courage, and went to meet your grandfather."

"You went to the cemetery?"

"Naw, not there. Seems Granma put a big one over on us."

"What do you mean?"

His father gave a dismissive hunch. "That's for later. What have you been up to?"

"I went to Juarez, spent all my dough on women and booze, and here I am."

"Well, good for you." Frank extended a hand. "Here, help your old man up. If the women are gone, we can have the house to ourselves—at least for a little while."

The front door swung inward and Allen called, "Ma? You here?"

When there was no answer, Frank said, "I told you so." He lurched left into the library. "Go get some ice, will ya?"

"Sure." Allen headed down the long central hall toward the kitchen and stopped cold in his tracks. His mother's bedroom door was open and across the hall an empty vodka bottle lay on its side against the wall.

Hairs rose on the back of his neck as his heart cranked up a few beats. He hurried toward the open door to see a pool of blood by the side of his mother's empty bed that was covered with sheets smeared in red.

Unable to contain the bile rushing to his throat as shock and his hangover joined forces, Allen vomited. He'd never lost consciousness before, but the whirl of the room and the black buzz were sure signs he had been close. Too weak to stand any longer, he had crumpled to the floor.

His father's footsteps echoed through the haze, then from above came a distant command. "Get a grip, Son. No time for you to pass out, hear me?"

Allen tried to focus through the blur, then waved in the direction of the bed and mumbled, "All that blood."

Frank grabbed his hand. "Get up, Allen. Act like a man."

Allen struggled to stand but his legs failed and he whimpered, "Ma's dead."

He felt his father squat beside him and an arm go across his back. This time his father's voice was soft. "No. No. Don't even think that."

"But the blood."

"Yeah. There's blood. But not enough for—I bet she cut herself or something. I'll call the hospital, first. Then we can panic."

"DID YOU hear me, Allen?" His mother's voice filtered through the nightmare.

Allen looked up, relieved to see she was alive. For a moment he had forgotten where he was. "Sorry. What did you say?"

"Is your father coming up here, or what?"

"He says it's too dangerous. Somebody could drop by."

Dolores nodded and picked up the watering can. "Okay. We'll go over there. Just let me wet these seedlings."

The two made their way to the small cottage by way of the barns, with Allen protesting all the way. "Nobody's around for miles, Ma, why do we have to go through all this rigmarole?"

"Better to be safe than sorry." She pushed him forward. "I don't see any cars on the main road. You go ahead. I'll follow in a minute."

Allen sauntered across the open space to the cottage porch, paused to surveille the road and opened the door.

His father sat clean-shaven and dressed in a freshly pressed shirt and jeans. His well-polished boots propped on the hassock in front of an easy chair. "Where's Agent Number One?"

Allen grinned. It seemed like old times again. "She's bringing up the rear. Can't be too careful, you know."

"Yeah. She's really into all this cloak and dagger shit." Frank gave him a knowing wink. "Women. You can't live with them and you damn sure can't live without them."

Dolores slid into the room and shut the door behind her. "Now what?"

CHAPTER 55

JULIA FOLLOWED Mac out of the Las Cruces Police Station into the glare of the late morning sun. "I can't believe Detective Garcia kicked us out before Palatia made her statement."

"I can't believe he asked us there in the first place." Mac shook his head. "But I'm no longer interested in what happens to Palatia after her shabby little performance. Right now, my main mission is to try to clear Frank. I've got to find Mama's letter."

Once they were on the interstate headed for Hatch, Julia brought up the interview again. "I can't see what help that letter will be. Doesn't it place the motive on Frank?"

"Maybe, but it's obvious Palatia's trying to protect Emaline. My guess is Steve Duke's in on the plan."

At the mention of Steve's name, the heat of that last meeting in the empty hospital room only days before replayed. His pleading eyes—his lips on hers. Now, those moments were negated by the damning photographs. Proof too real to ignore.

To know Steve was in Albuquerque when Ed Pierce was shot gave Julia some relief. He might be a rake and a liar, but in her heart she knew he wasn't a murderer.

Julia shook her head, hoping to clear her thoughts. What was wrong with her? She was sitting next to a man she loved and respected. Why couldn't she get Steve out of her mind?

MAC OPENED the front door of the hacienda and called, "Anybody here?" When there was no answer, he ushered Julia into the darkened hall and shut the massive slab of oak behind them. "Dolores? Allen?"

A sound in the back of the house drew them toward the kitchen, where Dolores stood at the sink rinsing dishes and Allen was slumped in a chair thumbing through a hunting magazine, both breathing much too rapidly for the activities they were performing.

"Hey, you two," Mac said. "Didn't you hear us call?"

Dolores turned to face them, her forehead glazed in sweat, a hint of a smile on her lips. "Guess the water was running. Drowns out most everything, you know."

She headed for the refrigerator and hauled out a large stew pot. "I was just about to reheat these beans. Want to join us?"

Allen, a beginning grin on his face, stood, waved to the empty chairs. "Have a seat."

Julia sank in the nearest chair. "Thanks for the invitation. I'm famished."

Mac settled next to her. "Something's going on here. For people hanging around the kitchen, you're sure out of breath; in fact, you both act like you've swallowed the proverbial canary."

"Guess the jig's up." Frank's voice filtered through the slightly ajar swinging door to fill the kitchen, then he appeared.

Julia's heart leaped, then quickly sank as the photo of Steve, headed for the bedroom with Emaline in his arms, flashed with grinding clarity. There was only one reason Steve followed Emaline to Mexico.

Mac jumped up, sending the kitchen chair skittering across the floor until it clattered against the cabinets. "Frank? You're alive? Thank God."

"Of course I am. Can't put a tough bastard like me down." Frank moved forward to meet Mac with a brotherly hug, then stepped back. "After what I did in the law office, I was afraid you might not be so glad to see me."

"You know better than that. Brantleys don't carry grudges."

Concern replaced the joy in Mac's voice. "But, where the hell have you been? You're in a lot of trouble."

Frank sat in the vacant chair beside Allen. "Sorry about the disappearing act, but it wasn't because I did anything wrong. I meant to let everybody know right away, but when Allen told me about Palatia pointing her finger in my direction, I decided to lay low until the dust settled."

"We came to find Mama's letter."

Frank leaned back, eyes narrowing. "What for?"

"Manny knows about it and considers it an important piece of evidence. Though the letter's somewhat incriminating, I think it can make the case against Emaline."

"You think Emaline shot her father?"

Mac filled in the blanks for Frank and added, "But your being here puts everything in a new light."

Dolores set the steaming pot of frijoles on a trivet in the center of the table. "I took the letter out of the desk and put it in a safe place the minute I found out Frank was back. I'm sorry I lied to you, but we didn't know how bad things might get."

"Guess you better leave it there for now, Dolores. I don't want to know where it is." Mac turned to Frank. "I sure would like to hear your version of what happened."

"I want you to know everything." Frank turned to his wife. "Maybe you and Allen should leave, Doro."

Frank's eyes were as soft as his voice. It was the first time Julia could recall hearing him speak to his wife in a civil tone.

Dolores nodded and put the pot back on the stove. "I haven't finished with my plants. Come on, Allen."

"But, Ma. I'm starving."

"It won't take but a few minutes to get through the details." Frank waved toward the door. "Go on, Son. You don't need to hear this. It really doesn't concern you."

He waited until he heard the door to the greenhouse close, then continued. "I left the law office, drove to Hotel Hatch and hit the bar. Guess I must of had a few . . ."

"Exactly how many?" Mac asked.

"Hell, I don't remember."

"The bartender told Manny you drank six shots of Old Grand Dad."

"But I wasn't drunk."

"Then you drove to Pierce's?"

Frank nodded. "I banged on the front door, then barged in and yelled for Emaline to pack a bag. That we were leaving."

"What time did you get there?"

"A little before eleven, I guess. It didn't take me long to down the booze; maybe it was closer to ten-thirty."

Frank stood and began to pace the kitchen. "I walked into Pierce's office. Guess he must have heard all the commotion because there was a pistol on his desk. I might have been a little drunk because I said something stupid like, 'Aren't you going to welcome home your long-lost son?'

"That old bastard's face went white and red all at the same time and he said something like, 'You're no son of mine.' And I said, 'Well, then I guess it doesn't matter I've been screwing your daughter since she was fourteen.'"

Frank lowered his eyes. "Pierce came at me with the gun pointed at my chest. I should be grateful to Palatia because she stepped between us and told him to put it down."

"She was in the room the whole time?"

"I suppose so. I might not have shut the door when I went into the office. Anyway, she told me to get out of there, that she would handle her husband. So, I went to get Emaline and we headed for the front door. That's when all hell broke loose. Pierce charged out of the office waving that damned gun with Palatia at his heels."

Julia saw anguish surge to Frank's face as his voice tightened.

"The bastard kept blubbering about how his little Emmy was his only true love. That she couldn't go with me because it was against the Bible. And all the time Palatia was begging, 'Don't do this, Ed. Let them go. Let her have some happiness.'"

Frank grabbed a beer from the refrigerator, opened it, then took a long draught. "We all stood there until Emaline finally said, 'What's against the Bible, Daddy?' And the old man threw back, 'Incest, that's what. This no good bastard is my son.'

"Poor girl stared at me like she didn't know who I was, then turned to her father, 'I've been going against the Bible all of my life, haven't I? First with my own father and now with the only man I ever loved.' She began to laugh. 'A man who turns out to be my brother. I ask you, is there a God?' And then I stood there and watched the love in her eyes die right before me."

Frank shook his head. When he resumed, his face was drained of emotion. "Finally, she said, 'It's over.'"

"Until that moment, I thought I loved her enough to live the lie, but once she found out the truth—well, the way she put it, I knew it was over, too. So, I set down the suitcase and walked out the door."

"That's it?"

"Yeah, I guess. I got in my truck and drove to Silver City. Stayed in some motel there. I was soused most of the time. Then, somewhere along the way, it occurred to me there was no place else to go but back to the Square B, and that being a chile czar wasn't half as bad as I once thought. So, I came home."

"What time did you leave Pierce's?"

Frank thought a moment. "Everything happened real fast after I told Ed about Emaline and me. The whole thing was over in probably ten—twenty minutes."

"Did you ever touch the gun?"

"No. I'm sure of that."

"There's been an APB out on you since Ed died," Mac said. "The fact that we know the whereabouts of a suspect wanted for questioning by the police makes us all accomplices. I think we should discuss our next move. Better get Dolores and Allen in on this."

Julia looked at her watch. "I'll get Dolores and Allen on my way to the study. I have to call Piñon Mesa and have Phyllis reschedule this afternoon's appointments."

CHAPTER 56

JULIA MADE her way to the study, settled at the large desk and called her office. "Phyllis, it's me. I'm running . . ."

"Thank heavens you called," Phyllis said. Julia could hear papers being shuffled. "Ah—yes, here it is. A Detective Garcia has been calling you every few minutes or so since noon. Says it's urgent."

Julia jotted down the number. "Please reschedule this afternoon's appointments for me. I might have to go back to the police station."

After Phyllis promised to do her best, Julia called Garcia.

She heard his relief. "Just in the nick of time. I was just about to contact Central Hospital and I didn't want to do that. Where are you? Can you talk?"

"I'm at the Square B, but as far as I know I'm the only one on the line."

"Okay, first question. Does Piñon Mesa have beds?"

"Yes. A few on the adult floor and several on the children's. Even so, we're mostly an out-patient facility."

"That's great. What about the staff?"

"Bob Sandoval is CEO and chief financial administrator. Max Blumfield is chief of staff. We also have two part-time psychiatrists. One is usually at the hospital during the day and on call at night. There are six full-time clinical psychologists and an adequate nursing staff. What's all this about?"

"They're flying Emaline Pierce and Doctor Duke to Las Cruces on a Medivac plane. Seems he went to Cabo in a purely professional capacity."

Julia's heart flipped. Steve went to Mexico as a physician, not a lover. Her voice quivered when she asked, "Did Palatia tell you this?"

"Nope. Dumas has her clammed up but good. We contacted Duke's ER group in Albuquerque and found out he called last Friday and asked them to cover for him. He went to Mexico because a woman was threatening suicide. His colleagues knew about it all along and have been in constant contact with him."

Relief flooded her whole being. "Was there an attempt?"

"Apparently a failed overdose. According to our contact, it was touch and go but since Emaline was in the care of a physician, the Cabos ER sent her back to the hotel.

"Duke had already ordered the plane to fly her to Albuquerque for treatment there, but my contact arrived just in time with the extradition papers. They land in less than two hours, so we have to work fast."

There it was. All she needed to know. Julia put her elation on hold. "I think we can arrange things, but I need to call Bob Sandoval first. What about an ambulance?"

"Too obvious. We've been able to keep the press out of this Pierce thing so far and I sure don't want to raise any dust now." There was a small pause on the detective's end. "I know Mac is there with you, but I'm going to ask you to keep this to yourself for now."

"I understand." She gave the detective the telephone number for Sandoval's direct line and hung up.

Julia leaned back in the chair, closed her eyes and took several deep breaths to slow the rapid pace of her heart. She had downed three cups of coffee within the last hour and knew too much caffeine often caused tachycardia. But that wasn't it.

In her mind's eye, she was wrapped in Steve's arms—his soft mouth on hers—pulling, pulling—his hands sliding over her body. Heat pulsed between her thighs and Julia let out a faint moan.

"Are you all right?"

Her eyes flew open to see Mac framed in the doorway staring at her.

She stood on trembling legs. "I'm sorry, I won't be able to stay. I have to get back to Piñon Mesa."

"Is there a problem?"

Julia came toward him, hoping her voice sounded light and unconcerned. "Nothing I can't take care of."

Once they were in the car, Mac said, "What about tonight?" The question in his eyes had nothing to do with dinner.

Julia hesitated, heart pounding, hating that she was unable to give Mac the answer he craved, knowing she needed to see Steve and find out her true feelings.

Mac's voice softly intruded. "Hey? Tonight?"

"I'd better call you." Then she lied, "I asked Phyllis to schedule appointments until six since I took the morning off."

He gave her a grimace, hunched over the wheel and glared down the interstate.

A few miles blurred past before he muttered, "What's going on?"

"What do you mean?"

Mac took a shuddering breath. "I can't forget how exquisite you looked a few minutes ago when we were in the study. The roses in your cheeks, that shine in your eyes."

Did thinking of Steve do that to her? Julia strained across the console and brushed Mac's cheek with her lips. A move to give the vise on her throat time to loosen its grip. When it did, she moved away and smiled. "I think you're making a little too much out of a caffeine rush."

The tension in his face eased. "Caffeine rush? Is that what it was?"

"Atrial fibrillations. They're benign but scary."

After Mac parked the Jeep, he drew her to him and kissed her with hungry urgency. It was as if he sensed something between them had changed. But how could he know when she hardly knew herself?

Julia shuddered, suddenly cold. She tried to return Mac's passion but all she could think about was Steve. In less than two hours she would see him again.

CHAPTER 57

JULIA TOOK the slim chart labeled "Emaline Pierce" from her secretary and headed for the adult wing on the second floor of the detached hospital facility. There she briefed the staff on what little she knew and assured them that Fred Bunting, one of Piñon Mesa's psychiatrists, would be there to cover the case.

An hour later Emaline was wheeled into the room. Although a chart written in Steve's hand lay on the gurney, there was no sign of him. After the first rush of disappointment, there was little time to think of anything or anybody except getting Emaline settled and comfortable. When that was accomplished Julia went to the small waiting room down the hall where Steve sat with Palatia.

The very sight of him sent tingles down her spine. "Hello Palatia. Steve."

Steve rose as she approached, but instead of the love she hoped to see in his eyes, a professional stood before her. Julia assumed it was because of Palatia and immediately adopted a manner to reflect his.

She sat in the chair across from them and waited until Steve was seated before continuing. "I'm so sorry about this, Palatia. Are you all right?"

Some of the hostility crowding the woman's face faded. "I've been better."

"Would you mind some questions?"

Palatia sighed. "Do I have any choice?"

"Not if you want to help your daughter. I already know a few things. A couple of weeks ago Mac told me about the sexual abuse. And I know Frank is your husband's son."

The hostility returned. "My God. Isn't anything sacred?"

Julia felt herself flush but kept her voice even and low. "I assure you everything I write on this page is confidential and will be placed in a sealed envelope kept separate from the meds schedule and progress notes. Only Doctor Bunting and I will have access to this information."

"Not the police?"

Julia turned to Steve, who nodded. "As far as I know, this would be regarded as doctor-patient confidentiality. I think Manny would have a hard time getting a court order to open the records."

He stood, then moved toward the hall. "I'm not needed here. If you'll excuse me, I need to check in with the ER at Pavilion."

Palatia answered his departing wave, then faced Julia. The silence in the room seemed to bind the two women in an unwilling alliance.

"All right. All right," Palatia said. "What do you want to know?"

"It would help if you could tell me about the sexual abuse."

The woman shuddered at the word, then straightened. "I hoped I would never have to talk about that."

The story was classic. What Palatia assumed was the natural affection between father and daughter had developed into something quite different as Emaline grew from infant to toddler to child.

The discovery had been made quite by accident. An early return from Palatia's annual visit to her ancient grandmother in Mescalero. Ed nude; the child nude and splayed across his body. Emaline was laughing like all children laugh, but the object of her amusement was her father's rigid penis.

As the story unfolded Palatia let her tears slide unattended, but her voice never quivered, nor did she take her eyes from Julia.

"I tried not to frighten Emmy or make her ashamed of what she was doing. My poor baby. She didn't know it was wrong.

"I remember saying, 'Surprise, everybody, Mommie's home,' then I swooped her from his belly and into my arms. Ed just lay there. I guess he was in shock.

"Emmy and I often showered together and I suggested that might be fun. Once there, I did the best I could to examine her without arousing her suspicion."

"Did you find any evidence of penetration?"

She shook her head. "I couldn't tell a thing. Later, after I gave Emmy supper and put her to bed, I went to find Ed."

Palatia smiled. "I went with a gun. To my knowledge Ed never touched my baby again. Emmy was never far from my side. I moved into her bedroom, then after a year or so, when I realized she should have her own space, I made Ed do a little remodeling."

Why did Palatia stay in the marriage? And why did Ed let her? No time to ask those questions.

Instead, Julia rose and crossed to sit beside the woman. "That was a brave thing you did, Palatia. Your instincts were right on. Protect the child so the child can remain a child." She finished the note she was writing and asked, "How old was she?"

"She was a few weeks away from her fourth birthday."

"Emaline must have remembered something about the sexual abuse," Julia said. "She told Frank about it early in their—" She searched for the proper word to describe that relationship but found nothing that seemed to apply.

Palatia bristled. "Emmy never told me a thing about Frank. She was just a teenager and he was in his thirties and married. I thought Emmy and Mac were the perfect couple, and all the time he was acting as a beard."

Julia covered the woman's trembling hand with her own. "Believe me, Mac knew nothing about Emaline and Frank until a few days after the party at Radium Springs."

"That may be, but I still can't believe this thing with Frank has gone on right under my nose for over twenty years. No wonder the poor thing was in such bad shape after he walked out."

"You didn't know that Frank was Ed's son, either?"

"I've seen Frank Brantley maybe three times in my life. When Ed and I moved up to Hatch from Las Cruces, the boy was a wild teenager. I think he went into the army as soon as he was old enough.

"But Emmy and Mac were childhood friends. When he wasn't at our house, she was at his. Then Frank came back here with that horrible woman." She sagged. "No. I had no idea that man was Ed's son."

"The news about Frank must have been a terrible shock to both you and Emaline."

"Of course it was, but their affair was a worse shock to Ed. He was going to shoot Frank in the back as he walked to his truck, but Emmy and I were able to get the gun away from him.

"Oh, the whole thing was dreadful. Like some horror movie. It all happened in slow motion. Like we were all trapped in amber. First, I got the gun but somehow Emmy took it from me. Then Ed went after another gun he had stashed in the bottom drawer of his desk and was barely down in his chair when she shot him."

Palatia smeared the tears from her face with the flat of her hand. "We just knew he was dead. The bullet went right through his neck and there was blood spurting everywhere. He was clutching his throat, gasping for air, then he collapsed on top of his desk.

"Emmy was screaming, screaming, screaming. I slapped her, then told her to wash up while I called Steve. When I told him everything, he suggested Cabo because he knew the people at the hotel. Told me they were almost like family. Anyway, he got the charter and I took Emmy to the airport. Damn Mac Brantley. If he had minded his own business, Ed would have bled to death and I wouldn't have . . ." She stopped. "I've told you too much."

Julia concealed her relief. Palatia finally told the truth. Frank was innocent. The only problem was she couldn't give that information to anyone.

She slid her notes into a large brown envelope and placed it in Emaline's chart. "Thank you for telling me this. I know it's been painful for you, but this will give Doctor Bunting someplace to begin therapy."

"How long will they keep Emmy here?"

Julia shrugged. "That's hard to say. The usual routine is to get patients on the proper medication so they can function on a day-to-day basis. Depending on how deep Emaline's depression is, it could be a week to three weeks."

She patted Palatia's hand. "Since there are no other adult patients, would you like to take a room here? That way you can be available when Emaline wakes up."

"Oh, thank you. I'll have Steve take me to get some clothes."

Both women stood and Palatia touched Julia's arm. "I want you to know Emmy didn't kill her father. She was long gone when Ed died. He was awake the second time I went in the ICU. I guess when he saw I was holding a pillow, he thought I intended to suffocate him and his heart must have stopped. Ed hated to be in tight places."

Julia heard footsteps and turned to see Steve standing in the door. "If you're through, I'll take Palatia home."

"Not for long. Julia's reserved the room across the hall for me."

Steve smiled. "I'll have her back here in no time." He shepherded the woman to the door, then turned. "Would you mind waiting in your office until I return? I have more information to add to Emaline's intake."

Julia nodded, then clasped the file to her chest in a small effort to calm her errant heart. Only an hour. Maybe less. From the moment she opened her eyes in the Pavilion ER and saw Steve, there had been a connection. She tried to deny the attraction she felt for him—to repair the relationship with Mac and make a life with him. But, even knowing how much Mac wanted her, she hadn't been able to return to his bed. And even though she stubbornly disregarded every red flag, the truth was now too obvious to ignore.

CHAPTER 58

I T WAS JUST past seven. Julia peered down at Emaline's inert form tucked beneath the sheets. The woman's once-vibrant jet-black hair formed a coarse and matted frame for a puffy face smoothed by drugs filtering through the IV.

When Julia checked the shunt in her arm, Emaline moaned then tried to shift to her side, but the drugs were too powerful and she sank back into the chemically induced coma.

Julia nodded to the nurse and motioned for the manila folder on the table. "I'll be in my office for a while going over these intake notes. Call if you need me."

She peeked in Palatia's room and saw she was already settled in bed reading. "Are you comfortable?"

Palatia gave her a tired smile. "I'm fine. Thank you for everything. I know you went the extra mile for me."

"Glad to help out. Sleep well."

She turned to go but Palatia's soft voice stopped her. "Do you have a minute?"

Julia returned to the woman's bedside and pulled a chair close. "I have all night," she lied.

The woman's dark eyes betrayed her desperate need. "I know it's going to be a long time before Emaline and I can reconnect." Eyes misting, she took Julia's hand and gave a gentle squeeze. "I sure could use a friend right now."

Touched by Palatia's offer, Julia squeezed back. "I'd be honored."

She rose, rearranged the pillows and smoothed the woman's forehead with her fingertips. "I'll stop by in the morning. Get some rest. It's been a long day."

Palatia smiled. "You have a good night, too."

Julia smiled back. What would Palatia say if she knew where she was headed and who she planned to see?

She hurried down the stairs, let herself out the side door and started toward her office building several hundred yards east of the hospital. The night air still held a slight crispness, and far across the valley the sun was fading from the lava flows just west of the airport.

In the darkness of the valley below, the Rio Grande still moved with some life. Mac was down there. Waiting for her call. Julia shivered. Not yet. She couldn't call him until—a small ripple of guilt was overcome by her anticipation of seeing Steve again and she quickened her steps.

The halls were quiet. Only the utility lights dimly outlined doors and other corridor entrances. She flipped on the switch in Phyllis's office and crossed to her open door.

Steve stepped into the light, drew her inside the office and shut the door behind them. His arms went beneath her open medical coat and she felt it slide to the floor as he brought her to him. Then his mouth covered hers, making her so much a part of him that she moaned at the exquisite pain of it.

CHAPTER 59

MAC HAD FELT the first sliver of fear as he stood in the door to the study watching Julia. She was leaning back in his father's chair, eyes closed, right hand over her heart, breathing rapidly. The rapture he saw in her face made her even more beautiful than he ever imagined.

When he spoke, Julia's eyes had popped wide in surprise but she quickly recovered her poise and the moment passed, but not before Mac felt the fragile fabric of their just-mending relationship begin to unravel.

The drive to Piñon Mesa brought little satisfaction. Julia dodged his questions, delayed answering his invitation to bed and wiggled out of his kiss to exit the Jeep.

After she disappeared inside the building, Mac drove north to Doña Ana then took a right on Shalem Colony toward his home on the Rio Grande. As the miles passed, the ominous gloom faded somewhat. Maybe there was something at the hospital that had distracted Julia, but deep in his gut the snakes were gathering.

He waited until after seven to call. Julia told him there were appointments until six and she would have to clear her desk before going home. When her machine clicked on, he tried Piñon Mesa, only to find the main switchboard closed at six. After the metallic voice referred him to the answering service number, he hung up, slid into his moccasins and headed for his Jeep.

Mac was hardly aware when he exited the interstate. Making the trip to Piñon Mesa from Hatch or his home was almost rote by now. Left off the feeder to North Main, left again at Del Rey and, after a few blocks, left at the entrance to the hospital. He repeated the mantra, "left, left, left," as he entered the staff parking lot.

To his pleasant surprise, Julia's Range Rover was still there. He pulled in beside it and walked across the empty parking lot to her building. He didn't know what his next move would be since he never visited Piñon Mesa after dark.

The lights were on in the main lobby of Julia's office building but the doors didn't budge. Security, he supposed. Her office was too far away from the entrance for her to hear him call out. Besides, it faced the inner courtyard. Damn. Then, recalling the arched opening between the connecting buildings, Mac headed down the dimly lit sidewalk toward it.

His moccasins muffled Mac's steps on the inner courtyard's winding walks edged with plantings of succulents and cacti and lit by ground lamps. Four stalwart cedars marked the shallow square pool in the center of the court where the light from Julia's window faintly reflected in the still, dark mirror.

Mac heard the noises first. Murmurings interspersed with low moans—sounds too familiar to be denied. He froze in mid-step, torn in two, knowing he should leave, but a morbid curiosity dragged him forward.

They were on the floor with their clothes strewn about them. Julia's legs splayed—Steve gliding between them. Rage caught in Mac's throat, cutting off his breath.

Julia's gasp commanded his attention and he watched as her hands began to trail up and down Steve's arms, slowly at first, then faster until she cried out and threw her arms around his neck.

No longer able to bear the ecstasy in their voices, Mac raised his hands to cover his ears. He wanted to turn away, lose the moment, but he couldn't. He watched Julia shudder beneath his longtime rival and move in agonizingly slow cadence until Steve collapsed on top of her.

When Mac lowered his hands, the lovers' sighs drifted through the open window to fill the night. A rush of heat between his legs signaled his own arousal and he silently cursed, hating that he was reacting to the seduction of his beloved like some geek watching a porno flick. He was about to turn away when he heard Julia give a low, breathy laugh and Steve laugh in response.

CHAPTER 60

THE ROAD BUCKED and heaved beneath the Jeep as it shot across the bridge over the Alameda Arroyo. Mac focused just enough to realize that in his pain and confusion he turned left instead of right out of the Piñon Mesa parking lot and was headed north on Del Rey. He had never turned left on Del Rey before and was surprised when, on the other side of the arroyo bridge, the two lanes abruptly narrowed to one. No problem. People would see his headlights and get out of the way, but he wasn't so sure about the jackrabbits.

Mac gripped the jiggling wheel and peered at the speedometer. Eighty-five. A little too fast for complete control, but what the hell? Who was in control? No one. It was his fault. He destroyed the perfect equation he and Julia once shared. He had put a curse on their *Nizhoni*, had driven her into Steve's waiting arms.

He knew she tried to fight the attraction, but she was just as helpless against it as he. Too late to stop the spirits. Too late to make it right.

He shook his head and focused on the road, but there was nothing ahead but a curb.

Mac heard himself scream, "Whoa," before the Jeep hit and tumbled end over end into the darkness.

When he woke, he was on his back. In the distance he could hear the motor rev, hear the wheels still turning. He stared up into a sky crammed with stars, then shut his eyes to see Steve and Julia bathed in a pale glow.

The pain filling every inch of his body was unbearable. Was this grief? This agony that pulsed through his entire being? Mac, eyes skyward, realized he was crying. Julia was lost to him. He would never hold her again. Never flood her sweet lips with kisses. Never experience her soft flesh surround him.

The explosion lifted his body off the ground as the sky domed orange and heat blanketed him. There was only one thing left for him to do. Mac prayed that he would die.

CHAPTER 61

A MUFFLED ROAR brought Steve out of his dream. He raised on one elbow to see the fine sheen of moisture on Julia's eyelids and the thick splay of lashes outlining them.

With his forefinger he gently traced the wing of her eyebrow, then her hairline and finally the side of her cheek, which brought a smile. In that instant Steve was sure he was lying next to a vision from a Renaissance painting.

The first moments they were together had been blurred by mouths connecting, hands searching and clothes falling around them.

Once freed they clung to each other, panting for air. He felt her breasts slick and warm against his chest and her trembling hands caressing his bare back. Finally, she whispered, "I love you."

He stepped away, light-headed, almost giddy at the sound of the words he had been so certain that he would never hear. Then he had drawn Julia to him and kissed her slowly and thoroughly. It was as if he had always known how to please her and that, in return, she would give herself to him, filling an emptiness no one else could.

Remembering how perfect their first joining had been, Steve touched his lips to her forehead. "You awake?"

Julia slid her arms around his neck. "What time is it?"

"Around eight. A little after."

She brushed her lips softly across his mouth. "We have lots of time."

Steve pulled her to him and whispered, "All the time in the world," then began the ritual again.

CHAPTER 62

DOLORES OPENED the door and stepped back. Manny Garcia stood there, a grim expression on his face. Did he know they were hiding Frank? She tried to conceal the fear that tingled through her body by smiling. "Good morning, Detective."

Garcia shuffled from foot to foot a few times before saying, "I didn't know who to call."

Dolores scrambled to think of something to throw him off. "Is it Frank?"

He shook his head. "No. I'm afraid not. It's Mac. He's been in a real bad accident. Real bad."

Dolores felt the floor warp beneath her. "He's not dead."

"Damn near. They coptered him to the Burn Center in El Paso. His Jeep caught fire but even though he was thrown free, his legs got it pretty bad."

Dolores crossed herself and opened the door a little wider. "Does Julia know?"

"I haven't been able to reach her. She was at the hospital last night but after that . . ."

"I'll find her. Thanks for coming all the way up here. I know you're fond of Mac and I appreciate your taking the time."

"I'd find Julia as quick as I could, if I were you." Manny turned back toward his car.

Dolores stood in the door for a minute before she shut it. "Did you hear?"

Frank and Allen stepped into the hall from the library and Frank said, "Let's go. I have to be with him."

"But, Frank."

Dolores's protest was cut short when Allen snapped his fingers. "We'll put you under a blanket in the back of Ma's Suburban. I'll drive with the lights blinking. If they stop us I'll tell them about Mac."

"Wait." Dolores stepped toward the library. "I've got to call Julia before we go."

Allen returned with a blanket from one of the beds. "Let's hit it."

"What about Julia?"

The two men were already at the door. "If she doesn't answer, leave a message," Frank yelled. "We don't have much time."

Julia's message answered after the second ring.

"This is Dolores. Mac's been in a wreck. We're leaving now for the Burn Center in El Paso. They don't think he's going to make it."

CHAPTER 63

I T WAS PHYLLIS who delivered the news. Julia was standing outside Emaline's room going over her chart when she saw her secretary pop out of the stairwell and run toward her.

"I'm so sorry. I thought you weren't in yet. I didn't know you were over here."

The woman was panting between each word, her hand clutched at her throat as if by doing so she could get more air.

"My fault," Julia offered. "I forgot to tell you I was coming here first."

Julia saw the anguish in Phyllis's eyes and her heart stuttered. "What is it?"

"They've been calling from Police Headquarters since I got here at eight. Mac's been in a bad accident. They helicoptered him to the Burn Center in El Paso. The detective told me he might not make it."

With each word Julia retreated, raising her hand to somehow deflect Phyllis's painful pronouncements. She wanted to run—escape the moment—rewind the tape.

Instead, realizing she was expected to act, she squelched the gathering tears at the base of her throat and pushed the chart into a nurse's hands. "Get Doctor Bunting. I have to go."

She covered the stairs in seconds, then rushed to her office. The room bore no signs of what had happened there the night before. When passing sirens had awakened them a second time, Julia and Steve dressed, straightened her office and were leaving the building just as a security guard passed.

Julia had hailed him. "What's all the commotion?"

The burly man shrugged. "I guess it was some sort of brush fire, Doctor Fairchild, though it seems a little early for that. Mesa's still green. Anyhow, it's almost out."

At sunrise they dragged themselves from her bed. While Steve showered in the guest room, Julia put on the coffee, then dressed and drove him to the airport for a 6:55 flight to Albuquerque.

The plane was an hour late.

Julia sagged against the steering wheel. "I can't wait, I'm sorry."

Steve drew her to him for a goodbye kiss. "I know. You have Emaline to think about."

He rubbed his face with both hands and groaned. "I don't know when I can get back down here. The trip to Cabo screwed everything up. I owe my associates about a million hours and my car's stuck in the short-term parking lot in El Paso."

Julia found his lips. "We have last night. It's a beginning."

"And we'll have lots more beginnings, won't we?" His eyes bored into hers, begging for a promise.

She traced her finger down the deep line that ran from his nose to his jaw and made the sign of the cross on his brow. "I promise you. We'll have forever."

Julia shook the memory away and hung her white coat on the hook, then searched for her purse. She stepped to retrieve it from the back of her chair, just as the bits and pieces of information finally came together. Burn Center. Helicopter. She had heard a helicopter in the distance but was too involved with their lovemaking to pay more than a passing thought. The fire was Mac's Jeep. Did he come looking for her at Piñon Mesa? Did he see them? At that, Julia's knees buckled beneath her.

Through the haze she heard Bob Sandoval's voice above her. "Are you all right? You're pale as a ghost."

Tears, pushed by a mountain of guilt, finally came. "It's Mac. Did you hear?"

"I just talked to the Burn Center and I won't sugarcoat the facts. Mac's hanging by a thread. Lots of internal injuries. Ruptured spleen. Broken ribs. Perforated lungs. All complicated by the burns."

Julia bit her tongue to keep from wailing that it was all her fault.

Bob put his arm under hers to help her up. "Let's get going. Myrt's waiting in the car. We want to be there for him, too."

CHAPTER 64

JULIA PEEKED through the narrow window of the ICU to a scene from a movie. Behind Mac's bed, bags hung from several poles with tubes disappearing into the heavy swath of bandages covering Mac's head and upper body. Two more were inserted into veins in his outstretched arms, taped to boards, giving him a crucifix-like appearance. From the side of his taped chest and beneath the sterile tent covering Mac's lower body, drainage tubes emptied into bags hooked to the underside of the bed.

Julia turned away in anguish and pushed past the silent Sandovals to collapse on the couch in the waiting room.

It should have been a relief to be in Myrtle's comforting arms and hear her soft commiserations, but each hug and kind word brought a spate of drowning guilt. Julia longed to scream the truth—that she had betrayed Mac with Steve and most probably Mac had witnessed the act then raced to his destruction.

Instead, she remained mute—unwilling to speak to anyone until it was her turn to don a gown, cover her head and face and invade the sterile environment.

The tap and whish of the assisted breathing apparatus accompanied by the shrill bleep of the heart monitor filled the cubicle with the urgent sounds of a life on support.

Julia moved to read the chart at the end of the bed. Mild concussion, cracked ribs, ruptured spleen, minuscule perforations in right and left lungs but no note of spinal involvement or other broken bones. That was the good news. But his legs—.

Her tears skewed the print following a note to delay the removal of the spleen until the trauma unit could re-assess the severity of the burns and initiate the proper protocol.

Julia used the sleeve of the sterile gown to dry her eyes, then leaned toward Mac's pale, still face.

His bruised eyelids were swollen shut, evidence of the blow to his head when he had hit the sand. The rest of his face was untouched—nose still straight, mouth unblemished though distorted by the breathing tube taped in place.

She gently stroked his open palm, hoping for some response. None. Then, standing, she touched her lips to his forehead. Cool and clammy, a symptom of shock, not a good sign.

The minutes she was allowed to spend with Mac passed far too quickly. At the sound of the opening door, she turned to see Mac's attending physician motioning her.

"They called me back to go over his stats. I'd like to talk to you after your next visit."

After Julia's second fifteen minutes with Mac, the doctor pointed her to the couch in the waiting room and settled beside her.

"Would it be too much to ask you to stay in the room? Quite frankly, he could go sour on us any minute."

"But, I'm not his nearest relative," she stammered.

The doctor nodded. "True. But when you were with him, we noticed Doctor Brantley's vital signs stabilized."

"I'm really glad to hear that, but . . ." Julia shook her head. "Frank is Mac's closest kin."

"I've already spoken with the brother. He said to do whatever it takes."

The man placed his hand on her arm. "Believe me, Doctor Fairchild, it's going to take a miracle."

CHAPTER 65

FOR THE NEXT five days Julia hunched in the small visitor's chair next to Mac's bed, holding his hand in hers, leaving his side only when the medical team arrived to assess his condition and minister to his inert body.

Food was out of the question since Julia's stomach was squeezed shut with fear compounded by self-loathing. The only thing she could swallow without retching was ginger ale, and the minute she finished one bottle another would appear.

Her inevitable exhaustion and ragged emotions brought uncontrollable tears that covered Mac's hand as she whispered again and again that she loved him. Julia wasn't lying. Part of her loved Mac and always would.

Sometime during the string of seamless days, Dolores had pulled Julia into the corridor. "You have to speak to Steve Duke. He's been calling for you practically every hour on the hour and people are starting to ask questions."

Julia jerked up. "What questions? Who?"

Dolores shrugged. "Well, it's really Frank who's been nagging the hell out of me. You know how he hates Steve."

Mind racing, Julia tried to find some reasonable explanation for Steve's calls, but all she could offer was a feeble, "I guess he must have heard about the accident."

Dolores studied her for a long moment, then shrugged. "Yeah, I'm sure that's what it is." She pointed toward a receiver dangling from one of the pay phones. "He's on that one."

It took every ounce of energy Julia could muster to get to the phone bank. She turned to be sure the waiting room was empty, then raised the receiver to her ear.

The sound of Steve's voice brought a fresh surge of guilt. "Julia. How are you? More important, how's Mac?"

"Not good." She leaned her forehead against the steely cool to ease the throb.

"I've been calling your place since I got back here last Saturday. I didn't hear the news until I called Piñon Mesa Monday. Didn't they give you my messages?"

"I suppose they did."

The uncomfortable silence was followed by Steve's subdued, "I see."

His obvious hurt drove her to blurt the sad truth. "Mac saw us. It's our fault he's in here."

"For God's sake, Julia, you can't know that for sure."

Steve's exasperation nourished her frustration. "Why else would he be driving north on Del Rey like a madman? They say the Jeep over-ended three times. It's a wonder he wasn't killed."

"But, he wasn't." Steve let out a long breath, then urged, "I know you're upset. Let me come to El Paso. Together we can . . ."

"I can't see you." Julia pounded the pay phone with her fist, then begged, "You have to stay away."

"But, I love you and I know you love me. Please let me help you through this."

"No one can help me through this except myself. I know what I have to do, and seeing you will only complicate things."

She heard the desperation in Steve's voice. "You're exhausted and not thinking straight right now. I'm begging you, please don't make any decisions—guilt is no excuse for a lifetime commitment."

Julia closed her eyes and felt the memory of Steve surrounding her only an instant before her stomach twisted with shame. Her final words came punctuated with explosive sobs. "It's over, Steve. What happened between us never should have happened. Do you hear me? It—is—over."

CHAPTER 66

I T WAS STILL DARK the morning of the sixth day when Julia heard Mac croak her name. She raised her head to peer into his half-open eyes, saw him attempt a smile and knew he was going to make it.

She searched his face, reading only love instead of the accusation she expected. Was it possible the accident had wiped those lurid moments from his mind? Julia finally caught her breath and said, "Welcome back, my darling. I'm here and I always will be."

For the rest of the day each time Mac opened his eyes Julia leaned toward him and murmured his name, saying she was there and she loved him. He responded with short, unintelligible sentences accompanied by ventured grins, then his eyes would roll up behind his lids.

The Sandovals, hearing the good news, raced to El Paso and were thrilled when Mac recognized them. When they exited the room, Myrtle took Julia in her arms. "It's a miracle."

"Yes." That's all Julia could muster in response. Her throat was so tight, it barely let the word pass.

Bob waited until Julia stepped out of his wife's embrace. "Do you have a few minutes? We need to talk."

After Myrtle left to retrieve the car, Bob led Julia to the vinyl waiting room couch. "I know this has been a hard time for you, but it seems like the worst is over."

Julia nodded. "Thanks for letting me be here. I needed to, you know."

Bob smiled. "Of course you did, he's your man."

She nodded, thankful no one knew what really drove Mac into the desert and near death.

Julia took a deep breath and changed the subject. "How's Emaline?"

"She's doing as well as can be expected." Bob rose and walked to the window. "The meds have kicked in and Bunting is having daily sessions. But, don't worry about her. I didn't plan for you to do any more than the intake and evaluation. Children are your long suit."

Julia waited for the shoe to drop. She knew she couldn't remain by Mac's side and continue at Piñon Mesa. Bob was a good friend, but he was an administrator first.

Bob must have read her mind. "How long do the doctors think it will take Mac to recover?"

"Since they haven't told me anything, I can only guess. Two to three months, maybe more, before he can be released to rehab." Her voice caught. "They still don't know how badly the lower leg bones were affected by the fire. So far there's been no infection, but time will tell."

Bob put his hands on both her shoulders and turned her toward him. "I think you should take a leave of absence this fall."

Julia shook her head. "Oh, Bob, that's such a generous gesture, but I haven't been with Piñon Mesa long enough. I'm not going to put you on the spot with the Board."

"Let me worry about that." Sandoval's voice was soft. "Mac needs you. He may be out of the woods but he still has a helluva long road ahead. That's the least I can do for him."

"I have a better solution for both of us," Julia countered. "Part-time. What about nine to two, three days a week? This gets the Board off your back and lets me live in both my worlds."

Bob smiled. "Always the professional, aren't you?"

Julia stuck out her hand. "I want to do this, Bob. Not only for you, but for me."

His grasp was as firm as hers. "Deal. But, no new patients until Mac is well, okay? Besides, as we both know, summers are always slow."

CHAPTER 67

THAT EVENING Dolores pulled Julia from her chair and steered her out of the ICU. "I'm going to take you home. If you don't get a decent night's sleep you won't be good for anything."

"I can't go now. Mac's just coming out of it. I can't leave." Julia struggled to free her arm but Dolores held fast.

"Frank's staying through the night. I promise I'll have you back first thing in the morning."

Julia was asleep by the time the Suburban exited the parking garage and was shaken awake when they reached her house. Somehow she was able to shed her clothes and crawl into bed before exhaustion won and pitched her into a dreamless night.

"WAKE UP, sleepyhead."

Julia raised to see Dolores standing in the doorway.

"Hi." She squinted at the bright light and rolled to her stomach in search of darkness.

"Sorry, chica, I was worried you might sleep through the whole day. It's almost three."

"You've got to be kidding." Julia pushed up on one arm. "Is Mac all right?"

"I spoke to Frank a couple of times," Dolores said. "Mac's doing real fine. They pulled the drains out of his lungs this morning."

"That is good news. Let me take a quick shower and we can head back to El Paso." She groaned as she sat. "Every bone in my body aches. That chair is murder on the backside."

"I fixed you a sandwich. You must be starved." Dolores turned to leave then paused to fish a folded slip of paper from her jeans and handed it to Julia. "Steve Duke called. That's his number."

Her heart skipped at the sound of his name. "I didn't hear the phone."

"That's because I unplugged yours and put the ringer downstairs on low."

Julia heard Dolores retreat and fell back, drawing the other pillow to cover her face. Steve's scent. She inhaled the smell of him until her lungs could hold no more, then clung to the pillow and sobbed.

They had made love again in her bed, exchanging few words, communicating only through the union of their bodies, then slept wrapped in each other's arms. It was as if they had both waited a lifetime for those precious moments and wanted to preserve them forever. Now, those moments were all she would ever have.

Julia dragged herself from the bed, pulling the sheets and the memories of her one night with Steve behind her to the utility room at the end of the upstairs hall. She shoved them into the washer and twisted the knob.

She listened to the water spilling over her sins, hoping somehow by that act she would be rid of the past forever. Mac had almost died because of her. There was a lot to make up for.

On the way back to El Paso Julia quizzed Dolores about Frank.

"Palatia pretty much backed up his story so Manny hasn't pressed charges, but they won't let him off the hook until they get Emaline's deposition."

Emaline. Julia piled another scoop of guilt on the heap. She had left her patient and never bothered to follow up. "Have you heard how she's doing?"

"Are you kidding? That bitch can rot in hell as far as I'm concerned."

"Sorry. I didn't mean to open old wounds. Guess I'm still a little undone over this."

"Is that what you call it?" Dolores sniffed. "Frankly, you're almost a physical disaster. Circles under your eyes. Khakis hanging on your hipbones. Didn't even touch that sandwich. I bet you've lost ten pounds."

"Thanks for the compliment. You're beginning to sound like my mother."

"Well, someone's gotta take care of you, at least until Mac gets back on his feet." Dolores turned to face her. "You want to tell me what's going on with Steve?"

"What about him?"

"He told me if you didn't return his call today he wouldn't be calling again."

"That's a relief. I have nothing to say to him." Julia looked away hoping her silence would end it.

When Dolores turned her attention back to the road Julia slid her hand into her pants pocket to touch the folded slip of paper with Steve's telephone number on it and crumpled it into a tight little ball.

They were just passing the prison at Anthony. Prison, that's where she belonged. She could see the papers now. Local psychologist jailed for betrayal of and physical bodily harm to a man whose only crime was to love her. She shook her head. No newspaper would print that headline. Too long.

The Suburban clunked over the speed bump at the entrance to the hospital garage. "Here we are, chica."

Julia patted the woman's arm. "You're such a good friend. Thanks for getting me out of the ICU and staying with me last night."

"Hey. What are sisters-under-the-skin for? You'd do the same for me."

They rounded the corner just in time to see a slender, dark-haired woman in a white coat enter Mac's room.

Julia touched Dolores's arm. "Who's that? I've never seen her around."

Dolores shrugged. "Maybe she's the burn person. I heard they were talking about skin grafts."

"No. I met the burn specialist. Male."

Julia peered through the glass to see the woman bend over Mac, say something and place her hand on his forehead. At that he opened his eyes and raised his hand to touch her arm. He muttered something, then his eyes closed as his hand slid to the mattress.

The woman turned and Julia saw an attractive face featuring wide, brown eyes and prominent cheekbones. It was obvious she was Indian and most probably Navajo.

The woman gave Julia a friendly wave and turned back to Mac once more before she exited.

After the door closed behind her, she held out her hand. "I'm Sylvia Chee. You must be Julia."

Her grip sent a small tingle through Julia, which faded as the Navajo's eyes crinkled. "I hear you make good medicine."

Julia smiled. "I don't know if it was my medicine that saved Mac but I thank God he's alive."

"Mac's a very special person. Everybody at Chaco Point was devastated when we heard about the accident. I would have come right away but I was on duty. This is my first day off. Joe Pinto flew me down."

So, Sylvia Chee came all the way to El Paso from the Four Corners to see Mac. Julia remembered the expression on his face and the pride in his voice when he told her about Chee. The words "brilliant" and "dedicated" were used. This doctor gave up fame and money to minister to her people.

Julia shivered the first time Mac spoke Sylvia Chee's name and, now, she shivered again. "I hear they took the drains out of his chest last night."

Sylvia nodded. "He's breathing unassisted now. A good sign. The ribs will give him some pain but the lungs are clear." She lowered her voice. "But his legs—I guess they won't know until . . ."

Julia couldn't bear to pursue the question of whether Mac would walk again. Her guilt was too great. "Is he conscious? I thought I saw him speak."

"Still in and out. I think he said, 'What the hell are you doing here?'"

Chee flashed a dazzling smile. "Well, I've run out of time. Got to get back north. Please tell Mac, I'll come again. I tried to tell him but I don't think he heard me."

"Of course I will. Thank you for coming."

"My pleasure." The woman turned to leave then stopped. "I'm glad everything worked out between you two. Mac's one of the finest men I know."

Julia watched the doctor turn the corner. She was just about to speak when Dolores said it for her. "Better watch your backside, chica. That gal could mean trouble."

CHAPTER 68

The day Julia and Mac's future began again had been a long one for both of them.

After two months of therapy Mac had taken his first steps. But with that victory came searing pain as the scars across his ankles screamed at the first weight they bore.

Julia began her day as scheduled: a morning of patients, then lunch. On the way back to her office she had seen Emaline across the quadrangle and was saddened to see that once-curvaceous figure bloated beneath a day dress, her hair pulled carelessly back into a ponytail. Though she was no longer suicidal and was making the expected progress on the drugs and therapy, Emaline was still deeply depressed and blamed Palatia for much of what had happened.

Julia had been able to follow Emaline's case through Fred Bunting's clinical reports, but the true boon was always her weekly lunch with Palatia.

Their friendship blossomed as Palatia assumed the non-judgmental motherly image Julia craved and Julia became her surrogate second daughter helping her through the sad and rough spots with Emaline.

Having taken an unexpected late appointment with one of her favorite patients Julia omitted the usual stop at her house for a fresh change of clothes and her mother's daily admonition that she was "ruining her health over that man." Usually followed by, "I'm coming west if things don't improve."

Even then, Julia had been late to pick up the dinner Cuca insisted on preparing each day. To her dismay the kitchen was empty. Cuca had been suffering from an ailing tooth and hadn't left her bed.

Mac's disappointment over a "Cuca-less" meal was as obvious as his fatigue, and though Julia was happy to hear his good news she had been strung-out and involved with her own lack of fulfillment. Both picked over the unappetizing hospital food and retired early.

Past midnight Mac's moans jarred Julia awake, pulling her across the room to lie beside him. Though the days were filled with a comfortable camaraderie, Julia dreaded these moments.

In the beginning she had lied to soothe him with each "I love you," adding more weight to the dull ache at the bottom of her heart. But over time those words came more easily.

"I'm here, I'm here," she whispered and stroked his cheek.

Mac's hand covered hers. "Sorry. Bad dream."

She knew it was about the accident and held her breath, waiting for the accusation. To her relief his next words were, "Stay for a minute will you?"

When he pulled back the sheet, she settled beside him. "I'm sorry I wasn't here when you walked. The pain must have been excruciating."

Mac leaned up on one elbow. "It hurt worse than—"

"The accident?"

"Yeah." She felt him shudder. "Worse than that."

Mac moved only slightly, but Julia realized he was contemplating a kiss.

Before when he tried to kiss her she would turn away, pleading his condition and returning to her bed. Once there she would stare into the darkness, a guilty witness to his restless turnings.

But this time, she didn't wait. She kissed him first.

Mac ended the kiss and reached for the light switch above his bed.

As a soft glow filled the room, Julia saw the question in his eyes. She put her finger to his lips. "I love you."

She kissed him again then drew away. "I love you more than I ever thought possible."

Each kiss Mac extracted drew Julia along with him until she was trembling with anticipation. It no longer mattered that they were in a hospital bed. Everything felt right for the first time since that night they spent beneath the stars months before.

To her surprise, Mac broke the kiss and rolled away.

"What's wrong? Are you all right?" Julia curled into his back and hugged him to her.

He pulled her hand to his mouth and kissed it softly. Through his back she heard, "Nothing could be more right." Then he chuckled, "But not in a hospital bed, okay?"

They slept until the nurses arrived. The only sign that passed between the two that something had changed was the grin pasted on Mac's face as Julia rushed red-faced into the bathroom to take her shower.

CHAPTER 69

I N LATE JULY Emaline's case went before the Doña Ana grand jury. Thanks to Fred Bunting's impassioned testimony on Emaline's behalf, and Palatia's owning up to her part in Ed's death, Emaline was no-billed by the Doña Ana grand jury and Frank was completely exonerated.

Manny Garcia made a special trip up to the Square B to personally deliver the good news, arriving just as Julia was having tea with Dolores. Frank poured drinks all around and decreed they take the party to Mac. After the Sandovals were alerted, Julia and Manny headed to El Paso followed by Frank, Dolores and Allen in the Suburban that carried enough of Cuca's chiles rellenos to feed an army.

Bob and Myrtle brought up the tail of the caravan with a large bowl of guacamole and chips to go with enough "serious" margaritas to wash down the chiles.

Mac greeted Frank's good news with an excited whoop, then insisted on serving the margaritas. Julia smiled at his first display of his usual enthusiasm. Now nothing but a little more healing time stood in the way of their future.

When the party grew too raucous the head nurse shooed them out and Julia walked the revelers to the elevator bank. The Brantleys and the detective caught the first car leaving the Sandovals and Julia alone.

"Mac seems really great," Bob said. "I hear he's walking a few more steps each day."

"Yes. He's making excellent progress but the scars still give him trouble. At least the bottoms of his feet were spared. Heaven knows how long it would have taken for them to heal."

Bob's smile faded. "Say, did you hear about the big HIV scare at Pavilion?"

Julia gasped. "The hospital in Albuquerque?"

"Right. Seems one of the ER group tested positive. A woman associate."

"Oh, Bob, she's not interested in all that gossip." Myrtle patted Julia's arm. "This hospital stint's been as hard on you as it has on Mac. You could use a little plumping up and a week's uninterrupted sleep."

Bob didn't wait for Julia's reply. "Well, it sounds pretty grim to me. I've tried to get a hold of Steve, but he's on vacation."

Julia went icy cold. "Why would Steve be involved?"

"He was dating the lady during the holidays. I met her at one of the parties. Isn't that so, Myrt?"

Myrtle launched into a lengthy description of the woman but Julia couldn't make out the words. Her heart fluttered in her chest like a helpless bird making it impossible for her to breathe.

Was it possible? Julia couldn't put words to her thoughts, the sentence was too dire. Not now. Not when things were going so right.

She thought back to that night a few weeks before. Since then each evening ended in Mac's bed and each evening there were passionate kisses and sensuous caresses but that was all. He refused to consummate their love in a hospital bed and for the first time she was grateful.

"Julia? Are you all right?" Her friend's voice broke through her beginning terror.

Hoping her face didn't reflect her panic, she tried to answer but the words stuck in her throat like stones.

When Myrtle's eyes widened Julia gave a small cough, then forced herself to smile. "Sorry, must be some left-over salt from the margarita."

Myrtle still seemed concerned. "You're so pale. I'll get you some water."

"No, no. I'm fine. Really." Julia took a deep breath, then climbed out of her fear to change the subject. "How's Emaline?"

"Relieved to be no-billed," Bob said. "You know she's moved in with Palatia."

It took every bit of energy Julia possessed to appear interested while her mind raced over the past. "I heard that. I'm glad."

Bob stabbed the elevator button impatiently. "Bunting says Emaline's doing well on her medication, but he doubts she'll be able to return to San Francisco. Odds are she'll probably stay in Las Cruces."

Julia, relieved to see the elevator doors slide open, made one last effort to end the conversation before she gave into her panic. "Thanks so much for coming. Drive carefully."

When the doors closed, Julia found the nearest couch and collapsed.

CHAPTER 70

JULIA'S INVOLVEMENT in Mac's daily care ended a few days after the party.

Still reeling from the news of the HIV scare, Julia threw herself into a frenzied house-cleaning attack. To her mind, she wanted to make the house livable for Mac's convalescence—if she were honest with herself, she would admit she was in denial.

When the report came that Mac was to be released the following week, Julia stopped by the hacienda to pick up Cuca's dinner creation and was having tea with Dolores while Frank leaned against the counter downing a beer.

The man Julia had once considered an enemy still bore the thatch of salt-and-pepper hair above icy blue eyes. But since Frank's return to the Square B, the flinty glint in his see-through eyes had mellowed and his attitude toward Dolores had certainly been more deferential.

The pleasant conversation came to an abrupt halt when Julia casually mentioned that she planned to have Mac stay with her until he could operate on his own.

To her surprise, Frank bowed his neck to announce his brother would convalesce in the small cottage at the Square B.

Julia protested. "But I've worked myself silly for the past week fixing the downstairs for Mac. I've even got a hospital bed on order."

Frank glanced at Dolores, who shrugged. "I'll be in the hothouse."

When Dolores disappeared, Frank asked Julia to join him in the library.

He pointed to one of the leather chairs. "Have a seat while I pop another beer."

Julia sat and glared. Frank wasn't making it easy for anybody by insisting that his brother stay with the family. He certainly wasn't going to nurse his brother back to health. Poor Dolores and Cuca would bear the burden. Finally, she said, "Don't you think this should be Mac's decision?"

"He's not in shape to make a decision."

Julia started to put up a fight, then decided she was too tired to spar with this man. Maybe it was better that she and Mac separate for a while. Maybe he needed the space. All she wanted was a few days uninterrupted sleep and an opportunity to get her blood tested.

Frank took a few swigs of his beer. "It's true Dolores and Cuca will do the major tending, but I need to have Mac stay here. It's a small way to make up for what happened at the reading of the will."

Before Julia could speak, he held up his hand. "I'll never be able to repay you for all you've done for Mac. I know it's been hell." He paused, then cleared his throat. "I guess nobody has the guts to tell you this, Julia, but I'd say you look like you've been rode hard and put up wet."

She sat up in indignation. "What did you say?"

"I see I got your attention so I'll try to put it a little more delicately. You're running on empty. Down to the last can in the six-pack. One step away from the cliff. Got the drift? If not, just check the mirror for the circles under those big beautiful eyes."

Julia felt tears spill as her fears rushed forward. Weight loss. Circles under her eyes. Fatigue. Only days before, Myrtle had made the same observation, and not long before that Dolores mentioned something about her khakis hanging on her hips.

After a few moments she stammered, "I suppose I am a little strung-out."

Frank gave her an awkward pat on the back. "Hell, woman, you've been on the verge of a nervous fit for weeks. Go home. Take a few days off. We'll move Mac into the cottage and set up a schedule that will certainly include you. Okay?"

CHAPTER 71

THE SEPTEMBER EVENING air was redolent with roasting chiles. To the group seated on the side verandah of the Square B, the heavenly scent of burning molasses meant the heat of summer would soon give way to the blue-sky days and crisp nights of a New Mexico fall.

Frank pointed toward the barns where Allen stood handing the last pay envelopes to the workers. "Harvest time. Can't beat it."

Though the Brantley chile harvest nudged the Labor Day weekend, an unusually heavy yield promised a prosperous return and guaranteed an even better crop the following spring.

Julia turned to Mac and offered up her own silent prayer. Without skin grafts, his lower legs were healing nicely and his lungs were at full capacity. Despite a small setback with the removal of his ruptured spleen, he had left the hospital weeks earlier than anticipated.

Bob Sandoval's voice broke her thoughts. "We can't wait for you to get back to Piñon Mesa full-time."

The Sandovals had been regular visitors at the Square B once Mac had settled in the little cottage.

Julia smiled. "I have to admit I've missed the daily grind."

Mac grabbed her hand. "Abandoning me for those kids? I can't believe you could be so fickle."

They both laughed an easy, knowing laugh. That was the good thing, Julia thought, they were laughing again despite the possible death sentence now hanging above her.

The summer had passed without either of them raising the question of what Mac witnessed that balmy April evening. Either Mac didn't remember seeing Steve and her together or chose not to—and Julia carefully avoided the subject.

"No complaining in front of the boss," she tutted. "Bob's promised me an abbreviated schedule until the Christmas break."

Mac turned to his friend. "That's real nice of you, Bob, but hardly necessary. I'm giving up the crutches for a cane tomorrow and I'll be moving back to the banks of the Rio Grande in a few days if everything continues to go well."

"That's great news. Great news," Bob said. "Can we count on a Thanksgiving wedding?"

Mac laughed. "That's up to Julia." His hand covered hers with a gentle squeeze.

Wedding? Julia couldn't think about that. She had put off having her blood drawn for a number of reasons—none of them valid. Suddenly desperate to escape, she stood and reached for Mac's half-empty glass.

"I think I'll have a little more wine. How about a refill?" She was across the verandah and inside the library door before anyone protested.

Outside, the conversation shifted to the coming November election, and Julia relaxed. Maybe her exit seemed smoother than it had been. Her hands were trembling, making it almost impossible to jockey the ice from the bucket into Mac's glass. When several cubes hit the tile floor, she slammed down the glass and stooped to retrieve them.

She must face the facts. Unprotected sex with a possible carrier. Not once, but four times. Julia stood, eyes darting frantically about. What was Mac drinking? Where was the wine?

Frank's voice was soft at her side. "I'll finish here. Why don't you go powder your nose or something?"

Julia saw concern in his pale eyes and protested, "Not to worry, Frank, I'm just fine."

"No, you're not, but you're doing a damn good job of covering it up. Now, go fix your lipstick or whatever it is you women do."

After dinner Julia and Mac stood on the porch watching the Sandovals' taillights flicker down the drive.

She turned. "Guess I'd better get going, too."

Mac balanced on one crutch and put out his hand. "How about giving me some help at the cottage? Dolores and Cuca are still tied up in the kitchen and it's been a long day."

She caught her breath. There it was. She swallowed hard. Mac had seen her with Steve, but she was almost positive he was blocking the moment. She didn't want to bring it up, but if she didn't how could she tell him she might be HIV positive?

They walked across the rutted road to the cottage in silence—Mac absorbed in making the trip without taking a tumble; Julia clambering through her tangled mind for an excuse.

Mac swung his frame expertly up the steps and waited while she opened the door so he could enter the small living room. He started down the hall to the bedroom, paused at the door and disappeared, leaving Julia alone, heart frozen, waiting for what she knew would come next.

"Hey, what's keeping you?"

"Sorry, I'm coming."

Julia moved down the hall to see Mac sitting on the edge of the bed, crutches in one hand.

"I'll take those." She slid them under the bed, then knelt between Mac's knees and began to unbutton his shirt with trembling fingers, carefully concentrating on each button, frantically wondering how she could gracefully extract herself from his tender trap.

There were two buttons left when Mac took her hands to guide them around his neck as his mouth found hers.

It was a slow kiss, a tender kiss, one filled with question. When it ended, he drew away to search her face.

Julia resumed her unfinished task, heart racing from equal parts of passion and fear. She couldn't tell him—didn't want to tell him. Not until she knew.

She felt his lips brush the top of her head and murmured, "Only two to go."

Mac pulled her to sit beside him. This time his kisses left no doubt about how he planned to end the evening.

She turned away, hating to break the moment, but the grim possibility of her predicament pushed her words into the silence. "I can't. I can't."

Mac drew her to him. "It's not your fault. I cursed our *Nizhoni* and threw you into Steve's arms. After the accident you never left my side and after those nights in the hospital, somehow I hoped maybe—"

"But I do love you." Julia kept her head against Mac's chest, afraid her eyes would betray her thoughts. "And I want to be your wife. I just need a little time to . . ."

She felt him stiffen, but his voice remained soft. "Don't make promises you can't keep, Julia. Guilt is a wretched substitute for love."

"Is that what you think this is? Guilt?"

"If it's not guilt, what is it?"

"Damn it, Mac, I love you and I want to marry you. I just need a little more time, that's all."

She tried to rise, but Mac held her to him. "The time is now. I need you, Julia. Stay with me."

Julia looked up, eyes pleading. "Not tonight. It wouldn't be fair. Oh, Mac. Please try to understand."

He released her and stood. When he spoke his voice was hard. "Forget it. Just give me a little help here and you're free to go."

Holding the bedstead with one white-knuckled hand, Mac unbuckled his belt, struggled with the zipper, and his khakis slid to the floor. The scars on his lower legs, in ugly red contrast to the pallor of his muscular thighs, still shocked.

All her fault. She turned away, unable to face what she had caused.

Mac's gruff voice broke her thoughts. "I can take it from here."

Julia turned to see the hurt she heard echoed in his eyes, and her heart squeezed. "Please, darling, it's only for a few days. That's all I need."

She finished unbuttoning his shirt, removed it from his shoulders and watched him slide beneath the covers.

He studied her for a moment. "A few days to reach Steve?"

Julia recoiled as if Mac had struck her. "How can you say that?"

"Sorry." He started to speak, then shook his head sadly. "Turn out the lights as you go."

CHAPTER 72

THAT NIGHT had been the longest of Julia's life, but by the time she showered and dressed for the day she had made a decision.

The slip of paper bearing Steve's phone number disappeared sometime during the summer, but that didn't matter. She knew where to reach him.

"Emergency Associates," the voice chirped.

"Doctor Steven Duke, please."

"Doctor Duke is no longer with the group, would you like to speak with someone else, or may I help you?"

Julia's heart flipped. "No longer with the group? Do you know where he went?"

"Who is this?"

"I'm sorry. This is Doctor Fairchild, a friend of his. I'm calling from Las Cruces."

"Oh, right." The chirp faded to sarcasm. "Well, to tell you the truth, I don't know where Doctor Duke went. You know how rumors go. First I heard he went to Uganda, then someplace in South America, and only yesterday it was India. Take your pick."

"Out of the country?"

"I believe that's what I said."

Julia ignored the gibe. "Can you tell me when he left?"

There was a long pause before the answer came. "Late June or early July, I guess. I went on vacation and he was gone when I got back."

Steve gone? She had meant it when she had told him it was over, but she had never expected him to leave the country. How would she be able to find out about the HIV?

The chirpy voice resumed. "Is there someone else you would like to speak to?"

"Is there a colleague of Doctor Duke's or a close friend who might have more information?"

Julia thought she heard the chirper snort. "Well, yeah, I guess you could say so. There's Doctor Driscoll, but I doubt—"

"I'll speak with him, please."

"She's no longer with the group, either, but I can give you her home phone if you want."

Julia took the number and hung up. A woman. Bob's words echoed. "He was dating the lady during the holidays."

Almost a year before. Months before she and Steve had met.

Thinking back, Steve had never mentioned any close friends other than Palatia and Emaline. Julia had surmised he was a loner, but now she knew she was wrong. She had never bothered to ask Steve about his past and he never offered to fill her in.

She checked her watch and sprang for her car keys. It was almost ten and she had promised to drive Mac to El Paso for his therapy. She'd have to break a few laws to make up for lost time.

JULIA OPENED the door to the cottage. "Mac?"

When there was no answer, she crossed the road to the hacienda and entered through the kitchen. Empty. She finally found Dolores in the greenhouse. "Where's Mac?"

"What went on between you two last night?" Dolores kept her head down, intent on her cross-pollination.

"I need to know where Mac is."

"He figured you weren't coming so he drove himself to El Paso," Dolores said. "I was sorta hoping things had gelled between you two, but when Mac came over for breakfast I could tell the evening went sour."

Julia settled on the stool next to her friend. "Frankly, last night was hell for both of us."

"It's Duke, isn't it?" Dolores spoke slowly as she tweezed a small yellow dot from the center of one plant and placed it in the center of the next.

"Yes, but not for the reason you think. Steve's left the country."

"No kidding? When did you find that out?"

"This morning. I called Albuquerque. After what happened with Mac last night, I knew I needed to clear things up."

Dolores muttered something under her breath and shook her head. "I was hoping Steve didn't mean so much."

"He doesn't." Julia stopped. There was no point in saying anything about the HIV—not until she was tested.

Her friend sighed. "I'd think Steve's relationship with the lady Pierce would've been enough for you to figure him out."

"If you know something, why don't you just tell me?"

Dolores gave Julia a knowing smirk. "They used to call Steve 'El Gato.' Does that mean anything to you?"

"The Cat?"

"He got around a lot. Get the drift?"

Julia's stomach caved. "I see."

She turned and started for the door when Dolores called, "Can we expect you for dinner?"

"I'll pass tonight. Could you have Mac call me when he gets back?"

CHAPTER 73

JULIA DROVE to El Paso to have her blood drawn at a small laboratory near the Burn Center. She had become acquainted with one of the technicians during her many breakfasts in the cafeteria and knew her well enough to ask the favor.

When Julia explained what she needed, the woman paled. "When was your last contact?"

"Late April. Almost five months ago." Julia shuddered remembering that night. She had been conscientious about taking the pill and knew pregnancy couldn't be a factor, but a sexually transmitted disease had never entered her mind.

The jab was followed by a sharp sting as her blood flowed into the tubes.

"How long?" Julia asked.

"Monday afternoon. You say your last contact was five months ago? Plenty of time to pick up antibodies. But even if it's negative, you should be tested again in six months, just to make sure."

Julia was back in Las Cruces by four, pacing the floor, waiting for Mac to call. Finally, when the sun was low in the sky, she picked up the telephone.

When Dolores answered, Julia said, "It's me. Is he there?"

Dolores's long sigh put a hole in Julia's stomach. "No. He came back from El Paso in time for lunch. Seemed real pumped up. The doctors told him he didn't need a cane. He didn't say much until after coffee. That's when he announced he was flying to Chaco Point."

"But he can't. He's not strong enough."

"That's what we thought, but when Frank tried to talk him out of it, Mac stiffed him. Told him the sooner he got back to work, the better. But I don't like this at all."

Julia knew what Dolores meant. Sylvia Chee was at Chaco Point. "Oh, Dolores."

"I know, I know. What happened between you two last night that would make Mac do this?"

"Nothing happened. I told you that this morning."

After a long silence Dolores asked, "You want to come out for dinner, anyway? It's lonesome without you."

Warmed by the entreaty, Julia thanked Dolores, begged off and dialed the Albuquerque number.

A sultry voice answered, "Driscoll."

"Doctor Driscoll, this is Julia Fairchild, I'm with Piñon Mesa Hospital in Las Cruces."

"Yes?"

"I'm sorry to bother you, but I'm trying to locate Steven Duke and the receptionist at the office was kind enough to give me your number. She seemed to think you might be able to help."

"You're talking to the wrong person. I haven't spoken to Steve Duke in months." The woman gave a mirthless laugh. "Besides, I'm no longer a member of that group."

"Then you don't know where to find Doctor Duke?"

"All I heard was that he left the country."

Julia felt herself curl inside. Mac warned her. Frank warned her. Even Myrtle had mentioned something about Steve's checkered past but she didn't listen. She was attracted to the doctor from the moment she saw him. Maybe Mac pushed her into Steve's waiting arms, but she went willingly. And now this.

The dial tone echoed in Julia's ear until she heard, "If you'd like to make a call, please hang up and try again. If you need help—"

Julia laughed at the irony of the message and rubbed the slight bruise in the crook of her arm where the technician had drawn her blood. Of course she needed help. But who could give it? Steve had left the country with no forwarding address, leaving her stuck in limbo until the test results were back.

She dragged herself toward the stairs, suddenly too tired to deal with the mess she had made of her life. Each step was an effort. Even the bed seemed out of reach. Once there, she fell across the comforter and slept.

CHAPTER 74

ASS THE SMALL PLANE gained altitude, the exhilaration of touching the sky once more eased the despair that had held Mac in thrall through the endless night.

He drew in a deep breath, surveyed the cloudless vista that lay before him, then headed the aircraft north toward Chaco Point.

Julia's behavior the evening before had hurt and confused him. In the hospital she had seemed so ready for love, her lips seeking his, her body eager for his caresses. Buoyed by the newly forged contentment between them, and those magical evenings that followed, Mac had waited until he was well-settled in the cottage to invite her to his bed.

He realized his mistake when he saw the pain in Julia's eyes and felt her pull away, leaving him sadly aware that, despite her professed love and the exciting moments in his hospital bed, she seemed unsure of playing a part in his future.

Her, "I can't. I can't," echoed like a clanging cymbal in the tiny confines of the cockpit, causing his head to throb.

When Julia asked him to give her a few more days, he lost it, positive there was only one reason for her hesitation.

He had blurted, "A few days to reach Steve?" before he thought it through, then watched her recoil as if he had struck her. He should have taken her in his arms. Asked for her forgiveness, told her to take as long as she wanted. Instead, he sent her away.

He let out a long, sad breath. The whole mess was his fault. He alone initiated the chain of events that threw them apart and brought him so perilously close to dying. She had made a simple request—a few more days. What difference could a few more days make?

TWO HOURS later, Mac taxied the plane across the tarmac at Chaco Point to a small shed topped by a faded windsock that hung as limp as he felt. He must have been out of his mind. He hadn't flown in more than five months and though there was no major head wind or weather, the flight took every bit of energy he possessed.

Putting out the blocks and tying the plane drained the rest of Mac's reserve, and he slid to lean against the tire. When he saw the dust rise from the approaching truck, he struggled to his feet and waved.

He had radioed the hospital that he was coming and heard cheers in the background. Now, as the truck neared, his smile widened. The rear bed was jammed with hospital personnel.

In minutes Mac was surrounded, pummeled and bear-hugged, and by the time he was lifted into the cab, he ached all over.

"Welcome back." Sylvia leaned to place a gentle kiss on his cheek.

Mac hid his reaction with a small effort at bluster. "Did you bring the entire staff? Who in hell is running the hospital?"

"We shut down in your honor." She wheeled the truck toward the road and stepped on the gas. "So, how long will you stay?"

Mac turned away, hoping to hide his sudden fatigue. "How long do you need me?"

At least that's what he thought he said. The next thing he knew he was flat on his back in a hospital bed and a voice above him was saying, "Call Sylvia."

A COOL hand on his forehead preceded the admonishment. "We need doctors up here, damn it, not more patients."

Mac opened his eyes to see Sylvia Chee's doe-eyes inches away. "Sorry. Guess I out-maneuvered myself." He tried to raise his head but found even that was an effort. "What's wrong with me?"

"Nothing a few nights' sleep won't fix. You're a little dehydrated, but your vitals are normal."

He squinted at his watch, but his eyes couldn't seem to focus. "What time is it?"

"A little past eight. Hungry?"

Suddenly, he was. "Yeah, I could use a little food."

SYLVIA SAT with Mac until he finished the hamburger and fries she ordered from the local joint down the road and waited until he finished the second beer. She told him it was either two beers or an IV, and the beer won.

He let out a long breath and settled back into the pillows. "Thanks. That hit the spot."

The tense silence hung like a pall between them until Sylvia could stand it no longer. "Want to talk?"

Mac shook his head. "Not much to say."

She heard the squeeze in his voice. Something was eating him. It must be Julia.

"You better get some rest. I have a few dudes to look in on before I head for home." She stood and reached for his wrist. "And you can be the first."

Before she could move away, Mac pulled her down to meet his lips.

The kiss was all Sylvia dreamed it would be, soft but strong, tender but demanding, reaching inside her body to capture her soul.

Afraid if she didn't stop she wouldn't, Sylvia pulled away and, though her legs were rubber beneath her, found the chair.

After she regained her composure she asked, "Why did you come?"

"Why do you think?" His eyes were dark. So dark she couldn't read them.

Her antennae went on alert. Something wasn't right.

"I asked you first."

He said nothing.

"There must be some reason you kissed me but it doesn't make much sense. You have a woman who adores you. I hear she never left your side. So, what gives?"

Mac rubbed his face with both hands and muttered, "Why in hell do you females always have to over-analyze everything?"

He seemed to be mocking her and that made her angry. "Did you come up here for a quick fuck to ease the itch between your legs? Because if that's why you came, you can hop back in that plane of yours and fly south."

His eyes told her she had cut him to the bone. "If that's what you think I came for, I will. First thing in the morning."

Their eyes locked for a moment, then they both laughed as the tension between them dissolved.

Sylvia stood. "Sleep well. I'll see you tomorrow."

"Not if I see you first." Mac rolled away.

She pulled the door behind her and headed for her office and the telephone. "Information for Las Cruces? Doctor Fairchild? Julia Fairchild."

Sylvia wrote the number, then walked to the window. The parking lot was almost empty. At the far end she could just make out the Toyota that had carried her to New Haven and, after ten years, brought her home to Chaco Point and her destiny.

She had never expected to fall in love, but the minute she laid eyes on Mac her heart had done a slow roll inside her chest. Working side by side for the next few months had brought them even closer and the admiration changed to love. Though Sylvia knew there was another woman, somewhere at the back of her heart she still held out a small hope that the spirits might send their blessing her way.

She gave up that hope when she met Julia in El Paso and liked the pretty redhead immediately. It had been obvious that Julia and Mac were meant to be a couple. But something happened between them. Something that sent Mac to find comfort and maybe even love with her.

Tonight his kiss was filled with the same longing she had nurtured for so long. It would have been simple to lean a chair beneath the door handle, turn out the light and let things happen. But she wasn't able to.

Sylvia walked to the phone. She needed to call Julia. It was the least she could do.

CHAPTER 75

THE RINGING jerked Julia from a fitful sleep. She moaned, reached to retrieve the phone and dragged it to her ear. "Doctor Fairchild."

"Julia, this is Sylvia Chee."

At the sound of the Navajo's voice, Julia shot to full attention. "Is it Mac? Is he all right?"

"He's fine except for slight dehydration and moderate fatigue. I admitted him overnight just as a precaution. Mac should never have flown solo this soon. He's lucky to have made it."

"Thank God he did. Is he near? I need to talk to him. There's so much I have to explain."

After a brief silence, Chee said, "I knew something must be wrong."

"It's all my fault." Julia hesitated, not sure she should confide in this woman, then decided there was nothing to lose. "I really hurt Mac yesterday and I don't know if he can find it in his heart to forgive me."

"Then I must have been out of my mind to call you at all," Chee said. "But you better get here pronto."

Panic reigned. The very thought of Mac and Sylvia Chee together caused black spots to spire before Julia's eyes. It wasn't a ghost this time. A real person was walking across her grave. There was no one to blame but herself. Mac had tried to begin again and she had turned him away.

Dolores. She was her only hope. Julia cursed the unanswered rings and dialed again.

"What?" Dolores's voice was deep with sleep.

"Wake up. This is an emergency. You have to help me."

"Julia? It's way past ten. What's wrong?"

"I have to get to Chaco Point before morning or it will be too late."

"What do you mean?" Dolores's voice was clearer now, more alert.

"I just got a call from Sylvia Chee. She told me I'd better get there quick."

"Why? Has there been an accident?"

In the background Julia heard a rustle, then a deep muffled voice. "What's that about Mac?"

Julia couldn't help but smile. It was a miracle. Frank and Dolores were sharing the same bed.

"No, nothing like that. Doctor Chee told me Mac was very fatigued and she put him in the hospital for a few days. But Dolores, you and I both know why he flew to Chaco Point and it wasn't to tend the sick."

After a muffled conversation Dolores said, "You come here. We'll be dressed by then. I'll get Allen to come, too. That way we can take turns driving through the night. We'll get you to Chaco Point with time to spare."

CHAPTER 76

I T WAS JUST past six when the Suburban pulled into the Chaco Point Hospital parking lot and Frank's voice cut through the darkness. "We're here. What now?"

As light paled the eastern sky, Julia uncurled from beneath a pile of blankets to peer out the window. "Why don't you go for coffee while I find Mac? After I get the lay of the land, I'll meet you in the cafeteria."

The others groaned and stretched then, one by one, eased out of the car. Julia turned to give Frank, Allen and finally Dolores a hug. "I don't know anything else to say but thank you. I owe you all a big one."

"Just get that damn ring back on your finger," Frank barked. "That'll be enough for me."

It wasn't difficult to find Mac. He was in the only private room in the hospital. Julia cracked the door and peeked in to see he was turned away from her, sleeping on his side.

She tiptoed across the room, slid into the chair next to the bed and waited.

She didn't have long. Mac rolled to his back and opened his eyes. The delighted surprise she first saw was quickly replaced with pained wariness.

"What are you doing here?"

Julia sent up a fast prayer and tried to cover his mouth with hers. Mac pulled away. "Hold on a minute. What's this all about?"

Her stomach clenched. A single kiss couldn't bridge the widening gap between them. Mac deserved better than that. She would have to tell him the truth.

He leaned up on his elbow and looked at his watch. "It's just past six. How did you get here?"

"Frank and Dolores and Allen. We drove all night."

Mac's eyes receded beneath his brow and his voice was low. "Why?"

"Because I have to tell you the real reason I couldn't stay with you the other evening."

She stood and began to pace, tears pushing at the back of her eyes. "Oh, Mac, this is so hard. I've already hurt you so badly. I can't bear to open those wounds again."

Julia saw sadness fill his face and her heart staggered. "I know you saw Steve and me."

Mac turned away, then shook his head, his reply an almost inaudible, "Yes."

"What I couldn't tell you the other night was that Steve didn't use protection."

The room was hollow with Mac's silence. All Julia could hear was the rapid thrum of her heart.

She saw his hand clench into a hard fist, then he faced her, eyes dark with pain. "I love you more than I've ever loved anyone, Julia, but I'm not so sure I can handle raising Steve Duke's child."

A small spurt of relief got her through the worst and the truth tumbled forth. "Oh, no. It's not that. I'm not pregnant." She took a deep breath and blurted, "But it's possible I could be HIV. I'll know by Monday."

Mac stiffened. "Steve is HIV?"

"I'm not sure. He left in the early part of the summer and might not have known about the exposure. Bob Sandoval told me one of Steve's associates, a woman named Driscoll, tested positive sometime after he left. She and Steve were dating last Christmas."

"I never expected this." Mac seemed to be avoiding her eyes by searching the ceiling. "How often were you and Steve together?"

She felt the heat rise to her cheeks. "Does it matter?"

"Only that the odds of contracting the virus increase with each encounter. You need to contact him."

"Believe me, I've tried. But no one seems to know where he's gone."

"Oh, Julia."

She heard the anguish in Mac's voice and decided there was no point in driving the nails any deeper. If she were HIV positive it wouldn't matter how many times she and Steve were together, any chance of a life with Mac would be lost.

"It was just that once. That's what makes all this so painful. I'm so sorry."

Mac studied her for a moment, then opened his arms. "I'm not living in a glass house. Are you?"

Julia took a step forward, but renewed tears came as her initial rush of relief was stanched by the dreaded future she might face. "But, the HIV?"

Mac took her hand. "As long as I know you love me, I don't give a damn about HIV. Marry me. We'll face this together."

"But, you want children—a wife who can fulfill every need. I might not be able to."

"I never stopped loving you, Julia, not for a minute." Mac drew her into his arms as his words resonated against her ear. "I don't want to live without you. I can't live without you. We're getting married as soon as you can find a dress and get your family out here. That's an order."

Julia heard the comforting soft drub of his heart and knew she would be safe with him no matter the outcome. For the first time in months the world felt right.

CHAPTER 77

OCTOBER IN NEW MEXICO is famous for its teal blue skies and crisp days. This day was no different. The cottonwoods shading the couple were a brilliant yellow, the sun was shining and the air was temperate.

Mac slid the heavy Navajo ring on Julia's finger, then raised her hand to his lips and whispered, "Now we are *Nizhoni*."

For a moment it seemed time stopped. There were no other sounds except for their breathing, no sight other than the love reflected in the deeps of Mac's azure eyes.

When "You may kiss the bride" echoed above them, Julia raised her mouth to meet Mac's, who held her to him until applause drove them apart.

The mariachis began to play and the couple walked through the crowd to the broad, covered porch as waiters carrying trays of hors d'oeuvres and drinks began to move among the guests.

Myrtle's voice came from behind. "You look radiant. I'm so happy for you."

Julia turned and opened her arms. "Thanks for being so understanding about Dolores being Matron of Honor. Family politics, you know."

Myrtle returned Julia's hug. "As far as I'm concerned, I was standing there right beside you." She stepped back, then whispered, "I know you want a family; care to clue me in on your plans?"

"Not right away. Mac wants to get back to work as soon as possible and I owe Piñon Mesa a few months as well. I'm guessing that particular project won't go online until early spring."

Julia's answer seemed good enough for Myrtle, but there was a more important reason for delaying their family.

Though her first HIV test had been negative, and the lab technician assured her that the chance of a subsequent positive read was almost negligible, Julia and Mac decided to wait the six months for a second confirmation.

PALATIA PIERCE was just accepting a glass of champagne when Julia's hand covered hers.

"Thank you for coming. It means a lot to me that you're here."

Palatia couldn't help but think of Emaline. Though their relationship was slowly being cemented, she knew her daughter would never be the beautiful, vibrant woman she once was nor would she love another man as much as she had loved Frank.

It pained her to look into such happiness, but Palatia managed a smile and squeezed hard. "All the best to you both."

Julia leaned to lightly kiss her cheek. "I know you mean that." She was gone before the mist in Palatia's eyes cleared.

A GLINT from across the river caught Julia's eye. A lone figure stood on the far bank—a familiar figure, but before she could put a name to who it was, her mother materialized, dragging the minister behind her.

Glowing with excitement, Lucia Fairchild clucked, "Father Shepherd has to leave now, darling. Sunday at Saint Bart's calls."

Julia said all the proper things to the minister that her mother expected, then waited until the two faded into the crowd. When she searched the far bank of the Rio Grande a second time, the man had disappeared.

CHAPTER 78

IT WAS PAST MIDNIGHT when Palatia woke to find Steve Duke slumped on the edge of her bed.

"Where have you been? You were supposed to meet me here after the reception."

"Sorry. I was hankering for a bird's-eye view of the Valley so I drove up to the pass." He sighed. "The Valley never really gets out of your blood."

She gave a small chuckle. "You mean that sad trickle called the Rio Grande?"

"It may be a sad trickle now, but just wait until the spring. But I miss the mesa almost as much. The Kenyan savannah creates a grand vista, but it doesn't smell the same after a rain.

"Mostly it's those damn mountains. Of course, I missed them when I was in Albuquerque, but I comforted myself knowing they stood only a couple of hours south. Now that I'm half a world away . . ."

Both were silent for a while, then Steve said, "Thanks for the binoculars. I saw her kiss your cheek—I'm glad you've become friends."

Palatia heard the catch in Steve's throat and reached for his hand. "Why do you torture yourself this way?"

"Don't ask me, I just needed to see her."

She let out a long sigh. "I should never have told you about the wedding. I didn't dream you'd come so far."

"To see her again, even from across the river, was worth every hour I spent in the air."

"But Nairobi is another world. Couldn't you at least have located in the States?"

"I need distance to cut down on temptation."

Palatia sighed and touched his cheek with her lips. "I never realized how much you loved Julia."

"From the moment I saw her."

"Then why didn't you stay and fight?"

The silent darkness grew heavy between them, and though she couldn't see his face, Palatia winced at the anguish she heard in Steve's next words.

"Because I always knew I would lose."

ACKNOWLEDGMENTS

I'm most grateful to Ellen Reid of Smarketing, who together with Dotti Albertine, Laren Bright, Michael Levin and Brookes Nohlgren brought this book to life.

www.louisegaylord.com